The Gravity of Guilt

Timothy Reynolds

Cometcatcher Press

First Edition: 2023

Front Cover Image: iStock: bestdesigns

Back Cover Image: iStock: chaluk

Cover Design: Cometcatcher Press

Library and Archives Canada Cataloguing in Publication

Reynolds, Timothy G. M. 1960 -

The Gravity of Guilt

Science Fiction/Timothy G. M. Reynolds

ISBN: Paperback print: 978-0-9939631-8-6

ISBN: eBook: 978-0-9939631-9-3

ISBN: Hardcover: 978-1-7380328-2-2

1. Fiction 2. Science Fiction I. Title II.

Title: The Gravity of Guilt

Cometcatcher Press

Calgary, Alberta, Canada.

For Barbara Novak,

the first to guide this story back in the late eighties.

Fuck Cancer.

Special Thanks to:

Barbara Novak
Craig Venables
Deborah Easson
Andrea Mercer
Lynn Jennyc
Kate Salter
Jennifer Rahn
David B. Coe
Sue Campbell
The When Words Collide Workshoppers
Ann Cooney
Naomi Davis
Virginia O'Dine

ONE

**103rd Year of the KOSHARI COLONY
in the KOKOPELLI SOLAR SYSTEM**

THE SLIVER OF LIGHT provided by the smaller of the two moons over the planet Koshari was barely enough for Zeke Hayz to count his own gloved fingers, but between the light-magnification of the darkscope perched on his forehead, and the tendril of invisible psionic sensory power he reached out with, darkness wasn't an obstacle the thief worried about. It was, in fact, what was keeping him safe from the heavily armed killers in six cruisers parked on the street below.

The building was small, not much more than a series of rooms on two aboveground levels. It was one of a hundred such residential cubes making up Kepler City's larger rental district. Twenty-two percent of the units were vacant, according to the data his AI was feeding to the DataLenz image projecting from the tiny brow-mounted unit onto his right eye. The data feed also said unit 22A was vacant, but the thief knew the information was at least a few hours out of date. It wasn't worth further risk without a little reconnaissance... he hadn't earned his nickname of The Psilent One by taking careless chances. Maybe no one was on the record as a renter, but there were six men and two women—all armed as well—paying rapt attention to the auction they were participating in.

With a silent tap and flick of two fingers, the digital control overlays on Zeke's fingernails relayed a command and urged his tiny drone forward. If he could get it far enough down the ventilation shaft before the countermeasures killed it, the drone's four highly sensitive microphones should pick up some of the pre-auction conversations. The unit, modelled after one of the planet's eight-winged native insects, wobbled forward on its six rubber-tipped metallic legs. The voices in Zeke's headset became clearer by the centimetre. He extended a filament of his psi power to the headset's control panel, the warm current soothing him as his seventh sense reached into the physical world and his entire parasympathetic nervous system vibrated gently. He smiled, then used the psi filament to initiate two sound filters. He paused while the filters activated, then nodded when the conversation came through loud and clear.

"Ladies and Gentlemen, we are at nine hundred for this beautiful Old Earth music box. There are only three like it in the entire colony, smuggled in by an engineer on the second colonization ship. Am I bid nine-point-five...?" A loud buzz and pop interrupted the auctioneer, followed by pure silence.

"Dammit," Zeke mumbled.

His AI responded in his earpiece, as if on cue. "I have an idea, Zeke."

"Anything will help, Shaelagh."

"The specs show that there are glass ceiling-mounted lighting fixtures in each unit. If you extend a psi-probe into the suite and make contact with one such fixture, it should amplify the conversations sufficiently for you to 'hear'."

"Brilliant, S. Have we got an update on the arrival of the Peace Force 62 team? I want to be gone before they can act on your tip."

"Their own drone will be overhead in eight minutes-and-fifty-three seconds, with the team following two minutes later. You need to hurry."

"No shit. Going in." Zeke closed his eyes and concentrated on the telekinetic power swirling through his body, delightful electrical currents skittering along his nerves. He drew his power to his centre, tightening it up quickly and efficiently, revelling in the warm-comforting-stone-glow heat centred in his chest. He wasn't just a seasoned expert, he was an industrial designer, an educator, and *the* psi expert of psi experts. This was what he had trained to do. He formed a probe the size of his fist, and 'pushed' it out and away, an appendage of invisible power reaching out almost indefinitely. He moved the probe down into the ventilation system, pushing it as fast as he could. He reached the little drone and took a moment to drag it back from the auction's electronic dampening field so Shaelagh could retrieve it.

His probe reached the slotted cover over the end of the shaft. Without missing a beat, Zeke grabbed the cover with the probe, slid it up and off of its mounting bracket, and pulled it inside the shaft. After a beat he directed the invisible probe across the nearby ceiling, sweeping it back and forth until he encountered a ceiling lamp. Only the leading edge of a probe was stimulus receptive, so Zeke flattened the edge out and placed it up against the lamp's glass shade. The conversations in the room continued, though with less clarity than the drone's mics picked up.

"...three times...*sold*! To bidder Number 4 for nine-and-a-half." There was shuffling and mumbling in the room as people shifted around, bidders grumbling about losing the item. "Next up, is such a one-of-a-kind item that bidding starts at two million. What we have here is a solid-brass ship's bell, fifteen-centimetres-tall, including its wall-mount bracket."

Zeke didn't need to hear anymore. The bell was why he was risking life and limb in the middle of the city in the dead of the night. "Ready, Shaelagh. In two, one, *go*!" His probe didn't sense light and dark, so he didn't experience it himself when Shaelagh knocked out the power to five entire residential cubes just to get this one, but he *heard* the shouts of surprise and made his move.

He quickly swung the probe down from the ceiling and aimed it for the place he guessed the bell would be, against the wall separating the two rooms. Organizers liked to keep auction items hidden until it was their turn to be revealed. This apartment was so small that there was only one place the unseen items could be, and that was in the smaller of the two rooms on this level. The probe bumped into someone. He couldn't hear anything they said, but he sensed their arm pass ineffectively through the probe as the woman tried to swat it away. He sensed she was a psi-12, strong, but nowhere near his 24. He was running out of time. He widened the probe's sensing face and swept it across again, bumping into a wide pedestal. He pulled the probe upward, to the top. There it was! His grandmother's bell. He wrapped the probe tightly around it, lifted it off the pedestal, and withdrew his mind's appendage as fast as he could, carrying the bell up to the ceiling and toward the vent.

Faint gunshots reached his ears, echoing through the ventilation shaft, and the probe felt the bell vibrate loudly as a slug grazed it. He didn't have time to worry about damage to the Old Earth relic. He withdrew the probe to his position on the roof, opening his eyes and catching the bell in his hands as it rose up out of the dark shaft. "Got it, Shaelagh."

"Then get the hell out of there, Lover Boy. The 62s are three blocks away and their drone is thirty seconds from spotting you."

Zeke ran to the edge of the roof and jumped across the two-meter gap to the next roof. Without breaking stride, he sprinted into the unit's rooftop garden and froze. "I'm here."

"I know. Curl up in a ball. Quick. By the way, you left my relay antenna on the other roof by the vent."

"Shit. Melt it down."

"Of course. But not until I'm finished with it. The drone is passing over your position in six seconds. Don't move. Your suit *should* hide your heat signature, but we've never tested it against a new Series 4 drone."

Zeke kept still and silent, waiting.

"Be ready to move in five...four...three...two...sprint! Stick to the path we picked out! Now left! Into that garden, behind that shed and... *hold!*" He did as he was told. They had plotted his escape route meticulously, with twenty-two variations. He hadn't memorized more than the main route, trusting the best artificial intelligence on the planet to monitor pursuit and optimize his escape path.

"Go!"

He went. Once he was tucked in under the wide array of solar panels, he took a moment to shove the bell into his heavily padded pack and stuff a small towel inside the bell to mute the clapper. He hardly needed the bell itself leading the pursuit to him. The 62s catching him was a concern, but it was the crime bosses he'd just ripped off that were the biggest threats. Shaelagh had determined that both Bruge Blue and Ray Addox had representatives at the auction, and neither man was one to screw with. Fortunately, neither of them had a clue of the identity of The Psilent One, so as long as he stayed ahead of them, he should be safe.

"The drone is circling the building and the 62s have arrived, catching everyone with their pants down, so to speak. Uh oh."

"What 'uh oh'?"

"The lead 62 is Marisol."

"What's *she* doing here? She's supposed to be in Aldrintowne."

"She's taking prisoners, is what she's doing."

"Then while she's distracted, let's get me out of here."

"I am. I moved your cycle to the base of the cube north of your position. One short jump, a ten-metre jog, and down the service ladder you go. *Now.*"

Zeke moved quietly out from under the solar panels, slipping the bell-laden pack on once he was clear. He took a moment to orient himself and took off for the dark gap at the edge of the residential cube. The gap came up fast, and at the last second, he realized it was the widest one so far. It was too late to stop without tripping over the edge and dropping ten meters to the laneway below, so he put on a burst of speed and as his left foot lifted for the leap, he pushed off with his right foot and a boost of raw psi, straightening his body and slamming his arms down in a forceful redirection of power.

He cleared the gap but came down hard and stumbled, nearly colliding with another solar panel rig. Deeking around it awkwardly, he grabbed the top of the maintenance ladder and scrambled down to his waiting cycle.

"Leave it on auto, Boss. I've plotted a course that will feel wrong but will avoid 62s, fleeing thugs, and as many surveillance cameras as you can. You'll switch to the cruiser over on Lilly Way, so be ready. ETA, ten minutes of casual, zig-zaggy riding."

"Thanks, S. Let's do it." He leaned forward and held on, letting Shaelagh do the driving.

oOo

An hour later, the bell was locked in his safe and Zeke was tucked into bed, leaving Shaelagh on high alert so her human could get some much-needed sleep.

oOo

(Fuck.)

"Dad! Such language." Lexis' 3-D projected image shot Zeke the sharp look he knew she'd learned from her mother, and he looked up apologetically. Deckard, his robotic PKD beagle pup—sniffed around in the background, his synthetic paws tapping softly on the beech-wood-laminate floor.

"Did I say that out loud? Sorry." He kept staring at a smaller 3-D projection hanging in the air in front of him.

"No, but you let your shields slip and you might as well have shouted."

"Sorry." He tapped his right forefinger and thumb together twice, saving the file. "You really caught that thought? All the way over there in Aldrintowne at your Mom's place?"

"Yeah, but it was just one word and you're frustrated so you put a lot of power behind it. Could the solar flares have helped?"

"The relay chip in your neck shouldn't be affected, but since the whole thing is beta-stage I can't answer that without more tests. Again, though, I'm sorry."

"It's okay. I'm sixteen. I've heard it used once or twice before. Hell, I've even used it myself, but I've never heard *you* use it."

"You still haven't." He smiled, his dark mood lifting.

"The Kokopelli Senate would disagree with you on that."

"You were reading my mind—that's a crime." He looked at the camera and smiled.

"I was *not* reading your mind, you were projecting. They ruled on that last week—projecting with intent is punishable." He watched as she saved her own file then flicked her wrist to clear something out of her visual.

"Then there's the flaw in your reasoning, Lexis. I did not intend to project that word. It slipped out. It was a stray thought. I can't be responsible if you aren't wearing a no-psi collar and pick up my ramblings."

"Ramblings? You said 'fuck', like a space-dock worker. Deckard might not have noticed, but I did."

"I *thought* it. Not the same. And the dog has heard me say worse, out loud. So, tell me why did I bother to invent the collar in the first place if my own daughter refuses to wear one? We're not specifically testing the chip so you should be wearing the collar, to be safe."

"You invented it for weak-shielders to protect them from mind-attacks and head-invasions. My psi-13 pretty much lifts me out of the category of weak-shielder."

"Not by much, young lady. Your last three assessments have been inconclusive. You might be a lot higher than a 13, but you're still vulnerable. Does your mother always let you walk around unshielded? No, I don't think so."

"But Dad, they're so limiting. Maybe when I'm wearing it no one can use psi against me, but it also keeps me from psi-ing with my friends. How am I supposed to have a private conversation with Jessica if I can't use my power?"

"But—"

"'But' *what*, Dad?" She leaned forward in her flexible body-sack chair. "It's not *my* fault my father has the only known perfect 24 and my mother is a near-perfect 23. Mom never hassles me like this. Gawd, you'd think *she* was the psi master engineer and *you* were the cop." Lexis leaned back and Zeke noticed her clenched jaw as she tried to keep a tighter rein on the temper everyone said she'd inherited from her mother.

"I'm sorry, Sweetie-o."

"No problem, Daddy-o." She looked back over her shoulder, out the window where it appeared to still be raining, her long red bangs dropping over her eyes. Her hair was another feature she'd inherited from her mother, though she'd once confessed she was prouder of her locks than she was of her temper. "This all started with 'fuck'. What's up?"

In his lab residence in Kepler City, Zeke grabbed the smaller image with his hand and his nearly invisible fingernail-overlays latched onto the file so that he was able to hold it up where Lexis could see it clearly, half a continent away. 3-D images didn't translate perfectly over 3-D videofeeds but hopefully, she could still make out some of the details.

"What is this, Dad? It looks like a bell."

He took a deep breath. How could he not trust his own daughter? "It is. It's a brass ship's bell from Earth."

"An Old Earth relic? There are laws, Dad!"

"It's a family relic, a solid-brass bell, and belongs to your great-grandmother."

"*Real* brass? Sweet!"

He was proud that she knew the value of the Old Earth alloy. He spun the image so she could see it a bit better. "Engraved on its waist is the name of the ship, *Nichevo II*. Family legend says the *Nichevo II* was a simple ferry on North America's Great Lakes in the late 20th century, but I never heard why it had once been cherished by one of our ancestors."

"Dad, personal OE relics are banned. They're all supposed to be in the museum on Yaponcha."

Oh, God. "Now you sound like your mother." Was he wrong to trust her?

"She's right and you know it." She reached out with her fist and opened her hand, probably trying to zoom in on the fine detail of the bell. "It's too fuzzy. Can I see the bell, please?"

"You *are* seeing it, Lexis."

"No, Dad, I'm seeing a digital of a digital you took, and judging by the acid burn on the bench in the image, you took it there in the lab. It's at the house, isn't it?"

"Lexis..."

"You said it's a family relic. *Our* family. *My* family. If that's true, then I have a right to see it at least one level clearer than this."

"There's a fresh scar on the bell, but my scans show there's something else wrong with it, though. It's emitting a frequency it shouldn't be." He grabbed the image with both hands then rotated it and tilted it, examining it from a different angle.

"Dad, that's a digital. You need to examine the real thing. Trust me. Where is it? Go get it and we can take a closer look. Wow, a real relic, in your house."

"I'm not..." He gave in to her, as he always did. "Fine. Fuck."

"I heard that."

"You were meant to." He left the lab with mechanical Deckard trotting patiently along behind him, and Lexis probably following him on the live feed through the cameras in the hallway.

Rather than go to the actual wall safe, Zeke stopped in front of a digital reproduction of one of his mother's paintings on the wall next to the safe door. He reached through the image to a cavity Lexis didn't know was there and she gasped in his ear. Confident she could neither see nor sense what he was doing, he grasped the cool metal handle in the cavity and turned it ninety degrees counter-clockwise while sliding a tiny lever up with psi. A section of the wall behind him slid back and another secret space was revealed. With simultaneous retinal, palm and psi scans, it opened, air hissing out as the climate-and-pressure-controlled vault was unsealed. Zeke tapped a code into the keypad on the inside of the door and the turntable within spun with a soft whir, stopping when the bell was in reach.

With a last look up at the camera he suspected Lexis was observing through, he shrugged. "One brass bell coming up, Sunshine." He removed a Plexi-encased bell from the vault that a moment ago hadn't been there.

"What else is in there, Dad? Can I see?"

"Just more family relics, Lex." With his hands full he used his mind to give her access to his own first-person view and set the turntable on a slow spin to reveal its treasures. "Take a good look, kiddo, but don't get any ideas. No one can open this safe but me, and if anyone tries, the entire thing drops down a shaft into a time-locked, nuke-proof vault in the building's foundation. If you ever say a word about this little treasure trove to your mother she'll have me buried deep in a cell on Anguta Lunar Prison, never to see the light of day again. You know she would."

"Is that a bottle of sand?"

"Coral pink sand from Utah, USA."

"And is that pottery?"

"The collar of a Mesoamerican clay jar."

"Mesoamerican?"

"Mayan. Central America. Sixth century CE."

"Dad, that's not OE, that's VFOE"

"VFOE?"

"Very Fucking Old Earth."

He laughed and stepped back from the little secret vault. "So true. Now let me close this up and we'll meet you back in the lab. Please set the lab scrubbers and filters to 'Clean Room Level 3'." He psied the vault closed and reset its defensive measures. "Come on, Deck, back to the lab, boy."

As he and the mechanical beagle reentered the lab, Lexis shouted in his ear.

"*Dad!* You've got company from Mom's work. Two Peace Force 62 hover-cruisers have pulled up in front of the house and six, no *eight* 62s in assault gear are piling out."

Rushing back to the lab, Zeke checked the monitors to confirm what Lexis was seeing and nearly dropped the bell's case. He turned, carefully placed it on the workbench, then addressed the cameras feeding his image to his daughter over in Aldrintowne. "I'm shutting off my feed of you. You'll be able to see me but they won't know you're watching. Deckard. Closet. Standby mode. Now."

The realistic PKD obeyed immediately, scampering off-screen to the recharging station tucked away in the kitchen.

"What do they want, Dad? Is this Mom's way of getting back at you for not calling her on her birthday last week? She didn't say anything to me, but I think she was hurt."

He took a quick glance at the array of monitors and confirmed that the 62s were spreading out through the waist-high grasses to cover the exits. "It's been ten years since she divorced me, Lexis, and I didn't call because I was over at a mine site on the far side of Moonstone."

"Aren't you going to lock the bell up? If they find you with it you're done."

"No." He smiled up at the camera and gave a short shrug. "That's sort of why they're here."

"Dad! Did you *steal* the bell? You said it was Great-Granny's."

"No comment. Shutting down now, for your safety. I still have your audio, though."

"Like it or not you'll owe me answers when this is over."

"Of course." He turned his attention to the house's AI. "Shaelagh, don't resist the 62s. Unlock all doors and let them enter, but back yourself up and go to Secure Mode Delta. Also, back up and erase Deckard's memory."

"Yes, Boss. And it's.... all done."

Zeke went down on his knees and placed his hands on his head, heartbroken Lexis had to see what was coming. He considered cutting off her feed completely, but a moment later two heavily armed 62s charged into the lab. The lead 62—a captain like his ex-wife, judging by the pair of bright green stripes on his helmet—pointed his arm at him. The telltale buzz warned Zeke, just before he was shot.

The last thing he heard was Lexis scream in his ear, "DADDY!"

oOo

Bossy stood at attention, her eyes focused on a distant point beyond the armoured windows filling the wall behind her commanding officer, Colonel Eduardo Stihler.

"I'm keeping you off the Level-Playing-Field terrorist investigation for another week. The current team can handle the LPF anti-psi bombers a little longer. I have a *treat* for you."

Bossy raised an eyebrow in response to her CO's comment, careful to concentrate on his eyes, and not his horrific burn scars. "Sir?"

"Since it was *your* investigation that led to the capture of The Psilent One, I'm placing Ezekiel Hayz into your custody for immediate and swift conveyance to Tereshkovaburg."

The arrest of her ex-husband as the famous thief was the high point of her shitty month, so getting to be the one who escorted him to trial was going to be the icing on the cake of his capture. She risked a smile and Stihler reciprocated, his burn scars twisting his face to a grimace. She flinched. She hadn't meant to, but his hideous smile was so unexpected that she hadn't been able to stop herself. She held her breath. She'd known him for years and knew that the rumours he had once assigned a man to prison detail on Irido Island for staring too long were completely true. The offender, Lansing, had been in her training squad. Why Stihler didn't have corrective surgery, she had no idea, but she had to admit that seeing his deep brown eyes staring out from the twisted, discoloured skin was not something she could do every day. Stihler's eyes narrowed. He'd seen the flinch, she knew it. It didn't matter that it was involuntary. But the sliver of emotion in his eyes looked more like sadness than anger.

"With your rating of 23, Captain, you should easily be able to complete and maintain an implant-assisted psi-lock on the prisoner, even at the height of a crippling psi-storm."

"Yes, sir. I'll assemble the necessary equipment. What's our time of departure, sir?"

"1200 hours, tomorrow. Your team is prepping as we speak."

"My team? I hardly need help escorting Hayz to T-Burg. With the implant, he'll be as controllable as a baby. In three days I'll drop him off and be home for dinner."

"You're certain? He can't be trusted. He'll cut your throat or stab you in the back the first chance he gets."

"He can try, but Hayz was never much of a fighter. He's more likely to try and lecture me to death. I suspect a simple choke hold will put an end to that and be quite satisfying at the same time."

Stihler laughed. "I'm sure it would. Now, there's been chatter amongst the LPF cells that The Psilent One will be moved soon. Your mission is classified, but keep your eyes and ears open en route. It's just a train ride through the desert and an airship ride up and over to Tereshkovaburg, but still. I ask again if you're sure you want to do this solo. I'll trust your judgment on this, as usual."

"Thank you, sir, but the two of us should be able to travel quickly and quietly. A crew of armed 62s will draw the LPF like copper-flies to blood-wax. I'll deliver him to the 62s in T-Burg in one, big, lying, not-quite-choked-to-death, thieving piece."

"I have no doubt you will. Dismissed, Captain."

Bossy saluted sharply, about-faced and exited the office, her mind quickly shifting to duty and compiling a list of the equipment she would need. On the way to the Quartermaster's Stores & Armoury, though, her first task was to check the solar-train schedules and book passage for brother and sister *Lester and Delia Bender* south to the shuttle port. It was her last unused undercover identity, but she could make more when the trip was done. She psied her DataLenz down in front of her right eye, logged on to the web, and got it done while she walked.

TWO

"**W**ELL DONE, HAYZ."

"You say my name like you never shared it."

"Right now, in this cell, might not be the best time and place to bring that up."

The echo of the words rang long and cold and Zeke didn't see that as a particularly good sign.

"Are you deaf as well as stupid?" She still stood in the doorway behind him, out of sight. He made no effort to turn. "No smart-mouthed comeback?"

Zeke raised another layer of psi-shields to block the thought-whip she was using to punctuate her words. Despite the throbbing pain at the base of his skull, he could almost hear her mind's poorly disciplined efforts snapping like gunshots against his mental armour. Most people could barely summon enough kinetic power to unlock a door, but an angry high-psi like Mari could do some serious damage when she concentrated her power into what he called 'the third arm".

"I didn't think being a thief precluded your still being a gentleman."

Zeke began a second examination of the fine print of the recruiting advert projected on the otherwise sterile wall, but he wasn't going to look at the doorway. "Always have been, always will be."

"Which? A thief or a gentleman?" The whip cracked again, testing him. His defences were nearly back to maximum strength. He needed them.

"The latter."

"Then shouldn't you stand when a lady enters the room?"

Beneath his trim beard, Zeke's lips curled into a suicidal grin. "There's just me and a 62 here. When a lady enters, I'll stand. But until then I prefer to read about the benefits of becoming a 62 here on Koshari." He pushed back, testing her patience just as she tested his shields. He sensed, rather than heard, her approach from the doorway—her anger a wave rolling over him with tsunami strength. The greater the anger became, the less focus her power had, and without focus, she had no hope of breaking his shields. She was good, but she still hadn't mastered the control he'd once set out to teach her. He nodded at the poster. "Do you know why you're called 62s?" He didn't wait for her answer. "Because this star system was discovered by the Kepler telescope and designated Kepler 62."

"Thanks for once again Zekesplaining what every cadet learns on Day One." She sighed, but it was another simple sound that told Zeke just how fine a line he trod. Her holster unsnapped. Then it snapped shut. Open again. Shut. Open. She'd been able to bluff her way out of many situations, but once his ex-wife started snapping her holster, Zeke knew to give her room to move—or to head her off at the pass.

He stood. The holster snapped shut and stayed shut. Unconscious habits in anyone with a weapon made Zeke more than a little uneasy. "Belated happy birthday, Marisol." He turned slowly to face her, waiting for the whip to start up again. She held it back, barely. Her pale blue eyes were devoid of expression, but her left hand hovered over her holster. Zeke held his hands out, palms up.

"Truce?" he asked. "Do we need to start in on each other before even saying 'hello'?"

"Whatever you say, Hayz." She folded her arms across her chest and Zeke relaxed his shields, just a little. Mari shrugged. "You sure didn't put up much of a fight when they arrested you. I half expected you to use your almighty perfect 24 to get you out of this mess." Her gaze remained locked on his, unblinking, grinding, frost-rimmed. Zeke's shields went back to full.

He looked away, breaking the eye contact. "You know that violence isn't my way. It's too easy to..."

Bossy sighed audibly, cutting him off, "I know, I know. 'It's too easy to kill with psi—we Masters have a responsibility.' I've heard your lecture before—it's hypocritical crap. You won't use it for violence, but you've been using it to steal? We arrested Ray Addox's little brother and one of Bruge Blue's lieutenants in the raid on that black-market auction. If you're going to steal from the mobs, you might want to change your stance on violence. When they come after you they're not going to give a shit about your stupid philosophy when they put a bullet in your head."

"*Allegedly* steal, what was once my family's property," he interrupted. "Until proven guilty and all that. Last month I even launched a constitutional challenge to the law. It sounds like you've got me tried and convicted, though."

"Not me. That's up to a judge in T-Burg."

"What do you mean, T-Burg? What's wrong with the Kepler City courts?"

"The Psi-Crimes Court is in Tereshkovaburg and someone with pull got your charges bumped up to Psi-Crimes. Artifact Possession is bad enough, but you *allegedly* used psi in the commission of a felony and we've got you dead to rights this time. Your days as The Psilent One are over, and if you've somehow gotten Lexis involved in any of this I will personally lock you into your cell on Irido Island and drop the key in the deepest magma shaft I can find."

He shuddered. If they sent him to Irido he'd be dead in hours, but if going to Irido kept Lexis from being charged as an accessory after the fact, then he'd do whatever time they assigned him, in whatever facility they saw fit. "She had nothing to do with anything. You can tear out my spine and beat me with it for being a less-than-perfect husband, but we have the best daughter in the system, and it took two of us to do that."

"Maybe you should have thought of that before you stole an OE relic."

She said 'relic', singular. Which meant they hadn't found the others in the safe. He tried not to smile at the realization. "It belongs to my family—to *Lexis'* family."

"No, they were smuggled here by your great-grandfather. They belong to the entire colony. *That's the law.*"

Zeke looked quickly to the doorway. "I'll have to ask my legal counsel about that—she should be here any second. This has been a nice visit, but you'd better get back to your duties, Captain Boissiere."

"This *is* my duty. As the lead investigator and the only Psi-23 on the force, I drew this assignment." She snapped to attention, stomach in, chest out, shoulders back, and eyes front. "Prisoner Ezekiel Hayz, in accordance with the Kokopelli System Criminal Mandate, you have the right to..."

The Psilent One sighed. And so it began.

o0o

Zeke was confident his defence was in good hands. The cell's door slid shut behind his lawyer as Jillayn went off to get started on sorting the mess out. The psi-master stirred in his chair, trying to work the circulation back into his numbing ass. He was caught and caged, and even his much-lauded "perfect 24" was of no real use—with the door shut and locked, the room was shielded, sealed. Even the air ducts that drew out the hot, moist CO_2, and pumped in the cool, metallic air were equipped with spot disrupters.

Hungry, thirsty, and exhausted all at once, Zeke lurched to his feet and moved to the centre of the room, shaking and stretching the stiffness out of his limbs. Hours ago he'd located the complete array of sensors watching over him and he'd even recognized one of his own designs, but because of their shielding, undetected tampering was out of the question. This single cell must have cost more than the rest of the building, he marvelled. The shielding consisted of pulverized crystals from the Pahana Asteroid Belt, and they were worked into a net of nano-strands that were integrated into the walls when they were poured.

He had a hunch the extra power needed to keep him contained was making Colonel Stihler damn anxious to have him gone. Zeke suspected that in the small, ill-informed, low-psi mind of the colonel, The Psilent One was just waiting for an opportunity to summon his 'demon powers' and go on a killing spree throughout the facility. Zeke chuckled. In truth, if he wanted out, he'd just use psi to turn out the lights, pick the lock, and sneak out a back door.

Since he didn't intend to escape, though, he was more than a little curious to see how they planned to contain him for the trip south to the shuttle port. They could hardly ship him in a shielded box—to be portable it would need banned nuclear batteries. A disrupter was fine, but if extended use didn't cripple him, then a psi-storm would cripple *it*—too unreliable for travel. If he were Stihler, he would probably try stasis. An armful of drugs and a suspended animation helmet would be safest, provided they weren't aware high-psi masters could work free of stasis with a little preparation and some effort.

Putting an end to his conjecturing, Zeke pushed the chair to one side. Using a quick psi-echo to determine the exact centre spot of the room, he lowered himself down into the lotus position. He closed his eyes, placed the backs of his hands on his knees and carefully brought his breathing to a rate synchronous with his slowing heartbeat. One breath for every ten heartbeats, and fifty heartbeats for every minute.

Ever-so-gently, he sent out a force sphere to the shielded walls. When the echoes returned he adjusted his position slightly and sent a second sphere out, a smidgen faster than the first. The third sphere was faster than the second and the fourth was faster still than the third. The arithmetic increase continued until Zeke was enshrouded in a psi-cube defined by the shielded walls.

The sensors were knocked offline by psi-data overload after the seventh sphere, although that hadn't been Zeke's objective at all; he was simply relaxing and regaining his balance because he detested being contained in any way. While he hoped they didn't put him in stasis, the sheer magnitude of the force he projected around himself slowly reassured him that he was indeed a psi-master, and no prison or stasis cell could ever change that.

He basked in the warm strength of his power and with the return of his self-confidence came the sense of peace and acceptance that was the foundation of his Antarian training. The force spheres slowed, each half the speed of the one before, and in brief seconds the echo of the last sphere was absorbed and Zeke stood up, ready for the future.

Unfortunately, the future arrived rather abruptly when the cell door slid back into its recess and four white-and-green-armoured, heavily no-psi-shielded 62s rushed in with a six-t-byte disrupter. They placed it just inside the door and one of them keyed in the arming code. Zeke froze, physically and psionically. The 62s departed, securing the door after them but leaving the disrupter to ensure The Psilent One's further cooperation.

oOo

With two spots on the solar-train booked and the time of the next morning's psi-lock procedure confirmed, Bossy sat wearily at the display in the Quartermaster's store. The brief list of supplies she wanted was nearly complete but there were one or two items she hesitated over. She didn't foresee any difficulties with the assignment once the psi-lock was in place, but this was Zeke she was transporting, not some low-psi ruffian up on charges of knocking a few heads together at a merquilium mine. She couldn't afford to underestimate his capability to take advantage of any opportunity that came up.

Her fingers flashed in the air and she called up the 'Restricted Equipment: Officer Eyes Only' list onto the wall screen. There were customized versions of most of this armament in the small vault behind the bedroom closet in her on-base quarters but just scanning through the available items might inspire her. She could just as easily have called it up on her remote, but she liked the quiet solitude of this part of the complex's sub-basement. The second time through the list she was interrupted by a familiar voice behind her.

"Bossy, is there somethin' specific-like you're lookin' for?"

She swivelled her chair around to see the quartermaster, Slim Wilkes, leaning over his counter, watching her. "The rest of your order's already on its way to your office." The burly officer nodded at the monitor. "If y'kin give me a idea who yer transporting mebbe I can make some recommendations."

Bossy looked back at the scrolling list, shrugged and stood. "Sure, why not, Slim? I've been given the dubious honour of escorting my ex-husband—The Psilent One—to T-Burg for trial."

"So, they caught Zeke. I'd heard a rumour-like. That musta bin some job." He shook his head in disbelief.

"You knew Zeke was The Psilent One?"

"I suspected it. I worked with him on a couple of projects a few years back when he was on loan to us. Man's a whiz, Bossy. Y'know, that disrupter of his is one of our most pop'lar items. I, uh, s'pose they ended up usin' it on 'im—best way to drop the only 24. Y'know..."

Bossy put a friendly hand on the quartermaster's arm, interrupting his verbiage. "Stop rambling, Slim. My weapon's still holstered." She smiled to put him at ease.

Slim returned the smile, reached into the computer's sensor field and with a few deft flicks of his fingers and a twist of his wrist, called up the restricted list. After a few seconds of scrolling, he flicked his wrist and froze it. He formed a fist and the display cleared. When it filled again it was with the schematic diagram of the very first device Bossy had added to her personal arsenal years before.

"The cell-scrambler—of course." She hadn't used one in years. Psi-immune, it could be set to scramble short-term memory to confuse an enemy or crank it up to just about melt a man in his boots. She turned away from the diagram. "But why such firepower? Zeke is hardly a killer and my psi-lock will keep him in line."

"Not for Zeke, m'dear. *Him* you can trust to be a good boy." Despite his security precautions, Wilkes lowered his voice to a whisper. "It's not him y'need fear. Just remember it was Bruge Blue that Zeke allegedly stole from. I'd be more'n a little surprised if Blue didn't already have someone on the way."

"Blue may be known for cutting the tongues out of informants and burning enemies alive, but he knows he's the first one who'll be suspected if something happens to either of us. I can handle the short, easy trip."

"You're handling this alone? If Stihler approved this, I'm not so sure I'd trust his motives entirely—"

"Slim—" She looked around, knowing there were ways to eavesdrop they'd never know were there.

"Let me finish, Bossy-girl. They may nail Zeke for this one theft they caught him at, but he's too good t'leave the courts much of a case with any other thefts. He'll probably do less'n a solar year's-worth of country club time right here in

Kepler jail. They won't even bother t'send him to Irido. He'll be back at work in no time, and that will make some dangerous people mighty unhappy. All I'm sayin', Capt'n, is that this little gadget may come in handy-like on your assignment."

They both regarded the schematic in silence. As quartermaster, Slim Wilkes heard much that escaped others. As a career officer, Bossy knew her duty and played by the rules. As one-time members of the same squad, they both knew how to read the other's signals. The quartermaster broke the silence first.

"Take a look at the name of the designer, Bossy, then go do some digging in that not-so-secret armament-filled closet of yours."

Bossy read the diagram's specs, looking for the name but knowing full well what it would be. She found it and knew Slim was right. Because Zeke himself designed the cell-scrambler, it would probably be a useful toy to have along, no matter which corner trouble came out of.

o0o

By the flow of energy in his cell, Zeke knew immediately when some distant technician reset the sensors, and a quick look at the readout showed him that the six-t-byte disrupter was keyed to blast him automatically should the psi-waves in the room go above a ridiculously low level. He suspected Colonel Eduardo Stihler was quite prepared to let The Psilent One set off the disrupter with no one around to shut it off after it knocked him out. Ten seconds of disruption would bring about unconsciousness, thirty seconds would induce a coma, and a full minute would shatter any human being unfortunate enough to be un-protected and within range. Locked in that shielded room, Zeke shut down all but the functions necessary to keep his body alive—his immediate plans didn't include satisfying the colonel's desire to kill another Hayz boy.

Three layers of psi-shields slid into place, not to keep anyone out of his mind, but rather to keep his own powers and anger contained within, where they wouldn't set off the disrupter.

oOo

The hours remaining before their scheduled departure passed relatively quietly for both Zeke and Bossy. The monitors showed her that he lay on the cot that eventually slid out of the cell wall, while she worked in her office, flashing through training notes on recent psi-lock developments. The more she read, the more she reluctantly concluded that none of the other prisoner-restraint methods were as reliable against a 24 as a psi-lock implant, even though it could turn deadly. It had a precise life of 144 Standard Hours or just over six-and-a-half days. After that, if the implant remained in place the victim's psi powers turned in on themselves and they died a spectacularly grotesque death, kinetic psi pulverizing their brain until the cerebral slop squirted out their ears, nose, and mouth.

The round trip was expected to take three days to turn Zeke over to her Tereshkovaburg counterparts and get home, so she wasn't worried about making it on time—it was just that technology had a tendency of going awry when you least expected it. As much as she believed her ex-husband had to pay for his crimes, the thought of watching him turn himself inside out tested even her alloy-lined stomach.

She saved her compiled summary to the sub-dermal onboard drive in her left forearm, her fingers flashing the signs the micro-thin overlays on her fingernails transmitted to the receiver beneath her skin. She then moved to the psi-center of her office. Sitting on the carpeted floor, with her hands on her knees and her eyes closed, she brought her breathing and heart rate into sync the way she'd been trained to. The rate of her psi-echo increased and she concentrated her focus and cleansed her psi-system. She didn't know if low-psi users experienced the same thing, but she and other psi masters tended to pick up stray bits of psi and emotions leaking from others. The 'stuff' stuck to their minds like sticky beach ooze to a bare foot.

Unlike what she'd heard happened in Zeke's cell, no alarms went off before she was finished. Cleansed, and mentally refreshed, Bossy stripped out of her body armour and stepped into the small shower stall in her office's en-suite washroom. Her mind floated serenely on the cloud of psi after-cleansing while the steamy spray washed the stale uniform stink from her flesh.

Oblivious to the passage of the minutes, it finally took the incessant chirping of her reminder alarm in her ear to bring her mind back to duty. She had half an hour to get to the psi-lock lab.

Twenty minutes later she palm-released the security lock on her ex-husband's cell and began what would be the easiest and most emotionally rewarding assignment of her career.

o0o

Zeke looked up from his mess-hall lunch and grinned. "Join me for a bite... or do we have a command performance before Colonel No-Psi?"

Bossy snapped to attention. Had it not been for the presence of the disrupter, Zeke suspected she would have sent his tray spinning into the wall. "Prisoner Hayz. From this point forward you will refer to my commanding officer only by his official rank and title."

"Which one? 'Lord High and Mighty' or simply 'Torchy the Firebug'?"

In one stride Bossy closed the distance between them. Zeke's heart gave a lurch. Whoops. He held up his hands in demonstration of regret, but she knocked him from his seat with the back of her fist so fast he didn't even have a chance to blink. It was the first time either one of them had ever struck the other. Heat burned up the sides of his neck. He'd goaded her into it and shame brought tightness to his throat.

Even had the blow not been lightning-quick, Zeke knew blocking it or even striking back would have been ill-advised—he was, after all, a prisoner of the colony, charged with grave offences. He rubbed his jaw, and when he spoke again, his mocking tone was gone. "Colonel Stihler, it is, then, Captain Boissiere." Their gazes locked and he held his ground against her hard, cold, blues, but the warning beep of the disrupter broke the contact off. It sensed the strengthening shields and rising psionic tension in the cell and was obliged by its programming to give out a warning tone three points before it was triggered. Bossy looked away first and pulled the small disrupter band from her belt. "We have five minutes to get to the other side of the complex. Sit down and I'll strap this on your head."

The beeping stopped, but the emotional tension was still strong. Wordlessly, Zeke planted himself in the chair and allowed the band to be placed and activated by Bossy's psi-print. Once she keyed in its frequency to the larger floor model all Zeke had to do was move even a pencil with his powers and a six-t-byte disrupt charge would be relayed to the band and shut him down, locking his muscles, and vibrating so violently and excruciatingly in his head he couldn't marshal his psi to even move a pin. Biting his tongue wasn't out of the question, either. Once again, he was at the mercy of one of his own inventions. If only he'd had the foresight to program in some personal access codes and safeguards.

o0o

Zeke watched in silence from the doorway as Colonel Eduard Stihler stopped his pacing and poked the inter-complex communicator on the wall, his back to the two of them.

"Control," he snapped, "Where are Captain Boissiere and that damned prisoner?"

The voice which answered came not from the unit's speaker but from beside Zeke. "Captain Boissiere reporting, sir—with the damned prisoner in question."

The colonel spun around. He nodded to her then scowled at Zeke.

"Prisoner Hayz, say goodbye to your freedom." Motioning to the strap-equipped operating gurney he nodded impatiently to the surgeon whose bowed head and slumped shoulders clearly revealed how much he didn't want to be there. "Let's do it, doctor. Proceed, Captain."

Justifiably wary of the power of the disrupter, Zeke hadn't spoken since the band had been placed on his head and, with difficulty, he maintained that self-imposed silence even as Bossy maneuvered him to the gurney. This was his first time in the same room as the colonel since Stihler was Stan's—Zeke's younger brother—roommate in military school. The last time Zeke saw Stihler in person was at Stan's funeral. The dormitory fire that gave Ed Stihler his ferocious scars had burned Stan Hayz to a crisp. Ed had been a nice, smart kid before the fire, but over the years Zeke learned through various sources that the good kid had become a heavy-handed, promotion-obsessed career officer whose temper was almost as harsh as the burn scars he'd elected not to have cosmetically repaired. Zeke nodded politely at Stihler, but there was something odd about the way the colonel glared at him. Maybe Zeke could have read what it was on the surface of Stihler's shields, but he didn't dare let even a smidgen of his psi reach out.

Since he couldn't pursue the conversational topics of either personal history or odd expressions, Zeke turned his attention to the equipment arrayed just for him. He knew what every single piece of gear was for and could probably list the specs of half of them from memory, but he couldn't figure out what they had to do with him in the here and now. And then he noticed that there were both a technician *and* a doctor in the room with them and he suddenly, grimly, understood what they had in mind to keep him in line for the duration of the journey planet-side. He should have seen it coming. His philosophy-rich, Antarian training had familiarized him with a great variety of psi-restraint techniques—most of which were useless on anyone over a Psi-20—but his instructors at Monastero di Antares had said only one thing about the psi-lock—don't. Don't do it, don't allow it to be done.

Zeke had never *had* it done, had never *seen* it done, and had only once witnessed a recording of death by psi-lock. After nine years his sleep was still periodically haunted by the images of the man's head simply exploding with the force of his unchecked powers as they attacked the biochip and sent bloody, hairy pieces of skull to stick to the one-way glass of the interrogation cell.

If Stihler was determined to use the psi-lock there was no recourse open for Zeke, so he merely held out his arm as the nameless med-tech taped on the anesthetic patch that would put him under long enough for the implanting, tuning, and recovery. If he showed even the slightest resistance, Zeke was damned sure

Stihler would have him shot on sight. He allowed them to place him face down on the gurney, his head cradled in padded supports, but his sweaty palms within his clenched fists betrayed the true state of his fractured nerves.

Marisol stepped where he could see her boots and she read what he suspected was the standard declaration on her heads-up. "Prisoner Hayz, the psi-lock implant is being connected to the neural pathway leading directly to the psi-center of your brain. Its control mechanism will then be tuned to the exact psi-wavelength of the custodian, each person's wavelength being as unique as their retinal pattern. Should you react in any way aggressively toward the custodian, your mind can and will be shut down with a single thought from that custodian. You have no defence, and if the custodian loses consciousness for any reason whatsoever—including sleep—you will be rendered unconscious as well."

As his mind succumbed to the drug, Hayz's last thought was a desperate prayer that anyone but Stihler be his custodian. Even Marisol would be preferable to his brother's killer, accident or not. Med-induced darkness wound around and through his mind just as a full-body shiver shook him.

oOo

Zeke wasn't sure whether it was the searing pain in the back of his skull or the vibrating steel vice attempting to shake his brain loose that brought him back from the darkness, but the result was the same—he was awake. As the black faded to grey behind the weak protection of his too-translucent eyelids, he reached past the pain and the shaking to find there was even greater motion involved.

"Hayz! Wake up, dammit. I'm not going to spend the whole trip watching you sleep. Open your goddamned eyes or I'll see if this psi-lock is as effective as they say."

Once he recognized the thunderous voice as Bossy's rather than some cruel god's, Zeke opened his eyes a sliver. Regardless of his feelings at the ungentle awakening and cutting pain, he was relieved to see his ex. It meant that Stihler hadn't taken up custodianship of the psi-lock and that in turn meant Zeke actually had a chance of surviving the trip without being thrown off the train in his sleep or being locked in some shipping container until the implant expired. Bossy was many things, but it was her unflagging sense of duty Zeke was most thankful for as he slowly sat up.

"It's about time, Hayz. You've been out for an hour longer than they expected. Stihler must have had them up the dosage. He really has a hate for you."

Her voice still thundered in his head, but with a slight concentration of his will, Zeke was able to subdue the pain and put it aside. He looked around. They were in a middle-class cabin on the solar-train and the motion was that of the train speeding along the elevated track at over a hundred kilometres an hour. Try as he might, though, he couldn't decide whether to read his custodian's expression as one of concern or as one of her usual irritated temper. He smiled and touched her uniformed arm with his slightly numb fingers. "Hi honey, I'm home. What's for dinner?"

Bossy pulled her arm back, a bit too slowly. "Are you still stoned, dammit, or can you carry half of a conversation?"

"You want to talk?" he queried. "I thought you had me drugged and in bed for more recreational reasons."

"Don't push me, Hayz."

"I was afraid you were going to try to have your way with me while I was still un..." He stopped mid-word as pain burst in his head. As quickly as it hit, the pain was gone, but it left him curled on the bed in the fetal position. Bossy moved from his side and nodded, satisfied.

"You're under psi-lock, mister. That tiny sunburst was merely a sample of what I can do as your custodian, so do us both a favour—don't piss me off. Unlike Stihler, I want you fit enough to stand trial, and I want no complications to keep me from delivering you on schedule. I was instructed to feed you every four hours for the first day—after you woke up—but I decided not to wait for nature to take its course. I'm hungry and the dining car stops seating for lunch in fifteen minutes."

She indicated to Zeke the small sink next to the mirror. "Clean the sleep gunk out of your eyes and get rid of your sedative breath while I add to my report that you're awake and the psi-lock is functioning." She stepped into the adjoining cabin, sliding the door shut behind her. Zeke uncurled himself slowly and rose from the berth, one wary eye on the door. Trapped on a train with a sunburst-happy ex-wife... it was going to be a long goddamned trip.

o0o

Bossy and Zeke slipped into the dining car a moment before the 'Closed' sign flashed red on the door, and she led the way to a table in the middle of the three rows. A quick glance told Zeke that two-thirds of the tables were full and a light psi-scan reported that nearly half of those were nearing the end of their meals. Even before Zeke was settled into his seat Bossy was signing her order over the sensor inset into the table's top. Ignoring her impatience, her prisoner casually flicked through the menu before eventually making his own choices, then he leaned back and lowered his shields enough to let out a blanket probe of the twenty or so minds around them. Bossy gave him a sharp look but he only shrugged and smiled, and she grudgingly withheld the touch of the implant.

While the Peace Force captain stared out the window at the patches of native grasses on one side and scraggy, tree-less coastline hurtling past on the other, The Psilent One closed his eyes and drew to himself the stray thoughts drifting from the many weak-shielders.

One older couple was returning home to the planet Yaponcha after visiting their daughter and son-in-law at one of Koshari's seaside resorts.

A pregnant woman—cautioned of the risks to her baby that came with exposure to Koshari's vital natural resource, merquilium—was leaving the planet to take up a new job on Yaponcha.

Five early-twenty-somethings enthusiastically conversed aloud on the subject dominating their thoughts—they were on their way to spend ten months travelling Yaponcha on their hoverbikes. Two of them were concerned about being away from home for the first time, and one of the young men fidgeted with a ring in his pocket, trying to decide when he should offer it to the girl who leaned on his shoulder. The girl, on the other hand, wondered when she would get the ring she'd been expecting for the last month. Zeke smiled to himself.

One of the lone travellers, dozing in his seat by a window, leaked thoughts of the clothing business he was temporarily leaving in his assistant's fumbling, but trustworthy hands.

Someone who was just leaving the train car thought of death and Captain Marisol Boissiere.

Zeke's eyes snapped open and he spun in his seat to look through the windowed door as it slid shut, but he sensed only strengthened shields and saw only a silhouette. He leaped up, dodged around the waiter approaching with their meal, and was nearly at the door when a sunburst slammed him in the back of the head. He dropped to his knees and crashed to a stop against the door. The screaming pain behind his eyes and at the base of his skull slipped quickly away, leaving him looking down the silvered barrel of Bossy's stunner. In her other hand was his worst nightmare—a cell scrambler. The one invention of his that heeded no psionic ability; a barely-legal weapon hated even in non-psi circles. He pulled back, shying from the memory of the first time he tested the scrambler on himself.

He'd been alone in the lab, not wanting to expose any of his assistants to the still-erratic tool. After only a short burst, he'd spent a month recovering at home before his memory returned to a level that would allow him to go back to work. It was a year before he and his superiors at the lab were certain the gaps in his memory were healed. That beta-model scrambler had been on a very low setting. Nowadays, unauthorized use of a cell scrambler was punishable by death. Even possession of one by a civilian was sufficient reason for the courts to put the offender away for a very long time.

"Choose, Hayz. Stand up slowly and return to the table or suffer another sunburst while I hold you long enough to scramble a few cells. We're drawing too much attention, so I suggest you come back and eat. *Now.*"

Zeke levered himself to his feet slowly. Bossy stepped aside to let him pass, but he tapped his temple and pointed at her in silence. She hesitated a moment.

(Go ahead. Make it good.) Her voice in his head vibrated at two distinctively different pitches, filling his head with a familiar warmth he'd never expected to feel again.

(I was not trying to escape, I was chasing someone who wanted to kill you. Besides, Captain High-and-Mighty, where the hell would I run to when we're moving at over a hundred klicks an hour? Damn it, I thought you'd ripped the top off my skull!)

(And I'll do it again if I think it's necessary. What possessed you to race off without a word to me? Did you forget that you're a prisoner in transit? How the hell was I supposed to react when I turned and saw you running away? Replay the thoughts you picked up and I'll be the judge as to whether or not we skip the meal to follow whoever you say you heard.)

Zeke lowered his shields as though he was opening a door to peek through, but when Bossy reached out and put her psi-hand on that door he instinctively slammed it in her face. The last thing he needed was her using this new state-sanctioned authority over him to dig and find what he'd been keeping from her for so many years. This was not how he wanted her to find out the truth if in fact she ever did. He suspected she could force her way through using the psi-link and was surprised when she instead reached out a slender tendril of psi and waited. An offering of cooperation.

Colours played across Zeke's shields like sunlight-dappled oil on water. At first, the colours tended to be blues and purples, but he concentrated on calming himself. The colours lightened and shifted to greens and yellows. Bossy edged her probe through the weakening curtain. Both psionically and physically, Zeke flinched, but she bolstered the tendril with power from the psi-link and Zeke relinquished control. Around the tendril, her shields shimmered in greys and blues with the occasional splash of red. Without the psi-link, the details of Zeke's shields wouldn't have been visible, but the link opened him up to her and trying to keep his dark core from her was draining his spirit. She followed the tendril in. Zeke's shields shuddered as she slipped past and his immediate memories opened to her.

THREE

THE HOVERBIKES WERE SAFELY strapped into the rigging that would keep them from rolling around the cargo car of the solar-train, so the young man leaned over and kissed the girl next to him. Bossy and Zeke relived the memory just as clearly as when Zeke picked it up from the stray thoughts of the boy behind them. The remembered tendril of psi then touched on an image of racks of business suits, then slipped back to a memory of a map of Yaponcha with a variety of cross-continent routes marked in red.

The image wavered and fixed on Bossy as the watcher stood and approached the table. When he reached her seat the image twisted and flashed streaks of smoking black acid. The watcher passed the table, approached the exit doors, and his dark mind called up an image of Bossy's ID card and dipped it in steaming blood. He passed through into the next car and his curdled thoughts were cut off abruptly when the door slid shut.

Zeke reasserted his presence, applying gentle pressure to her probe, and Bossy began withdrawing her mind from his. When the tendril finally slipped back through Zeke's shields the psi-barrier turned dark grey, rippling with purple. Zeke tried vainly to push the tendril and the link all the way out but it was impossible. He unclenched his fists and opened his eyes.

Bossy put a hand on her prisoner's shoulder and spoke softly. "Let's get to that meal. As you said, he's not going anywhere while we're moving at this speed. Did you get any sense he was LPF?" She helped him up and he stumbled back to the table where his meal waited.

"No. None. But that might not have been on his surface thoughts." Conversation in the dining car had subsided to murmurs so the only other accompaniments to Zeke and Mari's dining were the sounds of cutlery tapping and scraping quietly on plates while soft music whispered through the overhead speakers.

"You're not the only one I won't let in, you know, Mari."

Bossy didn't respond at first. "Really?" she finally asked.

"Before college, during the summer I spent at Monastero di Antares learning to use my psi, part of our instruction involved opening our minds to others to transfer or reveal complete, unedited thoughts. After a month of trying to get me to let them in, the masters gave up trying. One night, my overeager roommate, Lukasz, decided he'd try to do what six masters couldn't. Somehow he succeeded in breaching my shields on his own after I went to sleep, but my shields appear to have a mind of their own—no pun intended—and they held him imprisoned in darkness until the next morning when a master came into our room with our day's task lists. They couldn't wake Lukasz, and it wasn't until *I* woke up that he was released from the darkness. He immediately admitted what he'd done and when the masters punished him with a short term of silence and social isolation, he accepted not only the punishment but that entire way of life.

"As far as I know he remains in the colony and has never spoken, verbally or with psi, to anyone since that day." Zeke looked up from his plate and the fear in his eyes almost drew Bossy in. He held her gaze for a moment.

"Mari, I know I've said this to you a dozen times before, but I truly am sorry I've never opened up to you completely. I have this power I can't always control, even now, and that darkness inside me that I told you about on our wedding night is still there. You have such a beautiful mind, I couldn't bear it if seeing my soul made you close out the rest of the human race forever as Lukasz did."

Bossy placed her fork on her plate without taking her eyes from Zeke's, but he never heard her words. From beyond the train and even beyond the range of mountains they were now entering, a massive surge of pure, unfocused psi slammed into The Psilent One's shields and his world went black like the heart of a stellar anomaly where the force of gravity rips parts of the universe into unrecognizable sub-atomic particles.

The surge lasted for no more than a second, but the intensity was nearly enough to break through Zeke's shields, without the aid of the psi-lock implant. A moment later the darkness was pushed into a far corner and Zeke once more sensed Mari's presence, but this time she was adding the power of her own shields rather than trying to break through. The psi-lock performed its only useful service to Zeke as it allowed her to direct some of her psi-strength to drag him back to consciousness.

"What the fuck was that?" was all Zeke could say before the dining car lurched left, lurched right, and then broke free of the low, elevated track and violently corkscrewed toward the ground three meters below. The shredding of metal, screaming of passengers and crew, and low rumbling of the quake were lost to both Zeke and Bossy because, as the train did its death dance around them, Zeke performed the greatest feat of telekinetics he'd ever done in his life. He levitated.

He did it reflexively, but with a mastery only he could showcase. He shielded the two of them in such a solid bubble of psi, deflecting every piece of debris, that none of the folding, cracking, or shredding sides of the dining car touched them. He cradled them in place, floating them above their table while their fellow passengers ricocheted off anything and everything around them. Zeke strained to pull in the young man with the ring in his pocket, but even he had his limits and the lad spun past, end over end. Like a ragdoll in slow motion, he was casually tossed into the surprised garment-maker before both were impaled on a support rod that speared through the car's floor and into the midst of the devastation.

The wrecking of the solar-train was completed in less than thirty seconds, but the screams went on forever, it seemed. Zeke, still holding the two of them up with psi, floated them out through what was once a wide window, and onto the narrow service pad running parallel to the elevated monorail. Once he released the telekinetic force to return back to its source deep within his mind, he and his custodian sat, numb, in the sunlight. It was Bossy who moved first, and it was her military training that took control of the situation. Still sitting, he sensed her scanning the wreckage for the area that should have housed the crew. She located it, and pushed herself to her feet, heading off in that direction. Zeke started to follow her but a cry a few meters away got his attention. The young woman from the dining car was still alive and writhing feebly in pain.

He went to her with the hope of being able to do something—any-thing—but it didn't take a medic to see that her back was broken and her lifeblood was gushing through a hole in her left side. Her shields were shredded from the trauma her body was experiencing and it was a simple enough thing for Zeke to slip into her mind and silence the pain. Her eyes cleared and she looked up at the stranger who cradled her in his arms.

"I'm going to be married soon," was all she said. Then her eyes closed. Her psi-aura faded to grey, then broke up and scattered, adding to the stray energies keeping the universe turning. Zeke sobbed. She was barely older than Lexis, and yet she was gone. He couldn't imagine losing his 'little girl' in such a random, violent manner.

It took the cries of other survivors to drag Zeke away from the girl's body, and while wiping away his tears he moved from one to another, easing pain or even applying psionic pressure to contain or slow bleeding. Three of the five he helped died peacefully in his arms, and the other two, including the pregnant woman and her unborn—and miraculously unhurt—child, he comforted until real medical assistance reached and stabilized them.

One by one, survivors that could walk joined Zeke, and soon those with psi ability were using it to locate the remaining survivors and lead the others to them in the wreckage. Nearly all of them suffered from some degree of shock but many were able to push past it and help. The slow, tedious rescue effort continued.

"Hayz. It's time to go."

Zeke looked up from one of the survivors who would live to tell his friends about the day. A dusty but very alert Bossy motioned him to stand up. "Every-thing is under control here and there's nothing the two of us can do that a dozen others can't manage. We've got an appointment to keep, so go get our environmental suits and gather our kits, and I'll see if those hoverbikes survived the crash better than the kids who were planning to use them." She turned and marched off down the line of the wrecked train before Zeke could even think of a protest let alone voice it.

Blood and screams were everywhere and Zeke had no intention of leaving the wreck until everyone had been cared for, so he joined two surviving crewmembers as they pushed their way into the dining car where they had sensed a weak psi source. They quickly located the waiter who, having been in the tiny galley, was only slightly broken but severely concussed. They moved him out, away from the wreck. As he held back the peeled metal of the car's outer shell for the other two to carry the waiter through, he found the ring-bearer, the garment-maker, and the long rod skewering them in place. He helped place the waiter down and then climbed back into the dining car.

Gently, tears flowing, he tugged the lad off of the rod and awkwardly carried his body out of the wreckage to lay him beside his girl. With only a moment's hesitation, he reached into the boy's pants pocket and pulled out the box containing the tiny treasure. Gently, as if it were a soap bubble ready to burst, Zeke removed the solitaire-ruby-adorned gold band. The boy's dry, still-open eyes stared upward without fear or accusation. The Psilent One's seedier associates would have deftly dropped the ring into their own pocket and then gone on to other bodies to perform the same service for the dead-and-gone, but Zeke lifted the girl's now cold left hand, slid the ring home, and placed her hand on top of her fiancé's. Then he closed the boy's eyes. A sob escaped Zeke's shield of numbness he was desperately trying to erect and he suddenly missed his father and brother so much that he wished he, too, had died this day.

(Hayz! Give me a hand!)

Zeke expected Bossy to be standing a metre or two away but she was four cars down the line and he realized her voice had been telepathic. She repeated the call and Zeke reluctantly left the dead to help the living.

When he arrived at her side, she was trying to pry open the side of the freight car, but even with her psi, she couldn't force the crumpled metal to budge. Zeke grabbed hold of the bar she was using for leverage, added his own psi and muscle, and pulled. The door groaned, screeched, screamed, and finally fell to one side. Bossy hopped up into the compartment, but Zeke remained outside, staring down the line at the wreckage of both train and rail. The dead were starting to outnumber the living as damage won over life. The long train was more like a shredded snakeskin than a high-tech conveyance, and his anger grew at the thought of what he would do to the snake that had shed the skin and tossed away so many lives with it.

He didn't, for one minute, believe the devastation he'd witnessed was a man-made event. He was certain it was linked to the psi-pulse that had stunned him, and there was no way the gigantic pulse came from an artificial source. He turned his back on the horror and joined Bossy in the freight car where she was slowly maneuvering a two-prop hoverbike into a cargo sling. In silence, the two swung the cycle through the deformed doorway and lowered it to the ground. The power winch used to load and unload cargo was probably one of the few pieces of equipment to survive but judging by the screaming of complaining rivets and bolts Zeke didn't expect it to last much longer.

They climbed deeper into the car, over crates and bags and the wreckage of hoverbikes whose restraints had not held. In the back, under a pile of what appeared to be geological samples was the only other intact cycle. Its sling had snapped, but the cycle hadn't bounced around like the others had. There was no way the ceiling winch could traverse the twisted track this far back in the car so the Peace Force Captain and her prisoner slowly, methodically, cleared a path to the door. Kinetic psi and human muscle strained side-by-side and eventually, there was just enough room. Zeke sat on a cracked, grey, plasti-crate to catch his breath. His strength had still not come back to full after the psi-surge and the following act of impossible telekinetics.

"Mari, why are we struggling with these damned cycles when people are dying out there? We're obviously not leaving until a rescue crew arrives, so what's the hurry?"

Bossy turned slowly, her back stiffening. "We *are* leaving. The crew radioed for help before the power died and rescue should be here in four or five hours. Unfortunately, without the train's powered relay, my comm unit lacks the range and we can't wait for them to get the radio up and working again so we can send an all-clear. The best we can do is keep moving and make our flight. We can't help here any more than we have. There are fourteen healthy survivors each with more medical training than the two of us put together so we'd only be in their way..."

Zeke stood, furious. "But..."

She cut him off. "People are dead, Hayz! We don't know the source of the attack, but it's a good bet it was the LPF trying to eliminate The Almighty Psilent One! We're not hanging around here any longer so they can come and finish the job, not caring about collateral damage!"

He couldn't believe what he was hearing. "I wasn't the target, and it wasn't an attack. It was a quake, preceded by a continent-shaking psi pulse. You felt it. I *know* you did. I'm not leaving dying people just to save my own skin, and the Marisol I've known since we were kids would never ask me to."

With that, Zeke climbed down out of the wreckage and began walking back to the rescue operation. He never made it. A sunburst pulsed through the psi-link and past Zeke's shields. It was only another tiny one, but it was enough to make The Psilent One stagger and sink to his knees, the heels of his hands clapping to his temples in a futile effort to stop the pain. The agony ended only when Bossy said so.

Zeke rose slowly to stand and turn to face his custodian. Even with the psi-lock on her side and a psi-rating only one level below his, she flinched when Zeke's burning eyes settled on her.

"You, Captain Marisol Jessica Boissiere-Hayz, KEEP THE FUCK OUT OF MY MIND!" He took a deep breath and gradually unclenched his fists. "Since I don't appear to have a vote on this issue, let's get out of here before your LPF terrorists make Lexis an orphan. *You* go get the damned body armour and kits from our compartments and I'll get these bikes ready to go." Zeke climbed back up into the cargo car, pushed past Bossy, and got to work.

o0o

Mari wisely accepted her assignment and went off to gather everything for the long ride south. As she passed the dead and the dying, she kept her eyes forward. She was a member of the Peace Force first and foremost, and she had her orders to follow, but she was still very human. When she passed the broken body of a child, she stumbled but caught herself before anyone witnessed her weakness. She kept telling herself there really wasn't anything more the two of them could do here and the only way to keep the survivors safe was to get Hayz clear of the crash site, but that didn't make her decision any easier to stand by.

The once-flat flexicrete service pad had a few new humps and twists in it from the quake, but it was, for the most part, intact. Hayz officially deemed it definitely solid enough for the two hoverbikes, and they sped along in silence. Probably as eager as she was to get this whole damned trip over with as quickly as possible so that he could get the implant and her out of his head, Hayz took the lead and set such a pace that Mari suspected they might even arrive in T-Burg ahead of schedule.

She, too, wanted the implant removed, but only because she wasn't sure if the danger was limited to the recipient or could cross the link to kill the custodian as well. She had just seen enough death to last an eon and definitely wasn't ready to add her own to the list.

The air in the mountains was brisk and clean and light on humidity, unlike the three cities during summer, and the seaside resorts always. The psi pulse and quake must have chased all of the local animals into hiding because the usually active valley was devoid of signs of life other than the two angry humans. The deep blue skies were dotted with clouds and every now and then one managed to slip between the riders and the distant sun. The resulting shadows went unnoticed by Zeke, but Bossy would look up, half expecting to see a squad of the dirigible-like air-ships led by Stihler in the hunt for two fugitives. Air-ships couldn't fly in areas prone to psi-storms, but that didn't stop Mari's imagination from taunting her.

Zeke's anger cooled to a simmer as the kilometres of service pad slipped beneath the horizontal propellers of his hoverbike. He had to admire whichever of the youngsters had chosen the rental units—while they weren't quite the quality of his own machine, the two horizontal propellers kept the desired elevation of a meter and maintained the speed he was asking for without any undue stress to the electric engine. He extended a psi probe to examine the craft inch-by-inch and discovered a loose clamp holding the coolant line and a supply of energy bars and bottled water in the compartment beneath the seat. With a mental nudge, he tightened the clamp, sure it would hold until he could apply a few physical tools to the job.

The red-streaked cliffs and crags flew past, but not even the millennia-old hanging glaciers could keep Zeke from dwelling on the images of death floating around in his mind. For further distraction, he pulled his energies in and even while guiding the craft around bigger rocks and wide gaps in the pad, he sent out a tendril of psi. He boosted its sensitivity yet narrowed its focus so unless he actually touched Bossy's snug shields she wouldn't notice its presence as it probed her hoverbike for weaknesses.

Despite Zeke's anger at his ex-wife-slash-custodian, he knew there was strength in her argument. He wasn't probing her bike to find ways to hasten her departure to the afterlife, but rather was simply repeating the same routine safety check he'd just done on his own machine. The two of them had a responsibility to Lexis to survive this ordeal.

He retracted the probe after finding that one of Bossy's propeller drive chains was too slack, the seat was too low for her long legs, and there was a supply of energy bars and water under her seat, too. Those bars would definitely be an improvement over the Peace Force 62 rations Zeke saw in the kits Bossy had packed on the bikes.

More bright green hanging glaciers, a few rock-crumbling rivers, and more twisted native trees than any human could ever count were left behind as the two sped south, toward Hopi Terminal and the shuttle to Tereshkovaburg.

o0o

It was late afternoon when the first voice crept into Zeke's consciousness. He looked over his shoulder to see if Bossy was trying to get his attention but her eyes were on the pad that had long ago levelled out and become quite smooth alongside the elevated rail. Before long the first voice was joined by a second and a third and Zeke lowered his shields to improve his reception. Unknown to non-psi users, psi-shields seldom sealed off the entire mind. Unless the shields were set against a psi-attack there was always a small portion of the mind open.

Unable to decipher any worded message, Zeke could nonetheless catch the emotions behind the pleas. He listened and sent out encouragement to communicate and the signals altered slightly. He sensed fear, pain, and death, and it was the strength of the feeling of death that convinced Zeke he was somehow hearing the last psi-calls from the victims of the train wreck. They were calling to him for help and he had abandoned them. He was sure they wanted to know why, and he couldn't answer them.

The voices hammered into his mind. He swerved his bike to one side of the pad and brought it to a stop nearly as fast as he slammed up his shields to keep The Voices out. He dismounted the vehicle and stumbled off the pad, his helmet's visor rising automatically. Ignoring the rocks, he dropped to his armoured knees. He heard Mari take a few dozen more frantic metres to circle back to him.

He bowed his head. "I tried," he sobbed. "I'm sorry. You've got no idea how much I wanted to help. Forgive me. *Please.*"

"Hayz. Get up." He did and turned to face her, strength flooding back in.

"Lady, how the hell can you live with what we're doing? Is there any humanity left inside that emotionless machine Stihler has shaped and twisted? I hope the dead scream at you in your sleep! Let's get to T-Burg so I can get you the hell out of my life. Thank God Lexis doesn't suffer from your lack of heart."

Mari never got a chance to use the psi-lock and, if she were honest with herself, she really didn't have a reason to unleash it. Zeke stormed past her, mounted up, and sped off down the pad before she could even begin to fathom what had just happened. As she lifted off her own hoverbike, it occurred to her that maybe the psi-lock chip in Zeke's skull was already starting to have an ill effect. Worried, she followed him as the mountains slowly shrank down to foothills before being crushed by time into the sand of the desert.

An hour later, as the two vehicles left the last of the foothills behind, Bossy pulled up to ride beside Zeke. The speaker in his helmet clicked. "I know this sounds crazy, what with the sky clear all around us, but do you get the feeling there's a storm coming?"

Zeke shook his head and tore his gaze away from a spot ten meters in front of his cycle. It was all he'd seen since he'd slammed up his shields and visor and continued the ride. "What?"

"I asked if you could feel a storm approaching. Clue in, mister."

He lowered his shields and scanned both visually and psionically along the horizon from left to right. His mind found what his eyes couldn't.

"Psi-storm! Off to the west and approaching fast! We have to turn around and get back to the mountains! We passed a network of caves about ten klicks back. Mineral deposits in the rock will help shield us from the worst of the storm!"

Bossy made no effort to slow down when Zeke stopped his bike. "Forget it, mister. We're not going to be stopped by a storm. These suits are environmentally self-contained and if we slow down, these bikes can go through a monsoon. We continue." Zeke straddled his motionless hoverbike while Bossy rode on. He sensed a hint of psi-pressure from her through the psi-lock.

(Don't!) He shot back. (Have you ever been in a psi-storm? Stupid question. If you had, you wouldn't even consider flying into it. Lady, if we don't get under cover, your precious prisoner here may not survive even a little Psi-16 ripper because of a certain chip in his skull. And these suits you put so much stock in will only keep us from dying, not allow us to function properly.) Bossy finally came to a stop about half a kilometre away. Zeke switched to the helmet mic.

"Good thinking, Captain. What do you think will happen to your hoverbike's psi-assist guidance system when you fly headfirst into that much rogue psi-energy? You'll be riding at over 200 klicks an hour on *manual*. You'll make a very pretty smear on the pad." He turned his bike around and accelerated north at a pace that even the other hoverbike would find difficult to match. (NOW FOLLOW ME OR DIE! And if you try using the psi-lock I'll have just enough time to disable your bike and leave you alone before you make me crash. Dying isn't on my schedule for today.)

Zeke tucked his body behind the cowling of the bike and with a brief probe behind him determined his ex-wife was trying her damnedest to catch up with him. It appears she does have a few brains left behind that badge, he thought, as he looked to the foothills and began scanning for the caves that would hopefully be deep enough to keep the two of them from getting their minds torn apart. He sensed the psi-storm gaining on them and cursed Stihler for the implant that could bring the day to an early end, literally.

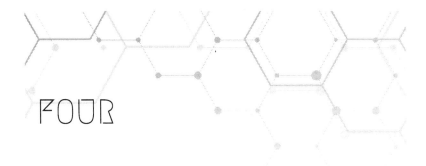

FOUR

W HAT BEGAN AS A feathery tickling sensation surrounding his shields grew to a mental sandblasting as the psi-energy of the approaching storm wormed its way through Zeke's shielded helmet and whirled around his mind, attacking anything that might be a weak spot. For the time being the implant posed no problem because Bossy had tightened her own shields and thereby narrowed the link to a thin thread, but that thread would eventually give the storm an entry into Zeke's mind if they didn't hurry.

When his shields shot to full, snug around the thread, Zeke switched over to a simple visual search for the caves. Just as Bossy pulled even with his hoverbike Zeke spotted what he prayed would be a safe haven. He flashed three directional hand signs at Bossy and, wrestling with the storm-affected guidance system of the bike, she pulled off the pad next to him. They abandoned the unpredictable hoverbikes and Zeke was off as fast as he could through a narrow cut in the rocks. He sensed rather than saw his guardian follow him.

Although the real danger from a psi-storm was in the damage it could do to their minds, there were definitely physical manifestations of the violence it held. The sand cloud swirled out of the desert toward Mari. The storm's telekinetic power didn't spin the sand in one huge whirlwind as a conventional—and almost as dangerous—sandstorm did, but rather it spun each particle in its own tiny dance of destruction. She clambered frantically over rocks and loose scree slope toward a dark slash in the cliff that appeared to be no closer than before.

They were cutting it too close! Adrenaline flooded her system, kicking her forward. She actually passed Hayz in the last few meters to the cave mouth but stumbled in the near-total blackness that engulfed them once they were inside. Reflexively she opened her shields and sent out a probe to give shape to the cave around her, but the pressure from the storm grabbed hold of her probing wave of psi and ripped open her shields. With a scream that nearly ruptured her helmet mic, Mari collapsed to the stone-littered cave floor.

Bossy collapsed so fast that Zeke was past her and at the back of the cave before she screamed and the blow was relayed through the implant. He didn't dare even a mental nudge to turn on the darkscope in his helmet so he stumbled back, groped around and found her, then dragged her, writhing and kicking, further back into the cave and into what gradually became a tunnel.

Seconds later the psi-storm was upon them and every loose particle in the cave became an airborne projectile. Zeke staggered on, Bossy still in tow. After the second turn in the tunnel he noticed that only the sand buffeted the two of them—the pebbles and rocks simply teetered in place, the smaller ones occasionally lifting a centimetre or two before dropping back. After the third turn, the battering of their body armour stopped altogether and after the fourth turn, Bossy regained her feet and could stumble along on her own. Zeke reached through a sliver of an opening in his shields and nudged on the darkscope in his helmet.

The next three turns were taken with more speed but with much less bruising as Zeke led the way deeper into the complex network of tunnels. Eventually, the pressure on his shields lessened to no more than a light buzz, and he sent out a wave-probe of psi, to sound out the caves around them and get his bearings.

When he finally turned his attention to her, Bossy was quivering both physically and mentally and her suit's respirator was working overtime to keep up with her hyperventilation. Zeke quickly adjusted her suit's in-take filter and her breathing slowed. A hesitant probe through the psi-lock link showed a conscious mind but one that was definitely unable to focus. Thankful his custodian hadn't lapsed into unconsciousness and taken him with her, Zeke pulled up a mental image of Lexis and held it in place for her to focus on.

Synapse by synapse Zeke sensed Bossy's mind and psi-powers latch onto the familiar image, and the swirling subsided. He gently lifted her basic shields into place, leaving only enough of a slowly closing gap to send in a command to sleep. Undamaged by the psi-storm, the psi-lock performed to spec, and at the instant Zeke pushed Bossy into sleep, he was pulled into the dark beside her.

o0o

Mari pulled the covers up to her chin but the appearance of Lexis' silhouette in the doorway brushed off the sleep. She tossed aside the sheets and got out of bed. After a moment she noticed that not only had she worn her boots to bed and there were rocks where there should be carpet, but it was also too late to slip back into sleep. She came fully awake only to discover darkness, dampness, and definitely no bed.

She triggered her helmet's darkscope manually, and Lexis vanished, replaced by a cave. Mari turned her head toward the sound of hardened polymer scraping on rock. Zeke was propped against one wall, slowly regaining consciousness. She resisted the urge to send out a probe to feel for the storm, preferring to wait for Zeke to give her the all-clear. She might not admit it to him, but she knew when she was ignorant enough about something that another uneducated decision could be dangerous.

Zeke was slow coming out of his forced sleep. While Mari waited, she wondered why she'd never received instruction about the danger of psi-storms. After all, it was her job to assure the safety of the colonists and visitors to the planet and something that dangerous shouldn't have eluded her training. She'd been an instructor as well as a leader and of what she could remember of the curriculum of the training center, there were no courses offered on psi-storms. Urban assault, yes. Merquilium pools and their hazards, yes. Even the use of twenty-one household items for subduing and restraining a prisoner, but nothing on surviving the psi-storms.

"Maybe because they know that if you're shielded you should live but if you're unshielded you don't have a chance. Course over." Zeke grinned back at Bossy's what-the-hell-do-you-think-you're-doing expression. "You were thinking rather loudly and the implant is having some interesting side effects. How're you feeling?"

She stood and stretched, working the stiffness out of her joints. "Not half bad, but probably bruised from head to toe. What happened? I remember reaching the cave and then pain. Not much more."

"You opened your shields in a psi-storm and got kicked in the teeth, psionically speaking. The storm is still out there but we're so far into the rock you should be able to lower your shields enough to send out a probe or to check yourself for injuries. If I try it for you I might get a reaction from the implant, though for some reason it let me touch your mind earlier." He shrugged. "Ah well, something to think about while we sit out the storm."

Zeke sensed Mari using a psi-probe to count and catalogue her multitude of minor bruises so he used a probe of his own to check his suit's battery level and general physical condition. The faded yellow of the probe's contact with the battery told him the power was good, but not full. His mind reached into the circuitry of the suit and followed the lines to each of the connections, reading the colours for hints of loss in integrity. It was all good. Now that it was safer to use psi, he shut off his helmet's darkscope to save power.

The air in the cave was damp but certainly breathable so he removed his helmet, thereby shutting off the suit's primary environmental controls. Although his experience with psi-storms over the years wasn't particularly extensive, he'd heard of storms lasting for weeks. He hoped this one would be of the shorter duration—the chip in his head would expire on schedule whether he liked it or not.

"I'm going to extend my psi out to map these caves so don't get the wrong idea if you feel my probe at your shields. I really don't need a sunburst in my head while there's a psi-storm raging outside."

Bossy nodded. "I appreciate the warning. At this point, I can't guarantee what the psi-lock will do but I'll keep it on a short leash if I can. Let me know if you find a fully stocked pantry... I could use a bite to eat."

"Wishful thinking. If you remember that meditation technique I once taught you, use it to lower your metabolism and reduce your need for food."

"62-training includes being able to withstand long periods of little food or water so I think I'll manage, thanks. Antarian meditation isn't exactly a proven way of doing anything but focusing your psi, and my hunger isn't psi-related."

Zeke shook his head, resigned. "Whatever you say, Captain. I'm sure the military has prepared you for every eventuality. Anyway, here comes the pulse," and he went silent. The pulse lightly brushed her shields as the wave of psi flowed around her, but the psi-lock stayed quiet.

The echo of the psi-waves returned to Zeke and he slowly pieced together a map of the caves they had passed through in their flight from the storm. The storm was sending mixed signals back when his probe ventured into the first chamber so Zeke altered the probe slightly and the echoes cleared for a moment. When the new echoes started to bring in their messages a voice added itself and once again the plea for help pierced his heart. In the confusion that resulted in their escape from the storm, Zeke had forgotten The Voices. Now they were back and this time he was bombarded by what had to be a thousand cries for help. The resulting message was so garbled that he strengthened his shields in an attempt to block it all out.

(HELPHAYZSAVEHELPDYINGDYINGHELPCOMEHELP-SAVEUSPOWERSHELPHELP!)

Since the implant maintained the thin link to Marisol, Zeke was sure the link was keeping his shields open just enough for The Voices to invade. The volume and sheer power of the sending slammed into him like a fist to his forehead. His concentration snapped, his probe ended when his shields started to close, and he could sense Bossy trying to reach him through the implant.

(Hayz, stop!)

(Can't! Help me close my shields to the voices! I...I can't do it... alone. Get them out of my head! *Please.*) Desperate for help, tear-blinded and his breath shallow and fast with panic, Zeke crawled over to Bossy and gripped her hands in his own. He sensed the anguish hit her like a backhanded slap and a sunburst building fast and hard in response to what the implant determined was an attack, but Bossy quickly added her own shields to his and commanded his mind to sleep.

o0o

Her long, digging claws made no sound on the sandy floor of the cave as she stepped out of the side passage to watch the humans. Her mate joined her after a moment or two and her three young soon followed. Within a hundred breaths, the gathering increased to fifty of their clan, but the human visitors slept on. When HayzZeke's mind was finally closed off to them they stopped calling to him, and now they were satisfied to just keep their saviours company. It had been a long wait, but the time had come.

She retreated to her home den further back in the caves and eventually the others followed. The tōh—the world's breath that stormed outside—was too strong to fight, and that gave her plenty of time to get through to HayzZeke. The humans weren't going anywhere for some time.

o0o

Accustomed to waking in his own sweet time, Zeke was not happy when his dream of a well-stocked dessert buffet was interrupted by the appearance of Mari's face.

(Hayz, wake up.)

(Get. Out. Of. My. Head. If I'd known that not even my dreams would be sacred, I'd have killed myself rather than let Stihler install this damned implant. Now get out.)

(As you wish, master-of-all. But you might like to know we've had company.) She left his mind as freely as she'd entered it.

Zeke threw the dream to the wind and climbed up to consciousness. He sat in the darkness a moment, letting his ears do the work, but there was only himself and a restless Bossy trying to sit still in dirty, sweaty body armour. Very gently he released a scanning pulse of psi that only had enough strength to travel a cave or two beyond their own before returning. Nothing. The two of them were alone.

Bossy broke the silence, her whisper sounding like a bellow in the darkness. "They're gone, but there were enough of them that I could follow their psi-trail to get a general idea of which way they went." Zeke stood and moved to the center of the cave. "Tighten your shields, I'm going to send out a strong probe." He latched on to an idea and changed his mind. "No. *Open* your shields and join your probe to mine, that way the psi-lock won't misinterpret my intent. Just follow my lead. Ride on the crest of my wave and hang on tight, so to speak. Actually, this will be less like a wave and more like riding on the outside of the solar-train. Remember everything you see and we'll compare notes later. This won't last very long but it will be intense."

"I can handle it. Get on with it. This is something I've done once or twice myself, you know."

"Sorry. I just don't want any surprises to cause the implant to react and I figured that the more you know what I planned, the smoother things will..."

Bossy cut him off. "Do it, Hayz. I'm right here and in control. Just shut up and go."

Mari knew people unaccustomed to psi got the idea that a score of Psi-8 is one step above a Psi-7 and in a way, they'd be correct, but what they often didn't grasp was that the Psi-8 has roughly one-point-five times the power of a Psi-7. That meant one-and-a-half times the strength, one-and-a-half times the range, and one-and-a-half times the speed. A Psi-24 had the same advantages over a Psi-23, and this was something she had forgotten until she was being psionically dragged through the cave network via her linked probe at a velocity and range that didn't so much as frighten her as stun her into respectful silence.

Zeke concentrated all of his energies into a directional probe and began the search. Accustomed to the speed of his own full-force probe, he mentally entered each cave, grotto, and alcove, covered every cubic metre of its space, and moved on in less time than it took his body to blink twice. He could sense Bossy's own probe nervously latched on, but she soon began enjoying herself and got into the thrill of the hunt.

Eventually, they discovered signs of habitation in the form of dried animal wastes neatly placed in corners and the occasional nest formed from what appeared to be sand pools covered in moultings or sheddings. The number of lived-in caves grew to ten before the probe caught up with the first creature. The probe came in low, close to the tunnel floor and just as Zeke's probe touched the fleeing animal it leaped into the air and he lost it. It wasn't until the creature's clawed fingers hooked over the sensing edge of his probe that Zeke understood, and he nearly shit himself. Stunned, Zeke froze the probe in place. The sudden halt was dizzying and he felt Bossy struggle to adjust.

The psi master tried to grasp what he was sensing but there was no precedent for it. Zeke's Psi-24 was roughly 16,000 times that of a simple Psi-1, but this creature had ridden on Zeke's psi as if the probe were indeed the solar-train. Not the creature's mind or an extension of it, but the little fellow's actual, physical being. Zeke was stunned.

With the probe motionless, the psiling—which Zeke sensed was a young male chalti named Chookva—gingerly climbed off the probe and dropped to the cave floor. Turning to face the probe he stepped into it, coming fully into Zeke's awareness.

A half-metre in height, Chookva stood on his hind legs like a human but his furred face was more like that of an Earth fox, though with two pairs of ears. He lifted what Zeke came to see were arms, not front legs, and the psi master noted the membrane running from elbow to ribs, not quite big enough to be a flight-capable wing.

Confusion reigned in Zeke's mind and he slowly withdrew the probe, but Chookva followed, staying within the probe's envelope as though he could see it with his flat, merquilium-grey eyes. When Zeke increased his speed of withdrawal the Chookva finally stopped and slipped from Zeke's awareness.

(Where do you think we're going?)

He ignored the question. (It just rode my probe like a goddamned hoverbike. Like it was a tangible, physical thing that could be touched and held.) He stopped the probe's retreat.

(So? Did you think you knew everything there was to know about psi, Hayz? You're a scientist—don't you want to know what we just experienced? You can't just walk away from a discovery like this. Follow that... follow Chookva! Without more information I'll be laughed out of the 62s when I put it in my report.)

(Is that all you're thinking about, Captain? Your damned report? Chookva just did the impossible and you're thinking of your reputation and the military applications of what we witnessed? I'm not charging in to confront a psiling who can see a probe with their *eyes*! What else can he do, and do I have to remind you that *we* are the trespassers and this is *their* home? That little fella was a lot shorter and uglier than Stihler but he might consider a Psi-24 to be a beginner level and decide to remove us from his cave, out into the storm. I'm not retreating. I'm taking a step back to re-evaluate the situation—something a military strategist should be able to appreciate!)

As Zeke's anger increased, he could feel the psi-lock warming up to counter the attack it anticipated. (Sunburst coming!) It was all Bossy needed to say to convince him to regain control.

(OK. Point taken. I... I'm sorry. The implant is affecting more than just my psi. I'm feeling an emotional drain and a weakening in my self-control. Thanks for the warning.) The probe swung about and started down a side passage they had originally bypassed. (What say we explore some more and come back later to visit our new 'friend'?)

(Fine, but let's find that pantry, soon.) He could sense her grinding hunger that mirrored his own.

Zeke moved the probe onward, the pace eventually getting back up to its original velocity. Whenever they came across a hint of occupation Zeke backed up and directed their course away from those caves and passages. Narrowing the search pattern of the probe also allowed Zeke to extend its range considerably and he estimated they had wound their way nearly a kilometre into the rock when he gave up. They'd long since left behind the caves that showed signs of animal occupation, so the long-cold campfire was no surprise. Zeke's hope of finding someone other than Bossy to keep company with was dashed.

(Sorry, Hayz, but you're stuck with me for the duration. It would be nice, though, to find a few humans to pass the time with.)

(Touché! I was thinking too loudly. Your point, but who's keeping score?)

(What?)

(Never mind. This is just an old campsite left by human explorers.)

(Hayz, I'm having difficulty with my probe. It's weakening. The... distance is too much.) Her probe wavered, the image in her mind of the cave fading. (Let's get back. There's nothing of use here.) Her probe started to slip away from Zeke's, but he tightened his mental grip on her, and together they withdrew slowly.

oOo

Chookva crouched against the wall of the cave, cornered there by his mother. He had contacted the humans alone and now his punishment was being described in great detail. He blew out a long breath. The new "duties" he was being given were going to keep him *very* busy. It would be a long time before his mother considered letting him out of her sight again, and an even longer time before he could again ride the storms with his clan mates. The thoughts now coming in from those same clan mates were a mixture of awe at what he had done, sympathy for how harshly he was being punished, and the derision typical of the young when one of them gets caught breaking the rules.

FIVE

B Y THE TIME THEY withdrew, Zeke was beyond feeling his exhaustion. He simply lay down on the rough stone floor and dove head first into sleep, saving the implant from forcing him in when his guardian slipped into darkness as well, her head cushioned by her gloves.

Zeke woke, confused and weak. Bossy stirred beside him. He lacked the strength for psi. "Pray that the storm has passed because we need the supplies on those hoverbikes. Without water, soon, neither one of us is going to give a damn what happens when my implant turns nasty." He rose stiffly from the rock and slowly stretched the kinks from both his armour and his body.

"Which one of us gets to volunteer to go back out into the storm?" She sounded as tired as he felt.

"Both," he answered. "We make it together or not at all. I had a bit of time to think while we were exploring and I'm sure we can create a protected link, together, that will last for a short time." He crawled to the opposite side of the cave. "Recently, I find I'm saying these words a lot more often than I'm used to but... trust me. Extend a strong probe that touches my shields solidly. Let me feel your presence there, but don't use the implant's link, yet."

The cave was black-hole-black but the moment Bossy's probe butted up against Zeke's shields, he was aware of every detail of her physical self. She stood lopsided, leaning on an outcropping of rock. Her eyes were puffy, and her red hair matted and tied back. Her once-pristine green-and-white armour was dull with dust but all the seals were intact and ready should she need them. Her suit's battery still held power but needed charging nonetheless.

They were as ready as they'd ever be. (I'm going to weave an extension of my shield around your probe. This will take a moment or two so monitor the implant link, please, and don't allow any thought of a psi-threat to enter your mind. Think pleasant thoughts, or at least as pleasant as you can in this hole in the rock. Whatever you do—don't let your probe through the opening I'm about to make until I tell you.)

(You said for me to trust you and I suppose I can manage that, for a while; but it's a two-way path.)

(Fair enough.) Zeke began weaving. (I'm constructing what amounts to a psi umbilical cord. The only difference between this and any other open-mind link is simply the shielding. Your part, the core, taps the power of the psi-link created by the implant, and my part is just a Psi-24 shielded conduit. Once done, it should self-sustain for a short period of time, which we need in our condition.) He continued weaving. Two bands of psi extended from his shields and he carefully wrapped them around Bossy's probe, like two bandages wound in opposite directions.

As he gave more concentration to the construction, his psi speech slowed. (We will...share...psi. Complete...shielded...link. Enough...to...withstand...a...storm...I hope.) He neared her shields and stopped talking to put all his thoughts into the joint. He sensed that she now understood what was needed, and she extended a ribbon of psi from her own shields. Zeke took hold of it and incorporated it into his weave. This reaching and wrapping continued until the seal was complete.

Zeke relaxed and took a few long breaths.

"Now, when I count three, slowly open your shields to me while I do the same for you. Let the psi trickle through the 'pipe' like water. This isn't just your probe, but a full lowering of our shields in one specific spot. Go slowly and tell yourself that you are in control. Take your time. Ready?"

"Ready."

"One... two... three." The cave fell into silence as they opened themselves to each other. Psi-sharing was something the two of them had done many times throughout their courting and then their marriage, but to protect his two dark secrets, Zeke had always kept an impenetrable shell around his core. Marisol had always opened herself up to him utterly and completely, but he'd blocked her access to his deepest inner world, where his darkest memory swirled.

They'd met as children, neighbours. Zeke was two years older than both Marisol and his own younger brother, Stan, but the three of them still managed to hang out together, right up to the death of Braydon, Zeke and Stan's father. A bomb planted in his small flyer blew the senior Hayz out of the sky, vaporizing him while his sons waited at home to tell them about their day. When the investigating officer broke the news to the family, the socially awkward Stan showed little motion, but Zeke was completely torn up. He vowed publicly to avenge his father's murder and was even arrested for breaking into his father's office in his employer's headquarters, but his mother convinced the corporation they were just the actions of a grieving son, and they dropped the charges.

It was at Braydon Hayz's funeral that life changed for his oldest son, the one with the perfect Psi-24 his jealous Psi-3 brother could never match. As Widow Hayz kissed her husband's favourite hat and hung it on the memorial in their backyard, Marisol's father, Ramon Boissiere, clutched his heart and fell over dead. Everyone at the service rushed to his side. Everyone except young Zeke, who smiled darkly and went off to the kitchen to find some lunch. Not knowing Zeke could 'hear' him, Ramon had been gloating silently about how easy it had been to kill Braydon after his neighbour and friend had slept with Ramon's wife, Mari's mother. Livid at this revelation, all young Zeke had needed to do was extend his psi and apply a little pressure to an artery for a few seconds, and his father's murder was avenged.

It was Zeke's guilt for his role in Ramon's death that he kept tightly locked away from Mari, as well as her own father's role in Braydon's murder. The day after Ramon's funeral she ran straight into Zeke's arms and professed her love. That was also the day Zeke vowed that he could never, ever, let her know the truth.

But the secrets buried deep in his core were too much for Marisol to take, especially after Lexis was born and the little girl bonded more with her creative father than with her military mother. Eventually, there was one you-and-your-damned-secrets confrontation too many and Bossy cut Zeke loose, ending their marriage in a storm of hurt and anger.

In the cave, fearing the psi-storm outside, they could each sense the other's private place where no intrusion would be brooked, but once the shielded link was complete there was still an intimacy of mind that caused them both to balk. Bossy spoke first.

(Wow. So this is the mind of The Psilent One. It's been a while.)

Zeke, relieved the conduit and shield were complete, cracked a grin. "Wow. So this is the somewhat disciplined mind of a Peace Force captain." Bossy's temper sparked weakly and Zeke knew instantly; Bossy was also privy to the light humour behind Zeke's statement and took the jibe in stride.

(Shall we see about our supplies then, Mr. Hayz?)

"Probably a good idea, as we have no clue how long this shared consciousness will last. Besides, what's the point of sarcasm when the other person can read behind it even as you think it?"

(Hayz?)

"Hmm?"

(Why are you talking out loud?)

Until that moment, Zeke didn't realize Mari's comments had all come through the link but *he* was still using his physical voice.

"Reflex."

(Relax, Hayz.)

He hesitated, then psi-spoke back. (I'm not particularly enthusiastic about facing the storm again. This implant is having some side effects.)

(Tell me later—we need food and water and *soon*. Lead on—the last time I travelled this route I didn't pay much attention to my surroundings, and, as I'm sure you see, while we're joined like this it's not possible to probe elsewhere.)

(I was wondering how long it would take you to notice we're locked in for the duration.)

(I knew when you knew. That's what this is all about.)

Zeke began working his way along the convoluted passages. His darkscope gave him a full view of what lay about them but it still couldn't see through rock walls so progress came in fits and starts as he hesitated at each junction to get his bearings.

Unlike a physical umbilical cord, the shielded link stretched and shrank and twisted with ease, and by the time Zeke led Bossy out to the star-filled night air, the link had become less a distraction and more an appendage. An intimate, shared appendage, but an appendage nonetheless.

Their darkscopes revealed, off in the distance, a propeller upturned in the sand where they'd abandoned their hoverbikes and it was only then that the two noticed the absence of the psi-storm. Rocks, pebbles and sand all sat, quiescent, and the sky was clear up and down the valley.

(It was fun while it lasted, Captain, but I think we can let go now.) Zeke began loosening his shield's grip but Bossy hesitated a moment. An image of the day Lexis was born flashed into her mind and emotional warmth flooded the link and Zeke grabbed at it and held on. (Thank you. Whatever faults we had as a couple, we made magic with her.)

Then the moment passed and Bossy, too, relaxed her hold. In a few seconds, the two minds were locked back up in their own shielded closets with just the implant's thread to remind them there was still a bond only a surgeon or death would sever.

While the two armour-encased humans dug their commandeered hoverbikes out from under the storm's dumpings, Chookva watched from his secret lookout not far along the cliff face. He knew HayzZeke would be moving on. His mother's wrath was formidable but she herself said there were big things at stake, so he had to do something about it. He needed to convince HayzZeke the Savior to help, and he had to do it soon.

Silent but swift, Chookva scampered back to his brother's den where chatter went on until the bright sky-light lit up the world.

oOo

Zeke's hoverbike finally gave up. It took four hours of hard flying but it was bound to happen sooner or later. He'd known about the sand-beaten air hose but they'd hardly had time to stop to work on it. Now they were forced to stop. It was repairable, even without all of the right parts, but it cost Zeke the use of his seat hydraulics and two hours of time to adapt parts meant for other tasks. Once fixed, the resultant loss of power cut the pair's speed in half.

They were flying along with dusk beginning to colour the sky red and purple behind their right shoulders when Zeke reached out for the first time in hours. "I can't believe I'm rushing to my own trial. I should have stayed in bed all last week." His suit's microphone clicked on at the sound of his voice and transmitted it. He was answered by silence, so they flew on. A short time later The Voices began intruding on Zeke's thoughts again but with the darkness of night making progress slow, he was able to push them away while still concentrating on controlling the cycle.

The two continued to ride on in the darkness until an unseen stability bar sticking out of the quake-ripped service pad caught Mari's front propeller housing and unceremoniously flipped the cycle end over end, tossing her twenty meters through the air, and onto her back on the pad. Even with her body armour on, she should have been seriously concussed, if not broken, but her trained reflexes took over, and the full power of her Psi-23 caught her and cushioned her landing.

Too busy with controlling his hoverbike and warding off The Voices, Zeke was alerted only when Bossy's stunned consciousness wavered momentarily and Zeke's mind grew fuzzy as the link to the implant reacted.

SIX

BOSSY PUT UP NO argument when Zeke insisted they take advantage of the forced break and get some sleep. Not even the possibility of the storm swinging around and coming at them from behind could convince Zeke to try repairing Bossy's hoverbike in the dark. He could tell she was exhausted when she readily agreed that operating the darkscope and applying psi to the repairs was too much after the day they'd had. They left the bikes on the service pad before finding a warm patch of sand on which to bed down, but despite the exhaustion, sleep remained out of reach for them both.

Bossy lay back and stared up at the dance of the stars, whereas The Voices slipped back in through the crack in Zeke's shields. His patience was tapped out and he was fed up—it was time to deal with the intrusion once and for all and then learn to live with the guilt their accusations would bring. Loosening a couple of the more constricting parts of his armour, he removed his shielded helmet and sat cross-legged in the sand. Without walls to reflect psi-waves, his cleansing took a different path as he pulled his power to him, drawing it into his center, his core warming up, and the hair on his arms standing on end. The psi-master visualized his energies as a hotly burning sun, but as happened periodically, that sun was marred by dark areas—sunspots as it were.

One by one he focused on the 'sunspots' and willed each of them to flare in his mind. With each bursting of darkened psi, the spots became brighter. Eventually, he pulled the smaller spots together to create one large spot, then he purified it even further with pulse after pulse of pure, concentrated, psionic power. Soon the only imperfection on the surface of the star of his psi was a single dark spot linked to a bright tendril stretching off into the distance. It was the one spot he couldn't cleanse, the one spot rooted in the very core of his power. It was the implant and its link to Mari.

As cleansed as he could be for the time being, Zeke finally opened himself to The Voices, ignoring passing Comet Bachman and the magnificent star canopy of the night sky over Koshari.

(HELPHELPHAYZHELPDONTHAYZGOPLEASESAVIOURPOW-ERSTOPHELP)

There were a thousand screams in his head but this time Zeke was ready. He listened closely and *heard* what he wanted—one distinctive voice, one that because of its pitch or its tone stood out. He latched onto it and pulled it to him. The other voices receded as that one voice was picked. It was as though they were all willing to let the one speak now that it had been chosen.

(We are the world and the world is us.) The emotion behind the words made them jagged and hot and hard to focus on.

Zeke concentrated and focused. He knew he had to take the situation by the horns and deal with his guilt. (Why are you harassing me?)

(We are the world and the world is us.)

(You said that already. Do you mean that when you died, your souls joined with the aura of Koshari? I find that hard to believe. I'm sorry I couldn't stay to help more of you. I don't have quite as much freedom of choice as I would like.)

The Voices all cried out, stuffed with impatience.

(NONONOHELPHAYZHELPWRONGSHUTNONOUPNOLISTEN-HAYZDEATHDYINGSOONHELP!) Then abrupt silence. After a moment the one voice re-asserted itself. (We are not dead, yet. We are not voices of death. We are the world. We need you. Your help.)

He rubbed his eyes with the heels of his hands, ground his teeth, and sighed. (*Show* me. I don't understand. If you aren't the voices of the dead come to haunt me, show me who you are. Give me an image. Give me *something*, goddammit.)

The voices came together again but to murmur in conference and Zeke was unable to understand any of it. A brief image flashed in his mind and for a moment he saw Chookva, the psiling who had ridden on his probe back in the caves, but the image was abruptly banished by a single (No) that escaped the murmuring. The silence returned, but only for a moment.

(HayzZeke, we will show you. Open and see the other way—with the eyes.)

Zeke did as he was told but there was only the moonlit desert and Marisol, still lying on her back with her hands pillowing her head while she continued to stare up into the sky. Zeke waited. And waited. Eventually, the sand in front of him moved. There was something under the surface and he tensed.

(It is the world. It is us. Wait.)

So, he waited. Grains of sand swirled and danced like bubbles caught in a little whirlpool caused by a curious child's finger. He stared wide-eyed, not afraid but instead fascinated. He could sense psi being used, but not on any level he was intimately familiar with. As they swirled, a mound grew, the soft whisper of glassy grains caressing each other as they shifted and found new positions. At twenty centimetres high, it sped up and he sucked in his breath while his pulse raced. The internal rhythm of the squirming, shifting mound changed and sped up, still shifting and growing. Zeke squinted at it, trying to see past the sand, but there was nothing within the sand except more sand. When the mound reached the level of Zeke's chin, roughly a meter high, it finally caught Bossy's eye.

With preternatural speed, the 62 stood, her pistol drawn, charged, and aimed. The mound stopped moving. Bossy held her fire and the mound remained quiescent.

The voice spoke in Zeke's head. (HayzZeke, tell BoissiereMarisol to relax. Her weapon cannot hurt the world. Should use her mind more. Psi is the greater thing. For psi-master-to-be, she has much to learn.)

Zeke laughed, unable to stifle it.

"Okay mister, quit screwing around." Bossy lowered her pistol. "I thought you were exhausted, but here you are making sand castles with psi."

"This ever-so-threatening mound is *not* my creation, Captain dearest. It's the planet's."

The pistol rose again. "What the hell are you rambling on about?"

"Mari, if you can manage to sit down and shut up, you might just learn something." Zeke turned his attention back to the mound as it resumed growing. When it was as tall as the sitting Zeke, there was a brief pause and then a reshaping began. Pistol still in her hand, Bossy sat.

The metamorphosis continued, slowly. Like individual living creatures, grains of sand shifted and crawled with a seemingly distinct goal in mind. The unsettling shaping went on for a minute or two longer. When it was finished, Zeke stared into the sand-carved eyes of himself. Every strand of hair, every whisker in his beard, every crease and scar in the body —it was *him*, at that moment in time. Flesh-Zeke lifted one arm and Sand-Zeke mimicked the motion. Flesh lowered the arm and Sand followed. It was a gritty mirror with an almost instant replay.

Then it spoke into his mind. (We are the world and the world is us, and you are one of us, now.)

Flesh-Zeke turned to Bossy but Sand-Zeke kept watching Flesh. "Mari, did you understand that?"

"How can I understand what I didn't hear?"

"You didn't...? Can you see it?"

"That much I'll admit to, but I don't hear anything except you, muttering in the starlight."

"Open your damned shields then and I'll relay it." Bossy glared at him and Zeke sighed. "Sorry. I need to know I'm not the only one who hears them. I'll lower my shields and you can read it from me." He let his shields dissolve to give Bossy access, but that also left him open to all of the voices clambering to reach him again.

(HAYZZEKEMARISOLHELPSTOPHELPDYINGPLEASEHELP!)
Then silence, followed by the conspiratorial murmuring and then silence again. Stunned, Marisol dropped her pistol in her lap.

Finally, a chorus of three voices joined to speak for all. (HayzZeke, we are sorry. We should have worked out the details of this communication before disturbing you, but some of our strongest voices are our youngest, and they lack both experience and restraint. They have agreed to let those of us who are more familiar with humans and your language speak for us all.) Sand-Zeke smiled and winked. (Sometimes their wisdom is astounding.)

Mari's shocked gasp told Zeke that she was now hearing what he did. "Who are you?"

(Such a simple question, but not such a simple answer. We are the world, the place you call Koshari. We are those who were here before humans arrived. We are those who live in the air, the sand, the caves, and the seas. We are what you call 'indigenous'. And we have a problem. The quiverings of the ground that stopped your journey—they were caused by you, by humans. They are not natural. Storms are natural, but these quiverings are a sign of death.)

(Humans are killing our home. They are destroying the flow of life. We need your help.)

Zeke sat, listening. Bossy fidgeted. He could sense her still wrestling with the idea that this was not one of Zeke's games.

The chorus continued. (Once, before humans came here, we were many and our mind was strong. We learned to feel the pulse and ride the breath of our home. Each creature, large or small, has some form of what you call 'psi'. The smallest creature uses psi to hide itself from the stronger probes of the hunters. The hunters can hunt and overcome prey using many ways, including confusion. A very effective weapon, confusion is. Projecting it into another's mind leaves many avenues open.) Sand-Zeke shrugged its shoulders. (But that discussion must wait for another time.)

(The blood of our home, the thing you call 'merquilium'... to you it is something to take and use. To us, to our world, it is what binds and bonds us all, and the flow is being disrupted and these wounds are creating waves of shock in our home's skin.)

Zeke interrupted with a mental and physical raised hand. (Not possible. We would see breaches with the monitoring satellites.)

(And so you have, HayzZeke. That place you call Moonstone, where pooling merquilium is collected, was attacked. Humans made explosions that ripped open the pools and pulled the flow away from the surface.)

(When did this happen? It wasn't in the news.)

Marisol finally joined the conversation. (Just after your arrest. It's been all over the news, but you haven't had access. The LPF terrorists took credit. Three mining crew were killed by the explosion and fifty more died when the destabilized merquilium got to them.)

(BoissiereMarisol is quite correct, except she only mentions the human losses. We lost an entire nursery of young. More than two hundred.)

Mari's shock hit Zeke like a punch, though it wasn't aimed at him. (*Babies?*)

(Yes. And there is an even greater wound under the sea. It centers around one of your machineries collecting pooling tyh—merquilium. More explosions ripped away the machinery and tore open the tyh. We have waited for your people to do something to heal this wound and seal the breach, thinking it must be noticed soon, but no action has been taken. Now we must act.)

(On the human scale of technological advancement, we are no more than animals, not worth human attention except to be illegally hunted or studied, so we need your help. We implore you to save us. For a human, your mind is exceptionally strong, and your understanding of human technology is quite sufficient. Your councils would not listen to the voices of 'beasts', but they will listen to you.)

A dry chuckle beside him reminded Zeke why he and Bossy were there.

(You've come to the wrong human. Hayz is a criminal. He has no valid opinion and no rights other than to a fair trial. The only human interested in listening to him is a judge sitting in session in T-Burg.)

The chorus cut her off, its tone one of amusement. (HayzZeke, is she always this difficult to reason with? You two are mates.)

(*Were*. Past tense. *Very* past tense.)

(What does our joke of a marriage have to do with these terrorist attacks?)

The slight pressure of the implant reminded Zeke who was in charge.

(It doesn't. But she's right. I have no influence, especially right now. There's nothing I can do to help.) Much to Zeke's surprise, the pressure of the implant subsided. He looked over at Bossy and she nodded, agreeing.

Sand-Zeke, too, had turned to 'watch' Bossy and at the signal of her nod it once again faced Zeke. (You are wrong, but perhaps you need to know more about us. We of the caves are called 'Chalti'. Air and sand dwellers are 'Malti'. Sea dwellers are 'Peralti'. The pulse of our world is 'tyh'. The breath is 'tōh'. HayzZeke, BoissiereMarisol, come with us and experience 'tyh'. Open yourselves and feel what it is to truly master the powers of your mind.)

Warmth surrounded their shields and Zeke sensed Bossy flinch defensively. But the warmth didn't back down or fade, so eventually he sensed her relax and let her shields melt away. With his own shields already down, Zeke dove into the welcoming warmth mind-first. Their minds were drawn in and down, moving effortlessly through the desert sand, going deeper and deeper, their bodies forgotten above.

Despite the black of the night above their camp, their psi-journey wasn't in darkness, but neither was it overwhelmingly bright. The warm presence projected a glow showing them the sand, and then the rock that held the sand. They flashed by fissures and sensed the change when the sedimentary, fossil-filled base gave way to the igneous rock, which, to the north, stretched and grew to form the mountains.

Zeke's mind had travelled by probe a hundred thousand times, but even for a psi-master, a psi-probe was always a slender, fragile thing that had to be monitored carefully. What they experienced now was like a rocket-boosted probe—they coursed through the physical substance of the planet, moving with the merquilium like a shuttle through the atmosphere.

In brief flashes, there were creatures around him that strongly resembled Chookva, the one they'd met in the caves. There were also occasional glimpses of short-limbed creatures whose bodies were those of elongated moles, and of half-meter-long, fully winged, foxlike cousins of Chookva. Bossy was a steady presence beside him, but the others flitted in and about, never remaining long enough to be seen clearly.

Their minds were as one. While Zeke tried to cope with the oddness by visualizing their surroundings, Mari made no attempt at rationalization. Emotions bound up for so long by both her sense of duty and her fury with Zeke, now exploded free of their restraints and she became like an electric current, a lightning bolt streaking on. At times she was aware of a powerful bolt surging parallel to her—Hayz, she assumed—but there was also the feeling of other currents with varied polarities guiding her and containing her energy, giving her confidence to shatter even more barriers.

There was no sense of the passage of time. Existence was everything and memory was long gone. The journey led them trustingly to an end, but just when the once-human Marisol was certain they'd reached their final destination, her mind went supernova. Every emotion she'd ever played with, every memory stored away, every psi ability she'd cultivated and trained, burst out from the core of her soul in an atomic, all-engulfing explosion...and linked as she was to Hayz, she knew he was experiencing the same thing. Then her memories, psi, and *awareness*, all returned, came imploding back in—cleansed, magnified and empowered beyond her wildest hopes and dreams. Eventually, their minds came to a halt within the artery of merquilium flowing through the planet.

At that moment, they ceased to be simply Ezekiel Hayz and Marisol Boissiere. Their essences merged for a brief eon-length moment and a deeper link than any implant ever formed was forged. Large portions of their pasts merged in no particular linear order. Together they were, alternately, Zeke as an unwelcome novitiate in the Antarian psi community; Bossy as a fresh recruit fighting off a rape attempt during her basic training as a 62; Zeke as a teen posing for the family portrait that was the last time the family would be happy and whole, Bossy first as a teen desperately seeking her mother's love after her father's death, and then both Mari and Zeke relived their courtship, marriage, Lexis' birth, the anger of keeping secrets, and eventually the divorce, all from one then the other's perspective.

It all flooded in so fast that it was over before the memories could be lingered upon, but each thought, feeling, and experience was as clear and vivid as when it had first happened. When it was all done they settled back into being Zeke and Mari, but with a wisdom and understanding no *one* person could have gained alone.

Zeke cringed, fearing that the dark core he'd protected so long from Mari's probes was now exposed, but his instincts told him he was still safe. The fact that he was still alive confirmed it. He cut off that line of thinking quickly and cleared his mind. A heavy pulse surrounded him and he suspected he was wrong about leaving their bodies behind. For a moment he thought he heard his own heartbeat, but it was a short moment. The rhythm was too slow and the beat too strong. It *was* his pulse but it was his psi pulse, not his blood beat. As the essence of the merquilium flowed through his psi, his power waxed and waned, waxed and waned, warm and cool. The presence that had brought them there herded them further along the flow.

o0o

Zeke flew. The sand danced and tumbled and gyrated but he maintained his altitude and speed. He pushed his arms out in front of his extended body and rocketed ahead through the teeming sand of the psi-storm, impervious. A field of psi energy encased his body and the sand flowed smoothly around him. He swung his arms out to mimic wings but his course and speed remained steady. He pulled in a small, almost immeasurable amount of power from the storm, willed himself a change in altitude and climbed rapidly, a human shuttle pushing to escape both atmosphere and gravity.

He relinquished some of the control and allowed himself to be buffeted lightly as he continued up. It was like the playful wrestling with a lover—there was energy, but no fear. At least, there was no fear until he shot clear of the storm and its psi power and into beautiful pink dawn skies high above the desert, while falling *out of control*. Gravity quickly reversed the momentum the storm gave him and Zeke went into a magnificent, tumbling, screaming freefall. Despite the small fortune he spent on lessons, Zeke's panic overwhelmed him and he forgot to extend into the simple arch all skydivers knew almost instinctively.

The Psilent One was a rag doll; plummeting back toward the storm he had so recently left behind. Fear may have been the dominant emotion careening around inside Zeke's mind, but he still had enough control to gather his psi energies and make one last effort to halt his fall. The blue sky receded, and the swirling beige of the storm rushed at him. Still, he did not stop.

If Zeke had still been exerting every point of his psi power when he re-entered the storm, he probably would have stopped with enough force to knock himself out, and then he would have continued to fall through the storm to his death hundreds of meters below. Fortunately, he gave up on his psi and was letting the energy slip away from him when he dropped back into the maelstrom, and this single act of defeatism saved his life. Although the desire to stop falling was still strong in his mind, the energy put into the command was greatly diminished and therefore, when the power of the storm was once more his to harness, Zeke decelerated at a comfortable rate. At least, the rate was comfortable until he saw what was happening and once again applied his full power. He came to a full stop then, but less suddenly, and with no mid-air loss of consciousness.

The storm began to move on and, sensing this, Zeke descended slowly to once again find terra firma beneath his feet. He pitched forward into the sand, exhausted and uncaring.

Reality was slow in returning to Zeke, and even when it did arrive he was loath to accept it. He opened his eyes to find himself still sitting cross-legged in the sand, and there was no sign whatsoever of a storm—their camp was as they'd left it, except that the sun was now coming up. Bossy still sat a meter away, in the trance state of someone deep in psi. His joints and muscles complaining, Zeke unfolded his limbs, leaned in, and reassured himself she was still breathing.

A quick probe of the surrounding area revealed only one surprise—in the sand directly behind where he'd been sitting, there was a small amount of blood and a tiny microchip. He was baffled, but only for a moment because he finally clued in that Bossy was unconscious but he wasn't. The psi-link had been severed. The implant lay dead in the sand and Zeke was free. Afraid of rousing Mari, Zeke restrained the impulse to use psi to crush the chip. Instead, he picked it up in his fingers and placed it on a rock. Checking over his shoulder to confirm his custodian was still in her trance, he hefted a second rock and dropped it on the prone chip.

Just when his most painful problem was about to be solved, Zeke's reflexes sent a last-second surge of kinetic psi at the falling rock. The nudge was just enough, and the rock missed the chip by a scant centimetre. Zeke remembered one small but important fact—the chip was still linked to Mari's mind and until it was deprogrammed, damaging it could damage her. He picked up the tiny piece of horrific technology and deftly sealed it into a compartment of his suit that was outside the shielded core. The absence of the implant would simply have to remain a secret between the psi-master and his benefactors. He resumed his meditative position and waited for Bossy.

Oblivious to wherever Zeke's dream was taking him, Mari flew within the psi-storm, mastering low-altitude, high-speed maneuvers. She was once again a pilot, but the craft she commanded now was her own psi-encased body. Unfortunately, the joy of flight was far too short-lived and she abruptly opened her eyes to find herself still sitting in the sand opposite an entranced Zeke.

Frustrated and pissed off, she got to her feet, slowly. Unclenching her fists, she probed her hoverbike to assure herself they still had a few hours' worth of repairs to do before they were going anywhere. She chomped on her first energy bar while clearing away the few signs of their camp, and just when she figured she'd have to fix her hoverbike alone, Zeke regained consciousness and quietly joined her.

SEVEN

THEY WORKED ON IN silence, each immersed in his or her own ruminations. The repairs to Mari's hoverbike went fairly smoothly, considering that most of the tools in the cycles' kits were nearly useless for anything other than light maintenance. It was a task best suited to very controlled kinetic psi and despite their being far off schedule and only a step-and-a-half ahead of the psi-storm, Mari welcomed the chance to observe Zeke at work.

The last day had brought her a great deal of enlightenment in terms of what psi was all about. Until this misadventure had begun, psi had been simply a tool for her. It was a tool she used with more power and skill than most, but it was, nonetheless, just a tool. As a 62, she was trained to trust her mind and body first, technology second, and psi third. Even during their courtship and marriage, her exposure to Zeke's psi-talents had been mostly limited to discussions of the passive Antarian psi philosophies and their influence on his thinking, versus the more practical and marshal psi-training she received as a Peace Force officer. She thought she knew psi because she had mastered its use during hand-to-hand combat, but from the moment Zeke had awakened on the solar-train after the implant surgery until her own 'awakening' here in the desert, sitting cross-legged here in their camp, she had come to realize she had been a stubborn, reluctant student of an education in being a psi master. She needed to give it the same respect she gave to her mind and body and stop seeing herself as something of a freak.

Zeke didn't switch his psi on and off like she tended to do but rather he existed *with* it. She could see now that to her ex-husband using psi was like using eyesight or the muscles of a hand—it was both a sensor and a manipulator, and he was truly a master. As a human being, he was still far down on her list of "People to Voluntarily Spend Further Time With", but watching him shape and re-shape the front end of her hoverbike, and then recalibrate the various controls and instruments, Mari appreciated the master she had shared enlightenment with. Her mind would be a long time dealing with the experience the psilings had gifted her with, but for now, she was content to let Zeke work while she mulled over the myriad possibilities her new knowledge opened up. She also concluded that Lexis would never have a better psi-mentor than her own father.

"Done." Zeke cracked the silence. "Give me a moment to eat something and rehydrate, and then we can get moving." He rose slowly to his feet and stretched his stiffening back. "Think you can send a light probe north to see how much of a lead we've still got on the storm? I'd hate to have spent all this time fixing the cycle just to get caught unprotected in the next five minutes because I was thirsty."

Mari favoured Zeke with an unexpected smile, knowing how much effort he'd actually put into fixing her hoverbike. Getting caught in the open now by the storm would not be good. "Two days ago, Zeke, I would have said we'd need at least a base station scanner for that distance, but today... I think I can manage. Eat something."

"Food sounds good." Zeke dug up only three food-imitating energy bars in his supplies so he limited his feast to one. Mari went winging along on a narrow probe and discovered that the storm was stalled.

"We've got some time. I'll check again shortly. Chew down some energy, and rehydrate yourself."

Her ex looked up at her from his spot on the sand and smiled. "You sound just like Lexis. When we're in the lab she always has to remind me to 'fuel up', 'increase my intake', and 'top up my fluids'. Half the time I wonder which one of us is really the adult in the room."

"If it makes you feel any better, she does the same thing with me, whether I'm at home or out in the field. I really wasn't keen on her helping you in the lab at first."

"I know."

She huffed at him. "Don't interrupt. I was going to say I wasn't keen on it at first, *but* since she started working with you her grades have gone up and she's more interested in her future."

"I'm glad I can do *something* right."

"Yeah, well she's also a lot more sarcastic and less patient with my technological shortcomings. She reconfigured my on-board system and snorted at me the whole time, saying things like 'Do a system purge once in a while, *Mom*', 'Try compressing more files', and 'Change your password at least once this century'."

"She's not wrong, Mari."

"I don't give a shit if she's right or wrong, I just wish she'd sound a lot less like *you*."

Hayz laughed long and hard, dropping his water bottle. "And I bitch at her for sounding too much like *you*."

"She does not!"

"Oh, but she does. I love it! It's as if—"

Mari didn't want to hear what came next. It didn't matter. She tuned him out, threw her probe back out, and discovered the storm was on the move again. "The storm is coming, picking up speed. Time to move."

In moments the duo were back on their much-patched hoverbikes and moving south along the service pad as fast as Zeke's hobbled machine would allow. As they rode they both made periodic probes to gauge their lead, but they didn't continue the conversation.

oOo

At about the same time the following storm blew over Zeke and Mari's abandoned campsite, the two came upon the remains of another fresh solar-train wreck. The damage to this one wasn't nearly as thorough as the first, but salvage would still take a long time. While the train they'd been on had flipped and corkscrewed, this second one had merely folded in half and wedged itself into a short tunnel cutting through a high rock escarpment. The hoverbikes had reached the limit of their usefulness. Nothing was getting through the blocked tunnel or around the escarpment, and the much-patched bikes didn't have the vertical power to go up and over.

Bossy dismounted and climbed up into the cockpit of the train to check on the condition of the communications equipment, so Zeke wandered off to survey the escarpment. He quickly came across the foot and handholds picked out by the crash's survivors caught on this side of the wall of rock, and even in his armour, he made quick work of the climb. The dark grey and red rock rose almost twenty meters above the desert. Zeke hauled himself over the lip onto the narrow plateau and took a moment to admire the view.

The escarpment ran in a more or less straight line to the horizons on Zeke's left and right. Smaller partial escarpments ran parallel to this one but they were off in the distance and didn't appear to have nearly the height of the one he now stood on. Ahead there was only desert and a clear sky. The storm only threatened from behind.

(Are you quite done impersonating a spider, Hayz?) Bossy asked with psi. (The radio is in good shape and as soon as I can hook it up to a fully charged power source I'll call for a pickup. The Hopi Terminal isn't far now and they're equipped to come get us.)

They're also equipped to shoot us on sight if Stihler has put out the order, Zeke thought to himself. (I'll meet you on the other side. See if you can find any food or water; it's not likely, but anything'll help. I'll see what I can find on this side.) He started a cautious descent of the south face of the escarpment. (Have the pickup crew bring a few gallons of water. Hell, if they're feeling generous have them make it Kokopelli rye. I think we deserve a good stiff drink after this trip.)

(I'm not sure Hopi Terminal's commander will see rye as rescue rations but I'll see what I can do. This round'll be on me. Find a shady spot and I'll dig up a battery to power this.) The almost cheery voice in Zeke's head went silent and he concentrated on finding solid footing for boots designed more for cycle riding than climbing.

Step by step he worked his way down, all the while thinking about the changes the psi-sharing had wrought in them both. Although years ago she'd hinted at the abuse she had suffered as a 62 recruit, now that Zeke had relived that memory from Mari's perspective, he had to admire the way she'd handled the sexual discrimination rampant among the Peace Force. Their psi-sharing showed him that a full third of the 62s were women, and Mari's thoughts on the subject revealed that twice as many women started the basic training as men but the women tended to buckle under the pressure applied by the male recruits and officers alike. Knowing this now both infuriated him and frustrated him. He wished she'd told him about all of this herself, but he was frustrated with himself for not seeing it. He thought of himself as perceptive and felt he should have seen signs of it all.

An overhang forced Zeke to drop the last two meters to the sand, but a lazy application of cushioning psi made it an easy jump. He found the exit the survivors of the wreck had used to break out of the mess, and a liberal sprinkling and splattering of blood around the portal told him that although the wreck may not look as serious as the one he and Bossy had walked away from, there had definitely been injuries and probably one or two deaths. He didn't expect to find any survivors, but he probed the mess for anyone alive or even recently alive. There was no one.

A sudden surge of anger exploded away from Bossy and rammed into him. He reached out and his probe reached her in the train's cockpit. She was safe, so he left her alone in silence. Silence. Zeke noticed the silence for the first time. The psilings hadn't been pestering him since he woke up in the desert that morning.

As if waiting for that thought as a cue, the voice spoke. (We were waiting, HayzZeke. We knew of this second place of destruction and death and believed it might convince you that you are needed. You no longer have the darkness in your head to keep you from helping. Save us. Save our world.)

Although he continued his search for any kind of supplies, Zeke kept his mind open to the plea. (How? I said before that no matter how strong my psi is,

I'm only one man. If I leave Bossy, I'll become a hunted man and she will follow me until she catches me or until one of us is dead. Her sense of duty to the 62s is stronger than that toward her family, as shattered as we are. Sorry, but there's no choice except to let me get to T-Burg and get through this farce of a trial so I can be free to help. Unless you can convince Captain Boissiere to grant me leave to save the world.)

(We tried, HayzZeke. She was rude. She ignored us. We will have to do something ourselves. Our choices are few.) The voice stopped. No further argument came. Zeke was surrounded by the silence again until Mari's mind touched his.

(Hayz, I sure as hell hope you found more supplies because we're on our own.) Her thoughts weren't particularly loud but the emotion—a boiling mixture of rage and frustration—was overwhelming.

(Okay, Captain, what's up? No luck finding full batteries?)

(That was the easy part. It only took me a few minutes to get through to the airship base at Hopi Terminal, too. They patched me right through to the commander but he was useless as shit. He agreed to contact Stihler and officially tell him we are on course, just behind schedule, but their last team just went out to pick up a survey team crippled by another psi-storm. He said it would be at least a day before he could get anyone here, but when I lost my temper with him he said it might be as many as four days.) Zeke sensed her take a long, deep breath. (I've got more water, and as soon as I get the energy bars and water from the cycles I'll climb over. Then I'm going to walk all the way to the airship base and kick that bastard in the nuts, for a start. He outranks me but that won't stop me from taking him for a walk in a passing psi-storm. Let's see how his Psi-6 handles *that*. I'm on my way.)

Zeke was left in silence, again. Considering Mari's foul mood, he was happy to end the one-sided conversation. He could still sense the powerful emotions pouring out from her and hoped the effort of climbing and descending the escarpment would cool her off.

o0o

Mari estimated aloud that the two of them had sixteen to twenty hours worth of walking to reach the airship base and, despite their meagre supplies, she translated that into two days at the most before they would be on their way over to T-Burg on Binder Island. When Zeke complained that his body armour was already rubbing him raw in more than one place, she stung him with a comment about using his precious Antarian philosophy to ease the pain.

Zeke followed with a remark about the Death Unto Duty motto Bossy seemed to have adopted for her own but lapsed into silence after that, fearing if he angered her she would resort to the psi-link and discover the implant was no longer where it should be. "Let the chafing continue, Captain dearest." With a final surrender to inevitability, Zeke picked up the sack containing the few water bottles and energy bars he'd scrounged up and left the dark coolness of the tunnel for the killing heat of the late-day sun.

As Mari fell into step beside her prisoner she was actually thankful for the few hours of sun remaining because it meant that the various solar-powered systems of her body armour would get a good charging. She wouldn't admit it to Zeke, but she was experiencing chafing of her own and a fully operational suit would at least keep her dry and cool.

o0o

Discipline—military and Antarian—got the pair through the next eight hours. Zeke suspected Bossy had spent so many hours in her body armour over the years that the weight and chafing could be ignored, but he hadn't, so he wove his psi into an almost physical padding where the chafing was the worst. By experimenting as they walked, he discovered that small, well-timed applications of kinetic psi pushing his armour just as it was about to hit the rawness reduced the pain down to simple irritation. It also wore him out. The rhythmic pulses of psi kept him from staying centred and after hour number four he was wishing for another psi storm to sweep over them so he could test the theory of his dream and try flying.

They trudged on. They'd used up all of their idle conversation in the first two hours and had begun getting into areas where contrary viewpoints only led to anger, so the talking stopped. Zeke began formulating in his mind ways to help the psilings and seal the merquilium breach, but he kept getting distracted by thoughts of the charges against him and the chance he might end up doing serious time.

And breaking Lexis' heart.

Leaving Zeke to his own thoughts, Mari spent her numbing hours rerunning various other scenarios in her head, including one involving the airship base commander and a six-t-byte disrupter. Her reverie was interrupted by a steady beeping in her head and when she withdrew from her thoughts it became apparent that the sound was her suit's time-elapsed alarm telling her that eight hours had passed. She slowed her pace and eventually broke the rhythm to come to a stumbling stop.

"Hayz. Rest time. We've been walking for eight hours which is what I estimated we'd need to do this first night while we had the strength." She sent out a brief, sweeping probe. "We're surrounded by sand so where we make camp isn't critical."

Hayz stepped off the concrete pad onto the fine sand and collapsed onto his back. He stirred only long enough to loosen parts of his armour and to remove his helmet. While the environmental system of his suit reduced its power dramatically when the helmet was removed, he didn't appear to care. He sent out no probes, said no "good night", and just faded quickly to black.

She, on the other hand, didn't even bother to remove her helmet when she curled up on the sand mattress.

Sometime during the night's march, Mari had set a second alarm in her suit. Four hours of sleep was all she'd allotted for them to recharge their human batteries and when the beeping of that alarm dragged her into wakefulness at the scheduled time the sky was only just beginning to lighten. It was too dark to make out much of the landscape around her, but it was more than enough light for her to see she was now alone.

"HAYZ!"

In the past few days, Mari had finally begun to believe in mankind again. She had seen another side of her ex and in that seeing revealed parts of herself once believed to be lost. But now a brief scan of the immediate area showed only sand, the elevated rails, and the service pad. Even with her darkscope on full, there were no tracks, human or otherwise. The Psilent One was now officially a runner, and within fifteen seconds Mari's estimation of mankind as represented by her thieving ex-husband dropped to a place on her list just below "flatworm". She didn't know if she was more furious that Hayz had left her in the middle of nowhere or that she'd failed to do the simple task assigned to her. Whichever it was, she was livid.

At first, she hesitated to use the psi-link to the implant because she actually believed Zeke couldn't possibly have run off, but the more she thought about it the more confident she was that not only had he skipped out but he'd always intended to do so as soon as her back was turned. She would send a full sun-burst of psi to the implant. Wherever he was, Ezekiel Hayz was about to become a cripple.

She focused on the always-present psi tendril, which led infallibly to the implanted chip. She wrapped her senses around the tendril, let the energy gather like a storm cloud behind the saw-tooth mountain range to the east, and when she estimated she had enough to halt even the vaunted Psi-24 Psilent One in his boots from any distance, she opened the sluice gate and released the burst. Right now she frankly didn't give a damn if she killed the bastard.

The nova of energy raced along the tendril and Mari braced herself for the telltale echo, which should confirm her psi had reached a destination. She waited. No echo returned home. She knew too little about custodial implants and cursed that lack of knowledge. She could only remember one contingency, which could break the link under these primitive conditions and it was the death of the implanted person. The thought of Zeke possibly lying dead in the desert somewhere disturbed her deeply but in her fury-filled state she told herself it was because she'd been robbed of killing him herself. Yesterday she might have told herself something else. Somehow she was going to have to break it to Lexis that her felon father was dead.

She checked both the charge on her pistol and the one on the cell scrambler still strapped to the other side of her belt. Then, concentrating on the tendril of psi still connected to the implant, she set off into the desert, grumbling to herself.

"Hayz, you jackass, you better've died close to the track because I'll be damned if I'm going to drag you all the way to the airship base. I'll haul your corpse back as far as the pad and then I'll just wait for our pickup in three days. There's no hurry, now, I suppose. Stupid thief of a psi-master ex-husband bastard."

The standard issue Peace Force 62 'Officer Class' body armour was designed to withstand repeated blows from a steel pipe, maintain a comfortable temperature under extreme conditions, be flexible enough to allow short-distance sprinting foot pursuit in the urban jungle, boost natural psi-shields two levels and even protect the wearer against a medium-range riot-gun blast, but it was not designed for extensive foot travel through ankle-deep sand. Dry, grating, shifting grains made for the most awkward walking surface and it took Bossy only a few steps to realize even a short walk was going to be a long walk. "Hayz, if you aren't dead now, you will be when I catch up to you."

o0o

A disturbance in the sand awoke the great predator from her month-long hibernation. The ripple was weak, but there was definitely prey to be had. Now that she was awake, her hunger cut deep. She banged her long claws together to shake off the sand and stood up on her back legs to scent the wind. The air told her only of the breath, the tōh, coming, so she turned her attention to the sand long enough to get oriented and start after her next meal.

EIGHT

ZEKE DREAMED OF FLYING again, but there were no acrobatic loops or rolls this time. There was also no uncontrolled free-fall, and although he saw no one as he rode the psi-storm, he knew he wasn't alone. He was sure he was being herded, and just like during the 'voyage of enlightenment', they went on to the merquilium pulse; but this time he had a bit more control over his movements. By experimenting, he discovered that as long as he didn't try to make any radical course changes he could play with fine-tuning his flight techniques—a reach of the arms here, a boost of psi there—but he still knew it was only a dream and therefore moot.

Visibility in this dream wasn't limited by the storm as it had been in the first imagining and, whether with psi or eyesight, he wasn't sure, he could make out a lot of the landscape a hundred meters below. By the light reflected from the crescent of the moon, Heyokah, above Zeke saw the desert give way to rolling hills. Moonlight glimmered on water in the distance and Zeke knew his dream took him to the Spinnaker Sea. What little control he had in the dream vanished, though, as he approached the shore and was brought in for a smooth if not graceful 'landing'. He had time to get one grand lungful of the tangy salt air before a command to 'sleep' insinuated itself into his mind and he lay himself out on the grassy knoll. The dream dissolved into blackness no longer illuminated by moonlight.

o0o

The time-lapse counter in Mari's suit said she'd been dragging one foot after the other for three-and-a-half hours but she was certain in her soul that it had actually been years. The sun struck down at her, but the harder it hit, the more power it gave to the armour's solar-powered environmental systems. The suit's exterior hovered somewhere just over 50 degrees Celsius, but sealed within the synthetic cocoon, the furious 62 pushed through the sand at a rather comfortable fifteen degrees. Even the blinding light of the sand's reflection of the sun was missed by Mari because hours before she had darkened the suit's face plate to allow in only enough light to show the shape of the land she struggled through.

She stumbled on. There was no question of stopping until she had to, which would only be when she was dead. The implant's psi trail—or maybe it was Zeke's trail, since she'd long ago forgotten which was which—was fading, so even when she was sure her legs were shredded beyond repair from pushing through the sand, she pushed on. Even when her vision blurred and her psi shut down out of sheer exhaustion, she somehow continued.

The auto-tint on her faceplate adjusted itself when the sun slipped behind clouds, so she wasn't even aware of the impending storm until it blocked the sun and she was left stumbling in the near dark. A light psi-nudge turned on the darkscope, but the unexpected moment of blackness knocked the wind from her sails and she folded down onto the sand. Disorientation struck her full force once she stopped moving and in a brief moment of blind panic, she clumsily drew her pistol and fired four rounds harmlessly into the dunes around her.

Discipline gradually returned. She fumbled her weapon back into the holster, slapped open her visor, and reached for an energy bar and a few swallows of water. While choking down the chewy, choco-berry-flavoured nutrition bar, she had the presence of mind to set her suit alarm for two hours time. Two hours would have to do, she told herself. She didn't dare rest any longer than that or she'd lose the trail.

Her stomach gladly accepted the mouthful of water that washed down the last half-chewed piece of bar. As if that swallow was a signal to the rest of her body, Mari slumped over, the bar's wrapper still clutched in her gloved right hand while her left hand semi-consciously triggered her face plate so that it snapped into place even as her head descended to the sand.

Not long after Mari stopped caring about such things, the natural winds that preceded psi-storms began in earnest, gradually burying her in a cocoon of shifting sand.

o0o

Zeke dreamed once again. This new dream was of salt spray and of creatures both on land and in the sea. Images flirted with his mind but eluded comprehension. The salt spray became gentle surf, which in turn melded into pounding waves. At the last all the swells and troughs came together to create, as their avatar, a single, all-crushing tidal behemoth. His awed dream self sat in the lotus position on a bluff overlooking this transformation. The power of the sea churned luminescent green and white and black and lifted itself up, so Zeke soon had to crane his neck to see its summit.

At the moment when he was most certain he was at the apex, it curled over his tiny patch of coarse grass on the jagged bluff and collapsed the power of the world onto him. It all happened so quickly that he didn't even have time to *think* about screaming. In a moment the sun's light was banished by the immensity of the world-wave, but Zeke's dream waited upon no catastrophe.

From the darkness of pre-death, Zeke was snatched up and his dream flight resumed. A current of urgency now surged through him, lending speed to the flight, but all pretense of control by the dreamer had evaporated. Once again, his dream took him back over the desert, although this time he flew not in the psi-storm, but ahead of it. The race was on and whatever force powered Zeke's flight pushed him on at a dizzying rate.

The psi-storm roiled and swirled but couldn't move its mass at a fraction of the speed Zeke achieved, so the psi master's lead widened. Thinking his dream was going to have him racing the storm in a circumnavigation of the planet,

Zeke was somewhat surprised to find his altitude suddenly plummeting at a breath-snatching rate.

His guiding force circled him around and down in a tight dream spiral and in doing so showed him the fast-gaining edge of the storm. Zeke rejoiced at the chance to dream-fly within the storm once again, but the ground rose up to greet him and in the blink of an eye the unidentified specks marring the continuous earth tones of the desert became the green and white armoured limbs of a 62. Zeke was deposited gently on his feet next to the body and the dream shredded in the wind. Reality arrived with startling clarity... this was no dream.

Control was returned to him and Zeke made quick work of digging the 62 out and flipping them over. The armour shape showed that the body within was female and with a very quick—the psi-storm was nearly upon them—psi-probe, Zeke confirmed it was Bossy he now held in his arms. He tightened his grip on his ex-wife and, as the spinning sand at the leading edge of the storm buffeted his armour, the psi master and his ward shot skyward, harnessing the stray leading energy of the storm itself to outdistance it.

oOo

Whatever controlled Zeke flew him up and over the storm, feeding on the tōh's power. He yearned to wrestle control of the flight and revel in the storm's energies, but the limp passenger in his arms smothered that desire. He flew on and eventually, his storm-extended awareness sensed the ocean ahead. He and Mari were taken down into the storm and onto solid ground. He laid her gently in the grass, then greyness clouded his mind, and Zeke slept.

oOo

The predator sensed a strangeness in the tōh, a power she was unfamiliar with, that made her feathered sensors quiver and vibrate with anticipation. Her prey was moving away much faster than she believed possible, but it moved with the power and the power was oh-so easy to track.

Eventually, she knew she was getting near, closing in, moving with an energy she hadn't known in a very long time. She was homing in on the power she could feel, hungry for its touch and for the taste of the soft flesh that housed it.

oOo

The storm swept in off the ocean and the water-bound peralti sent word to the malti who lived for and loved such psionic maelstroms—and the word was to ride the storm and stop the Ancient One that followed HayzZeke.

They sensed her hunger in the wind and knew her goal. If HayzZeke was going to be able to help save their home, they had to help him. Coming in off the ocean, the storm was water-vapour-filled energy above a vein of merquilium flowing far beneath the skin of the world. As the energy reached the shore it became less translucent as its kinetic energy brushed a layer of sand from the beach.

On the cliffs high above the beach the dozens of malti waited, their open arms pulling their wing flaps taut. The energy of the storm slammed into the cliff and coursed up and over, taking the psi-assisted flyers with it. The storm cleared the kilometre-wide strip of grassland and moved inland, fast, out over the desert, picking up more sand and small rocks, quickly becoming an opaque swirling dance of terrestrial 'stuff'.

The ancient one, claws held high out of the sand, moved swiftly on flat, webbed feet, designed by nature for speedy movement in the desert. The malti, tuned to the energies of the storm, knew exactly where to find her and dropped to the sand one at a time, forming three concentric rings around their quarry. Killing such an ancient one was not what they wanted, but if it was needed to keep HayzZeke safe, then it was to be done. Their leader hoped to negotiate peace. The largest malti stepped forward when the Ancient One halted.

She waited, rocking back and forth in her obvious impatience and hunger. The lead malti bowed her head.

(It is forbidden, Revered One.)

(Shick shick. Saying who says?)

(Consensus. The power you taste is last hope. You know tyh and tōh and pain.)

(Shick. A deep hurt. A new hurt. A hurt to end all.)

(All will not end. HayzZeke is with us. Will help. Leave it to the Consensus. Find your meal away from here.)

(Shick. Shick. You small ones ask much. But Consensus is Consensus. Will sleep again. This HayzZeke is to you. There will be others as tōh blows strong.)

(It is for us all. We share thanks. Sleep well, old one.)

The Ancient One burrowed down and down into the sand to a hollow the malti sensed with her probe. She watched with the probe as the elder tucked one claw under her armoured belly, then one behind her head, and slept. The malti, once satisfied the threat to HayzZeke was gone, launched themselves back up into the storm, and rode the tōh back to the coast.

The ancient peralti, Nnif, bobbed offshore, 'spy-hopping' every now and then in his frustration and impatience. A few strong thrusts of his tail lifted his head and upper torso out of the water and helped him see his two human charges. The spy-hopping was an old habit born of decades of dealing with the land-bound malti and chalti, and it was a habit that resurfaced when he became upset.

Upsetting Nnif took a great deal of effort these days, but the psilings' misjudgment of the situation with the two humans had shaken him. He had expected the two to quickly agree to help, but their alien priorities were in conflict with his own. HayzZeke very much wanted to help but he was determined to let BoissiereMarisol punish him for some unimportant human crime. The malti had even removed the tiny head-thing affecting HayzZeke's psi, but *still*, he resisted.

BoissiereMarisol, on the other flipper, was motivated by an overwhelming sense of duty to her job and anger with her former mate. At first, the peralti believed it was crippling the human's ability to see the whole picture. Now, after gently wandering through her mind for a hint of some way to convince her to help, he reluctantly agreed with her motives. BoissiereMarisol, too, very much wanted to help them, but unless she completed her task with HayzZeke, everything she had fought for would be sacrificed, and she, too, would be removed from their world.

Her logic was long-winded but it eventually made sense. Her thoughts revealed that she was prepared to make certain promises to help the psilings if they first helped her. Nnif's spy-hopping eventually paid off because when BoissiereMarisol awoke he was ready. So as not to disturb HayzZeke, the psiling touched a probe to the human female's shields to let her know he was there. Rather than open her shields to let him in, though, BoissiereMarisol slipped her own probe through her shields and the two probes joined.

(BoissiereMarisol, we are sorry.)

(For what? Last thing I remember I was dropping face down in the sand, alone. This stretch of coast is a bit more welcoming than that damned desert, and I've even tracked this bastard of a psi-master before he could complete his escape. If the implant was still working he should be dead, but this is better. We can figure out later why the connection between us is broken. No need to apologize for helping me catch him.)

(You misunderstand. HayzZeke is the one who brought you here, with a bit of help. No, I don't apologize for our part in saving you; I apologize for our interference. We have become desperate and some of us have acted rashly. We believed our problem was greater than your own, and that it gave us the right to interfere. Our problem *is* greater, but no less important, and that is no excuse for endangering the only two humans who can help save us. If we assist you now, will you promise to come back and help us? Without you and HayzZeke our world may not survive much longer. The tyh beats faster and the tōh blows stronger. These are not good signs.)

(Whatever happens to Hayz, I'll help. He may be gone for a long time.)

(We understand. We will try to be patient as long as we can until he is available. HayzZeke has made the same promise to himself, and that will be stronger even than a promise to us. He will not go with you willingly.)

(That's for sure.)

(There was a great danger to you in the desert but no longer. When HayzZeke is rested we will help you on your way. The tōh will blow in our favour again. As I said, HayzZeke does not really wish to leave us, so you will need to use your weapon.)

(My stunner? Shooting him isn't such a good idea and he'll only laugh if I try to force him to go at gunpoint.)

(Not the stunner, the weapon you call the 'cell scrambler'. From HayzZeke's mind, I have seen how it works. Set it on its lowest setting and there will be no lasting damage.)

(He'll be *so* happy to hear that.)

(No, he will not be, but that is unimportant at this time. We will do what we can while you are gone—you have both given us some ideas to try.)

(You said there was danger. Was it from other humans? What happened to them?)

(She was not human. She was the Ancient One, the Revered One older than even I. She listened to the tōh and tyh and she heard. This time you are safe. But she has tasted HayzZeke's power on the tōh and next time she might not be stopped.)

(I don't plan on spending any extended vacations here in the desert, so we should be safe.)

(Yes. We hope so. But you need to be on your way.)

Zeke stirred, and the 62/psiling conversation ended. The peralti sank back down into the Spinnaker Sea and Mari drew the compact scrambler and checked the charge level. She dialled in a low setting but hesitated a moment before taking the tool off standby mode. Hayz was slow in waking, and since he'd just rescued her from a psi storm that would have killed her, she was loath to use the weapon on him. On the other hand, as the psiling pointed out, Zeke probably wouldn't go willingly and she knew that for whatever reason, the damned implant no longer controlled him. Lexis was going to be almost as furious with her as Hayz was.

Her shields began to tingle and itch as the next psi storm gathered its energy. She looked back at the spot offshore where she last saw the peralti and his voice reached into her mind.

(Very little time remains. As the tōh again builds energy, so will HayzZeke. It pains me to say this, but you must use your 'scrambler', now.)

Boosted by the energy of the growing storm, Zeke opened his eyes and pushed himself into a sitting position. An unidentified click and hum caught his attention and he twisted around to see Bossy standing two meters behind him, an apologetic expression on her face. Why would she be sorry about anything? Then, she raised her arm and pointed the cell scrambler at him. As she triggered the weapon, the 62 and The Psilent One locked eyes. Just before his world went black, Zeke was sure there was pain where before there had only been anger.

oOo

Zeke awoke to the deep thrumming of three large engines and a sense of floating. He was on an airship. Full awareness was slow in coming and when it did finally arrive, he realized that not only were his wrists and ankles bound with Lite-Steel cuffs, but also his head was crowned with a disrupter band. The chalky taste in his mouth and blurred vision were bad enough greetings but when the voice cut through the buzzing in his ears, he knew a bad week just got worse. He slowly looked left and a blurry Bossy greeted him.

"Good morning, Chuckles. Please put your seat in the upright position as we're about to land."

"Ungh." Motor control was sluggish for the psi master.

"You're so articulate in the morning." Zeke reached up to the disrupter band, but Bossy pulled his bound hands away. "Yes, you're back on a disrupter. Now be a good boy for another half hour until you're in T-Burg custody, and then we can end this little excursion with both of us still alive."

Despite feeling like he was sucking sand from a dune, Zeke managed a sarcastic "Yessir, Captain, Sir" before lapsing into a dazed, depressed, confused silence.

NINE

ZEKE CRACKED HIS DRY knuckles painfully and gave an honest half-smile to two of the three people seated at the small table with him in the judge's chambers. The disruptor in the corner of the room beeped softly, an unnecessary reminder of the linked band around his head. "Madam Justice, Mister Prosecutor, while I fully appreciate the deal I am being offered and will be forever grateful for the reduced sentence, are we sure that avoiding a trial is a wise decision? A lot of people are going to be furious they're being denied the spectacle of The Psilent One's public humiliation, not the least of them being the media, my ex-wife, and her CO."

The very senior member of the PsiCourt Bench shook her head. To Zeke, she looked a little sad. "Normally, Mr. Hayz, I would agree that the trial of the solar system's most famous psi master would be beneficial to all, but the Prime President and his entire Cabinet agree that the expected crowds would just present too great a temptation for attacks from the LPF. We're not doing this for your convenience but rather for the safety of thousands whose only crime would be curiosity. Even if we held the trial at a secret location, we are still mandated to broadcast it live, and wherever people would gather to watch, they would be in danger."

Zeke's lawyer, Jillayn, put her hand on his forearm and squeezed gently. The gesture comforted him, though her words shocked him. "Please, Zeke. Everyone at the firm has been receiving death threats. My children have to be driven to school by a pair of armed 62s. If my team does the job you've hired us to do, this trial will take at least a month, and the risk is too high."

This was all news to Zeke, having been in isolation for the week since Marisol delivered him up to her Tereshkovaburg counterparts. With a nod and a deep breath, he placed his right palm down on the tempered glass screen set into the tabletop. It scanned left to right, then forward and back, the soft blue light oddly calming. He fought the urge to whistle a tune while the device repeated the scan twice more. When it was done, it flashed green and went dark. "What about my daughter?" he asked the prosecutor.

"I've received confirmation from Captain Boissiere that your daughter has been assigned two officers, hand-picked by her mother." He flashed his fingers over a sensor in the tabletop and a small camera rose up on the end of a delicate armature, looking to Zeke like an all-seeing eye on a stick. "Mr. Hayz, as part of the agreement we have all just become party to, you will now read the following statement both for the record and for release to the public, so that all may know who and what you are." He handed Zeke a small, simple tablet with the agreed-upon statement displayed on the screen.

Normally, Zeke would simply have called the text up with his onboard system and read it from the projection on the receiver DataLenz on his left eye, but all of his personal computing was deactivated the moment he was arrested. He accepted the tablet. "Thank you." The weight of his selfish actions, stealing the artifacts because of some stupid family pride, finally sat down heavily on his shoulders. It had all been just an adventure—until suddenly it wasn't. He was an asshole, and now he was obliged to admit it to the world.

The bailiff stepped away from his spot by the door, moving behind Zeke's chair, and facing the camera. "In the case of The People v. Ezekiel Samuel Hayz, this statement is being read into the official record on this time-stamped date, in the city of Tereshkovaburg. Presided over by Her Honor, PsiCourt Magistrate Sophie Hegler, and witness being bourn by Prosecutor Neelon Orenchko, and Attorney for the Accused, Jillayn Salter. Please proceed, Mr. Hayz." He stepped back to his spot.

Jillayn had briefed Zeke on what to do—simply read the prepared statement. Add nothing, leave nothing out. Asides or omissions will void it. He took another deep breath and read aloud.

o0o

Colonel Eduardo Stihler poured two hemp teas from the ever-present self-heating pot on his desk. "Bossy—*Marisol*—this reassignment is in no way a punishment." He placed a tea in front of Mari, and she accepted it with a smile. "The Espy Beach School is excellent, with the emphasis put on academics rather than psi-shit. Lexis can learn with other teens and not have to stay holed up in the house just learning online."

"Thank you, sir." She sipped the tea. It was a perfect blend of imported and local leaves. She really wished it was laced with something a bit stronger, but knew full well there was no alcohol in her CO's domain. His alcoholism was legendary amongst the 62s, but she knew he hadn't had a drink in fifteen years, after nearly drowning during a bender while the two of them were investigating a series of deaths at a merquilium filtration facility. She'd been the one who'd pulled him out of the tailing pond and resuscitated him, which is where she supposed they'd formed their bond. Once he embraced sobriety, he rose through the ranks quickly, and no matter where he was stationed, he maintained a soft spot for both her and Lexis. She never understood his burning hatred for Zeke, but then, Zeke blamed *him* for his little brother Stan's death, so maybe the mutual hatred balanced out.

"Since the Psilent One will be out of reach for a few years, you might as well enjoy this mother-and-daughter time without interference."

They most certainly would. "We'll both appreciate it, sir, though I hope there's enough 62 work to keep me busy. There's nothing I hate more than boredom."

"Except maybe The Psilent One?" He smiled, not unkindly according to his eyes, but his burn scars made it almost too gruesome even for her. "Don't worry, Marisol. There are three ongoing investigations and you will be inheriting lead on two of them. It is a small, but effective detachment." He tapped his desktop twice. "There. I've sent over the files so you can get up to speed before you arrive next week. Also, I see you've selected Corporals Axelrood and Tashna for Lexis' Aldrintowne detail. I've cleared them to remain with her until you're both settled in..."

There was a sharp knock on the glass door, and it shifted from opaque to one-way, revealing Stihler's aide, Lieutenant Habib, fidgeting impatiently. Stihler tapped his desk again and the door slid open. Indicative of their good working relationship, Habib didn't wait for permission to speak.

"Sirs, you need to see this." He turned to the west wall and the mundane artwork morphed into a screen filled with Zeke's face. "He's making a statement."

"... admit fully and of my own free will, that I am the individual known both publicly and privately as The Psilent One. I fully admit to misusing my psionic abilities in the commission of crimes against The People, and of unauthorized possession of an Old Earth artifact, as described in..."

On-screen, Zeke continued, listing the various laws he'd broken with regard to the brass bell. He then read a list of the various public services he would use his unique abilities as both an engineer and psi master to perform and assist society with when he was released from prison in a year's time. Mari wasn't sure whether she wanted to throw up or cry.

"I conclude by apologizing to The People of the entire Kokopelli System. My actions were criminal and selfish. As a high-psi citizen, it is my duty to use my abilities responsibly, for the betterment of all, and not the gain of a few, or one. I have brought shame upon psionics as both a science and a discipline, and vow to serve my sentence as agreed upon, without appeal. By the time you hear this, I will be en route to Irido Island Prison to serve my time. Peace be with you. I am Ezekiel Samuel Hayz, felon, and violator of your trust."

Damn him! She stood abruptly but was saved from being humiliated by her tears when Stihler smashed both of his fists down onto his desk with such fury that the glass shattered and both she and Habib scrambled back from the damage.

"Out! Both of you!"

Mari turned and followed Habib without another word. She marched out into the hall and around two corners before she dared to stop. She took a shaky breath. She was stunned. She was livid there would be no trial, but she was also relieved. Hayz was guilty, and he would do time, but it wasn't going to be a horrendously long sentence. She'd thought she wanted him to go away forever, but Stihler's comments about Lexis made her realize Lexis losing her father for so long would *not* be the best thing for her. Acknowledging his guilt, doing some time, and giving back to the community—were all good lessons for their daughter. It would have been even better if her father hadn't been a lying thief, but at least Lexis would see that 'crime equalled time'. Mari was also relieved because as much as Zeke pissed her off, he was no hardened criminal who could last five or ten years on Irido Island. He could probably stay out of trouble for the year, but not much more. Psi or no psi, he was no fighter.

o0o

Zeke shuffled along, his progress hampered both by the standard ankle re-straints designed to keep him from running and by the skull-rending headache he had after his 62 escort 'accidentally' triggered a two-second burst through the disruptor band embracing Zeke's head.

A door slid open at the end of the windowless corridor, revealing a clear gangway leading to a tiny Class 3 airship. Except for the autoguns mounted fore and aft and the lack of any windows in the small passenger compartment, it was like any of the dozens of private lighter-than-air craft Zeke had flown in over the years. Two other prisoners were chained to the benches, both at least fifteen centimetres and thirty kilos bigger than Zeke. He was a scrawny academic next to these mesomorphic gladiators. His escort chained him to a bench just out of reach of the smaller of the two giants, but that put him opposite the bigger behemoth.

If he'd not been shackled by both the disruptor band, and an industri-al-strength six-T disruptor in the corner of the cabin, neither his fellow prisoners nor the guards would have been any threat. Just because he didn't use his superior psionic strength offensively didn't mean he couldn't. He was only too aware of how easy it is to kill with psi. Since he was denied his only real weapon, when the big man opposite him leaned in and spoke, Zeke leaned back against the wall and listened.

"Mayor Addox sends his regards, *freak*. He wants you to know he'll keep an eye on your family while you're enjoying your Irido Year. He's especially going to keep an eye on that lovely, luscious, defenceless daughter of yours."

Zeke didn't even think. He just surged forward as hard and as fast as he could and slammed his forehead into Addox's messenger's face with a crunch.

o0o

The Psilent One woke up on his back in what smelled like a disinfectant-washed hospital room with a rough industrial white ceiling. The bright light stabbed at his two headaches—the one in the soft tissue of his brain from the disruptor, and a second centred on a point on his forehead just above his eyebrows, from an impact with something at least as solid as his skull. He reached up to touch the wound and feel the extent of the damage, but his shackles drew him up short.

"Oh, yeah. Irido." How could he forget?

"Yes, Hayz. Welcome to Irido. Don't get comfortable, because when I let you out of here, your last days will be counted on two hands."

Zeke pushed himself up on one elbow to see the speaker, expecting yet another thick-necked convict; but removing a tray of sterilized something-or-others from an autoclave was the narrow back of a lab coat. Zeke nearly reached out with a finger of psi to see whether the tools were more for torture than for surgery, but even if he hadn't been able to feel the disruptor band around his head, he was now fully aware of where he was and what anti-psi measures were in place.

The lab coat turned around and smiled as insincere a smile as Zeke had ever had the displeasure of receiving, including the many from Marisol. He couldn't tell if the scrawny old man was the prison doctor or just a nurse convict, but between the raw ice in his blue-green eyes and the smile of an apex predator, the man scared the shit of out of him. Zeke erred on the side of wisdom and said nothing. He gently lowered himself back down and closed his eyes to the bright strip lights in the ceiling. *What the hell have I done?* He wondered.

"The good news is, Hayz, to some of the residents here at Irido Resort and Country Club, you're a legend, a hero. Sadly, none of those fellas matter.

o0o

Lexis knew she was being followed again, but she wasn't worried as she sat astride her powerful RedWing three-wheeler at the only traffic light on the small campus. Two vehicles back in the line, a woman watched her. She'd seen her before, and Lexis recognized the psi-signature as one she'd come across previously. Maybe the woman knew that Lexis knew, and maybe that's what she intended, but what she didn't know was that Lexis's shielded riding suit held a few surprises from her Dad's private toy box.

Her left sleeve hid a miniature directional riot-spray gun, and both her gloves were the contact points for a small disruptor pack at her waist. The cop's daughter lurking behind the student's smile was always alert—strange events tended to gravitate toward her parents, and she had learned to always be at least a little bit on guard.

Her mother had suggested she stay close to school or home for the couple of days she expected to be gone, but when Lexis received the call from the university this morning asking her to come in for her entrance interview, she realigned her priorities, armed herself as semi-legally as she could, and hopped on RedWing. There was a big difference between being alert and ready for trouble and being paranoid in a hidey-hole, paralyzed by fear. Her mother always said that knowing what you were up against was half the battle, and Lexis was well aware her parents both had enemies who might focus their anger on her. She also knew that four cars back in line there was an unmarked 'ghost' cruiser with two highly trained, well-armed, very cute 62s, who were eager to help her mother out by being her protective shadows.

When they commenced their assignment, Dave and Bunji originally wanted to sit in the cruiser on the street and simply watch the house but Lexis had told them they were being silly and they should at least come in where they could keep an eye on her and keep her company. "Besides," she said to the men, "who's going to make sure I do my homework?"

When it came time for her to leave for her interview, though, she refused the offer of a lift in the cruiser. "Look at that blue sky and sun and then tell me I should be in a stuffy cruiser instead of on my cycle. I don't think so, guys. I'll be a good girl, though, and go slow enough for you to keep up." The two 62s, both cycle enthusiasts, couldn't come up with any argument Lexis would listen to, so they simply shrugged their shoulders in resignation and climbed into the cruiser while their young charge fetched her machine from the garage.

Now, sitting at the traffic light, Lexis was still on an emotional high in the aftermath of what was a 'killer' interview. She was feeling even cockier than usual and when the light changed in her favour she acted on impulse and rather than go straight with the rest of the traffic in her lane, she adroitly slipped RedWing through a gap in the lane to her right and zipped onto the cross-street. She knew it would drive her 62s crazy, but if her other follower reacted the way Lexis expected her to, the 62s would become aware they had company.

She'd driven almost a full block before she risked a look back. Damn! The woman was still with her, albeit some distance back, but the cruiser wasn't in sight, yet. Lexis let the car close the distance and change lanes to pull abreast of her. She then increased RedWing's speed just enough that as the car's driver pulled up even with her, they reached a side street and Lexis hit all three brakes, geared down and took RedWing off to the right, leaving her pursuer gaping in surprise while trying to maneuver her cruiser in traffic that wasn't letting her turn.

Lexis accelerated and kicked the trike up two gears before she slowed for a curve in the road, taking her back toward campus. A dark slit of an alley entrance came up quickly and she slipped RedWing into its shadow. Nudging on her comm-unit with her psi, she dialled her guardians' cruiser.

"Lexis? That you?"

"Yes...uh, Roger... or whatever."

"Someone's following you. She's driving a..."

"I know. I've lost her for now, but she may be tracking me."

"If she's any good she won't take long. Do you remember the lunch place we talked about before you went in for your interview?"

"Sure."

"Meet us there. If you don't see us standing on either side of our cruiser when you pull in, get out of there and go you-know-where."

"Okay. Five minutes, and you're buying."

"Yeah, sure. Smart-ass kid. Be careful and we'll see you there."

A light probe told Lexis she'd pulled into a dead-end alley and the possibility of being trapped in there was enough to spark her into action. RedWing's turning radius was short enough to be done in the narrow space, and she was soon back out onto the streets and zigzagging her way through the city's core on her way to the restaurant.

62s Axelrood and Tashna stood in plain sight on either side of their cruiser when Lexis came around the corner, so she figured it was safe to go in. Bunji tapped his ear with a finger while looking directly at her and she psi-nudged her comm-unit on as Bunji spoke through her earpiece.

"Miss Hayz, go twice more around the block and we'll scan for anyone who goes with you."

"Okay. Should I be casual about it or pick up speed to draw them out if they're there?"

"Casual. We don't need you getting a ticket for reckless driving."

"Roger, Bunj. See you guys in a couple of minutes." She took the corner slowly and lost sight of them as she drove past a low building.

She heard the 62s breathing in the two-way radio implants linking her to their cruiser's unit. It wouldn't take her long to get around the block, even at the sluggishly slow pace she was forced to do in traffic. Patience wasn't in her nature, at least when she was on the trike.

"Shit!" The road was blocked.

"Miss Hayz? *Lexis?*" Axelrood broke the silence.

"Nothing to worry about, Dave. There's been a small accident at the light here. None of the vehicles behind me is familiar, though. Hang on. Two guys just got out of the cruiser five back in line and they're walking this way." She dropped her voice to a whisper. As the two men approached, she panicked. "Uh, guys, I don't like the feel of this. The two big-and-thick types are coming my way, on foot. I'm about to break the law, again, so cross your fingers none of your 62 buddies are around."

"Lexis, get here now! And break as many laws as it takes. When you get here park your cycle in front of the restaurant and jump in the back of the cruiser. Don't look for Bunji cuz he'll be behind the wheel. I'll be standing watch. Move it!"

"I'm going as fast as I can! Those two guys have started to run and I'm having trouble getting out of line! Hang on! What's the penalty for driving in a pedestrian area, because I'm about to chase a few walkers."

"Do it, but carefully."

"The guys have turned around and are running back to their cruiser, but traffic is starting to move again. Shit! This is going to be close." Other than the sound of her ragged breathing, Lexis got quiet as she concentrated on negotiating the sidewalk on the trike. She went half a block, peeping her polite little horn to scoot pedestrians out of her way, then managed to get back on the roadway, just ahead of the cleared traffic. "Here I come. I'm back on the road and they're having trouble getting around the accident. We'll have maybe thirty seconds' head start on them. I sure as hell hope you two are ready."

"We are."

Their cruiser was easy to spot in the parking lot as she whipped around the corner. Bunji stood on the passenger side, with both doors open. One hand leaned casually on the vehicle's roof but she couldn't see the other. Hopefully, it held a big gun. She weaved in and out of traffic.

"I see you, Lexis. Watch the entrance to the parking lot—it's the exit, too."

"I see you, too, Dave. I'm coming in on your right but I'm going to stash the cycle in the narrow alley on the far side of the restaurant—let me pass you and follow me over."

"Got it!" As she approached, Bunji craned to stare past her at the traffic while slamming the rear door shut. "It looks clear behind you, but don't trust that."

"Of course not." She zipped into the narrow parking lot and shot past the cruiser. Sacrificing speed for safety so as to not hit any pedestrians or other moving vehicles, she slowly slipped through a gap in the parked rows and into the alley past the all-day vat-beef sandwich place. The electric motor shut off as soon as she dismounted. Dave pulled up across the end of the alley, and Bunji pushed the rear door open for her. She dove in, and Dave got them moving even before the door latch clicked and secured.

"Keep your head down, Lexis. We could tint the windows to hide you but that could draw their attention as quickly as speeding away. We'll take this casually so they don't have any reason to think you may not be hiding in the parking lot. Hopefully, by the time they find RedWing, we'll be out of reach. It's a shame you have to lose that cycle, though. I doubt it'll be there by the time we get back to it. Want us to have City Impound pick it up?"

Lexis pulled off her helmet, tossed a packet of guidance and programming chips onto the front seat next to Bunji, and lay down across the back seat, out of sight. "I wouldn't worry about it. RedWing isn't going anywhere without her brain, and there are only three sets of palm prints that can start her even if they transplant another brain. She's also got a subsonic alarm system to keep anyone from getting too close."

Bunji picked up the chips and examined them. "A *subsonic* alarm?"

"Oh yeah. Dad and I installed it when I was last at his place. It detects motion and sets up a vibrating sphere with a radius of only a meter. The vibration is so low it can't be heard, but it severely affects balance and creates nausea. The closer you get, the more you want to puke. We've never had a chance to field-test it, so let's hope it does what we planned. If we're lucky, it'll at least make them think twice about messing with Hayz & Hayz again."

Dave laughed. "Bunj, I think we have a fighter here. Good thing we joined her side."

"Agreed. Give me a second to get a drone in the air so that we can get a better look."

A little hatch opened in the back of the cruiser and a drone popped out and up. The cruiser moved gently into traffic. Between the seats, she saw Bunji flashing his fingers at the onboard screen.

"Dave, I've got a visual, I think. I'm tracking a cruiser moving slowly across in front of the restaurant, toward the alley. If we don't get further down this street in the next ten seconds we'll be visible. They've stopped at the alley. I'm seeing one passenger and a driver... and they're out of the vehicle." With Lexis slouched below window level and Bunji piloting the drone, the 62s' unmarked cruiser joined the flow of vehicles when the light changed.

TEN

THE CELL WAS BIGGER than Zeke expected, but other than what he'd seen through entertainment media, he really had no basis for comparison. He estimated it to be four square metres, with just enough room for the single bed, the bolted-down desk with the swing-out stool, and the sink-toilet side-by-side. The walls were plain drab grey, the lights bright enough to illuminate his life for the ceiling-mounted cameras, and the alloy bars welded so tightly in place that even *he* would need a cutting torch to get through them. If they'd at least been a form of military-grade glass he might have used psi to find a way out, but the bars were old-school effective. Of course, if he used psi, the small disruptor in the ceiling next to the camera would shut him down.

Or would it? He could tell from the faceplate that it wasn't one of his models, which made it at least five years old. His P-39 model had been standard for at least that long. Quasiox, his prime competitor five years ago, hadn't been able to keep up with his innovations and upgrades, so they'd shifted gears and concentrated their design efforts on consumer-level psi-assisted tools.

So, if the entire Irido facility was outfitted with Quasiox disruptors, Zeke suspected he might have a bit of an edge. Because psionics worked within a particular range of wavelengths, sensors only needed to be capable of detecting that range; but what Zeke had never bothered to reveal even to other ultra-high-psis like Mari, was that he could occasionally work beyond the expected range. He had long suspected such a thing was possible, but he was surprised when he discovered it wasn't upper frequencies he could access, it was the lower ones. He couldn't do fine detail work, like picking locks or adjusting a micrometre, but he could push, pull, and form dense barriers for brief moments, which could deflect both psi and physical objects.

It was a variation of this low-frequency manipulation he'd used to shield and levitate Mari and himself during the wrecking of the solar train. Accessing those wavelengths with consistency had taken a year of steady, daily training, but eventually, it became a reflex. Since he was never one for physical confrontations, he'd never really had much use for it. There were few limits to his regular psi, so playing at the low end was more of a cool trick he'd taught himself.

Zeke was a perfectionist, though, so when he designed his P-39 disruptor series, he included detection and reaction to those lower wavelengths. With anyone else, even his old masters, he had no idea how many high and ultra-high psi users had made the same discovery. He was the *highest* psi, but he wasn't the only one in the over-twenty ultra range. The unit above his head was a Quasiox model, though, and that's all that mattered. With the threats already coming in, Zeke was sure he was going to need his low pulse skills before long. His biggest concern was his physical condition. He was a little out of shape, and on an island prison of alpha males, his body needed to be as solid as his psi.

He got down on the cold floor and did ten push-ups, struggling through the last three. "I fucking hate exercise," he grumbled as much for himself as for the cameras he knew were being closely monitored, at least for his first few days of incarceration. He tried sit-ups next and managed a slow steady twenty. Well, he admitted silently, he had nowhere to go but up, so he bent and twisted and pushed and stretched. It all hurt like hell as he pushed himself harder and harder, but it would give the prison something to talk about when they talked about The Psilent One. What they *wouldn't* talk about was how the small towel under his cot first curled up in a ball by itself, and then gradually moved in a figure-eight pattern, around and around while the disruptor remained quietly unreactive. They might even discuss the odd smile he wore as he worked out, but only because it probably confused them.

oOo

Twenty minutes later, Zeke was deep asleep on his cot, oblivious to the chill in his cell, or the sour, not-laundered-well taint of the blanket he lay on. He'd only intended to lie back and cool off, but he was asleep the moment his eyes closed. How long he was out, he had no idea, but he came fast awake at the clanging of metal on metal.

"624182—come with me."

Zeke rolled over to see a guard he didn't recognize leaning against the barred doorway. "Um..."

"No. Not 'um'. Maybe 'yessir', or 'you betcha' or at least 'sure, whatever', but not 'um.'"

Zeke sat up, swung his legs around, and stood up. "You betcha, sir."

The guard stood a head taller than Zeke, had at least forty kilos more in mass, and could probably take the best punch Zeke could throw and then kill him with a simple backhand, so Zeke was caught off balance by the man's grin. "Call me 'Luger'." He stepped aside to let Zeke step out of his cell, then led the way down the beige-on-beige corridor. "Keep up."

Zeke had no problem matching the man's pace, but it meant he didn't have any spare attention to glance into the cells they passed. Through three barred, section-dividing, alloy doors, and past disruptor array after disruptor array they strode. He was tempted to test the reach of his psi on these devices as well, but he knew this was neither the time nor the circumstance. He may have been stupid enough to steal and then get caught, but he wasn't so complete an idiot as to think they wouldn't expect him to try something in his first few days. Messing around with the towel was one thing, but showing his hand too early would be reckless, possibly suicidal.

They arrived at their destination and it only took a glance for Zeke to clue in and let go of the tension he hadn't realized was building in his neck and shoulders. It was a square room with seats bolted to the floor, facing three of the walls. The fourth wall, the one with the door they had just entered through, was a mirror. More accurately, it was one-way glass, and he hardly needed his psi to determine that. On the wall in front of each seat was a number and a headset. Only three of the seats were occupied, by men in coveralls matching his own.

"You have a call. Number six. You've got five minutes."

"Thank you, Luger." He took the seat, lifted the headset off its hook, and put it on. The ocular piece was missing, so it was obviously going to be audio-only. "Hayz here."

"Daddy! Oh my God! You're really there!"

"Lexis? *What*?" He almost asked her how she got the number, but it was probably listed somewhere, being a government facility and all.

"I guess part of me wanted to believe it was all a mistake and you'd be found innocent or get off with a fine and probation or something."

Ha! "That's wishful thinking, Kiddo. Is everything okay there? They told me your Mom has arranged for a little protection."

"Bunji and Dave. They're great. I'm still trying to get used to the idea that I won't get to see you for a whole year, or even talk to you any time I need to." Her voice cracked a little and his heart stumbled.

Zeke had been thinking the same thing about not seeing her, too, ever since he'd recorded his guilty plea. It would be the hardest part of doing the time he'd agreed to. "It's only a year. I'll be out in no time and *Hayz & Hayz* will be business as usual. Maybe I can even move a little closer to you two, so I can see you more often." He wanted to say more and pour his heart out, but he knew the call was being monitored. Prison was no place to get sappy.

"I'd love that, Dad, but one, Mom's been transferred to Espy Beach and is there now getting set up; and two, I had my interview with the uni this morning, and since I'm sure my Hayz charm won them over, I'll probably be relocating to Kepler City Campus next year, where the engineering school is."

That news was just what Zeke needed to hear. "That's wonderful, L! How does your Mom feel about Espy Beach? A resort town is not exactly a hotbed of terrorist activity."

"That's kind of what I said, but she claims it's not a demotion and it'll be good for us to have a change. She also said she has some personal project she's working on that being stationed at The Beach will be perfect for. Colonel Stihler arranged for the whole transfer."

"Stihler? Well, no surprise there. I guess if your mom is going to have the support of someone on the force, it might as well be her CO. I just wish her CO wasn't Eddie the Torch."

"Daddy! That's *cruel*!"

"No, cruel is that *he* lived, and your Uncle Stan died in the fire *Eddie* started."

"I know, but it was an accident. Even Mom says so."

"That surprises me. She didn't always. She liked Stan, though not as much as Stan liked her."

"Uncle Stan crushed on Mom?"

"Deeply. And he was furious when she ended up with me."

"How could you do that to your own brother?"

"I didn't *do* anything to Stan. Your mother made the choice. At her father's funeral she was so distraught she grabbed hold of me and never let go." Zeke was certain he'd forgotten a few moments in his life over the years, but that funeral was as burned into his memory as his own father's. When Mari clutched his hand he almost pulled away, terrified she'd be able to read his guilty thoughts, but then he squeezed back, out of guilt. Eventually, she left and divorced him, because of the same damned guilt and what it kept locked away from even her.

"That's so sweet. Except she *did* let go, at the divorce."

"She did. And I've never blamed her. It was all me, and the fact that I'm in prison just proves it. Your mother is a hard-nose, but she's also a pretty amazing woman."

"Yeah, she is. I just wish she spoke as highly of you as you do of her."

So did he, but it would never happen. "I broke her heart and I deserve all the anger she throws my way."

"Sometimes I wonder how a by-the-book 62 and a philosophical engineer stayed together as long as you two did, Dad."

"Love. She'll never admit it, but by the time we both graduated, we were so in love that our own career choices didn't matter as much. Then you came along and sealed the deal. If Stan hadn't died three weeks after you were born, I think your mom would have quit the 62s for a quieter, safer career in security."

"Really? I always thought Mom was a 62 through and through. I'll have to talk to her about this."

"You go ahead, but if you mention you talked to me about it, she'll shut right down."

"She doesn't like secrets, Dad. It's her one rule."

He was more aware of that fact than Lexis would ever know. "True, but I won't tell her if you don't. Besides, she and her CO have a good working relationship, and it's best not to mess that up."

"That's sweet of you to think of."

"I'm thinking of *you*, kiddo. If Stihler is happy, your mother is happy, and if she's happy, then you are, too."

"That's a bit simplistic, but I get what you mean. He's actually pretty nice, unless the conversation touches on psi in general, or The Psilent One specifically. He sure hates *you*. He's been to the house a few times over the years and I've learned to steer clear of certain topics of conversation."

"Smart thinking. I expect the LPF is one of those topics. He's always in the news after one of their terror attacks, presenting us with updates of how many of them were caught in *this* raid, and how many killed in *that* raid."

"Not really. In private he's not as militant about them. He dropped by a few months ago, and we got to chatting. I got the impression he actually sympathizes with the terrorists. He even asked what I thought of their cause of making high-psi and low-psi more equal by banning merquilium and shutting down all mining and retrieval operations completely."

"What did *you* say?"

"Well, I sure as hell didn't tell him I was in business with my father, The Psilent One, working with merq to better the world."

"Smart move. Let him direct all his misguided hate *my* way. It makes no difference to me. The hatred is mutual."

"I know, Daddy. And I do understand why, but accidents happen."

He thought about two fathers buried, and neither death an accident. "They do, kiddo. And sometimes they don't."

"What do you mean, Daddy? Are you saying Uncle Stan's death wasn't an accident?"

"PRISONER HAYZ! Time! Twenty seconds. Wrap it up."

"Shit. Sorry, kiddo. I have to go. Thank you for the call. I love you to the sun and back."

"I love you, too, Da—." The line went dead.

Zeke took a slow, deep breath, and returned the handset to the hook. He wasn't sure if the call helped or hurt his mood, but he was sure he needed to maintain control while he was being watched. He was determined to give them nothing to use against him. They knew he had a daughter, and he knew they'd recorded the entire conversation, but they didn't need to know how completely wrapped around his heart Lexis was. He stood and turned. "Thank you, Luger. I appreciate being allowed to speak with my daughter."

The guard cocked his shaved head to one side when Zeke offered a weak smile, but the big man didn't quite smile back. Keep them guessing, Zeke thought. Keep them wondering where the hell he stood, and what his weaknesses in here were.

o0o

Zeke was allowed one night of peaceful sleep in his cell before his world was shoved sideways. It happened in such a cliché moment straight out of the movies that he actually saw the attack coming and was able to shield the blow to his gut with the low-frequency psi. He still doubled over from the immense inmate's punch, but the broken ribs he was supposed to get were reduced to just the wind being knocked out of him. He got caught between two behemoths and they each hit three times, hard and fast. He took the blows and made no attempt to fight back.

"This is for the head-butt, Hayz. And it's a message from Mr. Addox that even in here you're at his mercy. There'll be no more calls from your sweetmeat daughter. Your year of Hell has just begun, and when it's over, just when you think you see the light of release, I will personally end you. And that's a—"

The threat stopped mid-sentence, at precisely the moment when Zeke heard a meaty thump not directed at him. The man hitting him dropped to the ground, unconscious or dead, to be replaced by two men he'd never seen before. The hands pinning his arms back released him too suddenly, and his knees wobbled. One of the men facing him stepped up and took his arm to steady him.

"Bruge Blue sends his regards, Mr. Hayz. You're under his protection, safe. You keep your nose clean with management, and I'll cover you in the population. I'm Hunter."

Holy shit! Zeke was confused. Blue had to have been the one who turned him in in the first place. "Thanks, Hunter?" This made no sense. Zeke thought Blue wanted him dead.

"You okay now, Zeke? You need to see the doctor?"

Zeke forced a smile. His gut hurt like hell, but it could—and should—have been much worse. I'm good, thanks, Hunter. He wasn't trying to kill me, just sending a message."

"From?"

"The Mayor. Ray Addox."

"You sure as hell know how to pick your enemies, buddy. Well, hopefully, His Honor gets the message I just sent *him*." He pointed at Zeke's forehead. "I heard about the head-butt. Your bruise will fade, but you got your rep off to a good start before you even walked through the doors."

"Did I knock him out?"

The big man laughed warmly. "Not even close. But you tried and that's what counts. Just stay clear of him and his people." He nudged the man at his feet who was starting to stir. "Trust no one, Zeke. Even me. We all answer to someone else." Hunter grabbed the prone man by the back of his coveralls and helped him roughly to his feet. They were of similar size, which is to say they were each twice as big as Zeke. Hunter pulled the man in close. "The Psilent One is with

Blue. Pass it around... and make sure *Ray* gets the word." He released the man, who stumbled off, rubbing the back of his neck.

Zeke was impressed. "You took him down with one blow."

"One blow is all it takes if you land it in the right place."

"Will you teach me?" Zeke couldn't believe he was asking Blue's man for lessons in self-defence.

"Me? No. But I'll send someone around who will."

"He's good?"

"Good enough." He stepped to one side. "Now get going to wherever you were off to, Zeke."

"Thanks, Hunter."

"Don't thank me, thank Mr. Blue. If he'd given me the order to kill you, we wouldn't be having this conversation or *any* conversation. Like I said, *trust no one.*"

Zeke swallowed. He was so out of his element in this place. "Thank Mr. Blue, then, please." He too shuffled off, to finally get some lunch. The media had built up The Psilent One as such a badass, uncatchable thief that Zeke had started to believe the hype himself, except he was no badass by any stretch of the imagination. Marisol would do better in here than he would. Without psi, he was unarmed, untrained, and nothing really more than a soft-crime inmate wandering through a hard-max facility with a *Kick Me, I'm Fragile and Famous* sign on his back.

o0o

Using the full-access computer at the Espy Beach 62 Station, Bossy located a privately funded university satellite that recently made a series of passes over the area she suspected was hiding the merquilium vein. The information given to her and Zeke by the psilings was more visual than technical, but there weren't a lot of submarine canyons in the region they'd indicated, so it was relatively easy to deduce the location simply by pouring over the charts collecting dust in the station's storage room.

The chart she picked was old and not detailed enough to suit her, but it was only a matter of accessing the Marine-Net online library to get the degree of detail she needed. The rest of her on-duty crew were patrolling the town, wishing for some of the end-of-week excitement common to Kepler City; the station dispatcher had his own office, and she wasn't due to begin her street patrol for another two hours, so she was uninterrupted. She worked quickly, easily finding the files she wanted. The computer prompted her to enter the latitude and longitude of the central area to be mapped, and she obliged.

The chart was on the screen only long enough for Marisol to glimpse its colours before her whole system crashed. The screen went black, the various operating LEDs darkened and a shiver of alarm raced up her spine. Someone had denied her access. Someone had the authority to block a 62 inquiry. She didn't need the chart now—they'd confirmed her suspicions simply by shutting her down.

A quick psi-probe told her the dispatcher's system was still operational and the shutdown of her terminal hadn't set off any alarms. She decided to risk starting up again. She tapped the reset button on the floor with her boot and proceeded with the six-step start-up. Her first attempt was unsuccessful, but on the second try everything booted up as it should have.

Now that she was sure of the location of the LPF operation, she suspected some of the files she'd already examined had to be reviewed again in this new light. She started with arrest reports going back six months and from there worked over the records of cargo-capable seagoing vessels whose courses lay in the general direction of the canyon.

By the time the dispatcher called her to take her relief duty, Mari's personal onboard system was loaded with a score of files deserving detailed perusal. Before shutting her desk system off, she sent an innocently worded email to Slim Wilkes. To anyone else, the missive was nothing more than a casual greeting, but to the quartermaster, it said Bossy was finally onto something and he should expect to hear from her through one of the secure drop-boxes she had established with the 62s of her old unit.

oOo

The sky over Espy Beach was clear, and down by the boardwalk, the air was damp and chill, with a cold breeze blowing in off the Spinnaker Sea. Mari finished her foot patrol of the beach area, then mounted her hoverbike and began her last quick tour of the four main streets of Espy Beach before returning to the station to finish off the shift with two incident reports.

The streets were quiet. As she approached the Luxton Theatre's full parkade, she remembered that a new musical was premiering in town and anyone who was anyone was probably at the pre-curtain reception. Slowing to read the marquee as she passed the theatre itself, Marisol didn't see the gun-metal-grey pursuit buggy emerge from the shadows of the alley opposite the theatre. The buggy was nearly on top of her when her psi set off warning bells in her head. Reflexes tightened her hand on the brake and she swerved, reducing the impact to a mere nudge.

The hoverbike shuddered, but the buggy accelerated away. Easily regaining control, Mari steered back into her lane and the chase was on. Her psi enveloped the bike and within a heartbeat, she initiated the tracking system, pursuit lights, and claxon, armed the weapons, and keyed on her helmet mic.

"Patrol Cycle One-Seven to Espy Base, I am in pursuit of an unidentified buggy for reckless driving and speeding. No ID plate on display, invisi-grey in colour, full-tint windows. Number of occupants is unknown. Heading south on Tidal Drive. Request available units converge. Vehicle attempted to ram this officer's vehicle before fleeing." With the hoverbike's better maneuverability and speed, she caught up with the fleeing buggy easily.

"Espy Base to PC One-Seven. One unit is available to assist, but ETA is three minutes. Please keep us apprised of any changes in route of pursuit. We have you on screen. Record pursuit if not already doing so. We will attempt vehicle identification from this end. Word of warning—Tidal Drive at The Split reverts to one way and as this is an 'odd' day you will be travelling the wrong way if pursuit reaches that point. Air Buggy 3 is warming up. Go get 'em, Captain. Espy Base, out."

"Roger, base. I copy. I'm gaining quickly and expect electronic disabling guns to be in range in ten seconds. Keep Air-3 in his stall. This will all be over soon. One-Seven, out." The buggy swerved into a gap in thin oncoming traffic but slipped back after passing a slow-moving mini-bus. The bus pulled to the curb in response to the cycle's klaxon and lights and Mari passed it without blinking or slowing.

Traffic began to thicken, forcing both vehicles to slow. At the sound and sight of the 62 Cycle in pursuit, most vehicles moved out of the way, but Mari still couldn't get a clear shot at the fleeing buggy. Another alternative existed and she reached out with her psi for the buggy's power source. Before she could trigger the reaction she wanted, though, the buggy slipped through two lanes of oncoming traffic and down a side street leading out of the city.

"PC One-Seven to Espy Base. Suspect vehicle has switched over to Sanders Avenue, eastbound." She swerved her way across the two lanes and onto Sanders Avenue but the buggy was gone. She checked the tracker. "Pursuit now onto Luckhardt Lane, south. She geared down and rounded the corner into the laneway.

"I see him. Electronic disruptor armed, locked on, in three...two...one." What appeared to be a lightning pulse erupted from the nose of the bike's weapons array and struck the buggy broadside as its driver attempted another change of direction. The power systems of the buggy immediately shorted out and the buggy coasted to a stop.

"Got him. Closing in. My psi picks up two persons in the vehicle." She was twenty meters from the buggy and slowing when the emergency charges blew the buggy's doors off and two shots were fired from the dark interior of the vehicle. The first shot hit the bike's cowling and rocked the vehicle. The second shot blew out the whole front end.

"Goddamned explosive shells!" Bossy landed with as much grace as possible but even with the psi-cushion she managed to throw out, her roll became a tumble and she bounced along Luckhardt Lane to stop, stunned, a few meters from the gap-sided buggy. As she struggled to sit up, a third shot came from the darkness of the vehicle's interior and hit her green-and-white-armoured chest dead centre.

ELEVEN

NEWS OF THE SHOOTING of Captain Boissiere in Espy Beach spread quickly through the 62 Complex in Kepler City. The colonel's voice edged up in pitch as he shouted through the open office door.

"Get me an update on the Boissiere shooting, and get me the Espy Beach Hospital, now! Nobody shoots one of my officers and gets away with it." A moment later the comm-unit rang and he turned away to answer it.

"Stihler." His aide's face came on the screen.

"Colonel, I have the hospital's Chief of Staff, Dr. Eldon Winnicki. Here you go, sir." The face on the comm-unit faded to become a distinguished fiftyish man in a rather expensive imported suit. A strong, professional voice greeted Stihler.

"Dr. Winnicki, here. How can I help you, Colonel?"

Stihler forced his anger down and became the professional administrator he was. "I'd like a status report on Captain Boissiere, if you have a moment, doctor."

"Certainly. It may be a cliché, but this is a case of good news-bad news. The good news is that Captain Boissiere has only two cracked ribs and bruises on most of her upper body where she should only have a gaping hole and shredded organs. She should not be alive, but her Psi-23 saved her, apparently."

"Saved her how?"

"Well, we won't know for sure until she can answer a few questions—and at this point, we have no idea when that might be. We *assume* that in the fraction of a second before the blast hit her, the captain was able to surround herself in a nearly solid manifestation of psionic energy."

The colonel's professional mien faded quickly with the discussion of Mari's superior psi. "Impossible, doctor. It must have been her body armour that saved her."

The doctor shook his head. "We originally thought so, too, Colonel, but the armour doesn't show signs it took much of the blast. It's damaged, yes, but not as severely as we expected. So little is known about psionics that to say 'impossible' is unreasonable. 'Unlikely' may be a better choice. As I said, though, we'll have to ask Captain Boissiere herself, and that's where the bad news comes in. Her mind has retreated into what we are tentatively calling a psi-coma—her shields have shut *us* out, and *her* in. Other than the fact that her bodily functions are working fine, there is no indication of higher-level brain activity whatsoever. She has literally locked us out, Colonel, and there's not a damned thing we can do but wait for her to emerge on her own."

"Do you see a need to transport her here, to a city hospital?"

"No need at all, Colonel. There's nothing to do but wait, and we're equally set up for that here." The doctor glanced at someone out of range of the comm-unit then returned his attention to the call. "I'm sorry, Colonel, but I have to go. I'll send a full report to your office as soon as I can. Should you have any further questions please don't hesitate to call my office. They'll find me and put the call straight through."

"Thank you, Doctor. I'll be in touch." The screen went dark as both men broke the connection. Stihler called his aide. "Call The Beach and have them double security at the hospital. Overtime is authorized. No one fucks with the 62s."

o0o

Trapped and confused by the trauma, Mari's mind grasped at memories until it latched onto one of her time at DeepHole Lunar Prison on Anguta.

The tunnel split but First Lieutenant Boissiere didn't hesitate, taking the darkened left fork at a run. With her psi extended in front of her, tracking the

Breaker was easy, even if she hadn't been able to hear his big-footed stumbling ahead of her. Had she not been armed, she wouldn't even be chasing this serial killer trying to vanish into the depths of the prison colony, but he was a pivotal witness in a trial and her CO implied that if she didn't bring him back she might as well stay down in the caves herself.

Her probe showed there were no more branches off of this tunnel for almost half a kilometre and then the splits came by the dozen. It became a foot race for 500 meters but she still had a few tricks up her armoured sleeve. She slowed her pace for a few strides to tighten her psi concentration on the terrain ahead of the Breaker. Timing was the key to her plan and just as the convict moved into the narrow section of the tunnel, Bossy punched his shields with her Psi-23.

(LUDWIG!)

She caught him off guard and Ludwig turned, probably expecting to see 'that Peace Force bitch' right behind him. It was this moment of distraction Mari was watching for and, in that split second of time, she narrowed her psi and used it to shove a head-sized rock from the edge of the tunnel into his path. His feet followed a map his own psi probed and constructed in his mind as he went but, as Mari knew, the obstruction was now behind the probe head and, therefore, not seen. The toe of the Breaker's left boot jammed into the face of the rock and, in a tangle of arms and legs, Ludwig caromed into the wall and bounced to a stop, facedown in the dust. A moment later, Mari was there, spraying a sticky, moist, steel-strong restraint web over her prisoner's body to pin him down.

"Move and you're a dead Breaker, Ludwig."

"I go back to the cell area and I'm a dead man anyway. Either kill me now or let me up so I can get at my body-pouch. There's ten thousand credits in it and it's yours if I get cut loose and vanish."

She increased the charge in her pistol until it was humming audibly. "Or I could blow your damned head off and take the money anyway. If I kill you in the next few seconds I'll even have time to find the other ninety-thousand you have wrapped around your body."

"You fucking *bitch*." The Breaker struggled against the web but Mari's probe showed that the restraint was holding fast.

"You calling me names is limiting my choices, Ludwig. I may just kill you in anger and walk away. My tour of duty here is up next week and it'll be at least that long before they find your ugly carcass if the cave beetles don't just strip your bones clean and make a nest of what's left. We found one of those yesterday in H Sector. The queen beetle was quite proud of the brood she'd raised in the skeleton and she put up quite a fight. We only needed a DNA sample for an ID, and then we let her back in."

"Fuck you!"

"Yup, the two or three thousand beetle babies literally hummed with pleasure when they reclaimed their home. It's too bad Prisoner Speckler couldn't share the overwhelming joy the new inhabitants of his carcass were experiencing." She slipped a pair of Lite-Steel cuffs out of their pouch and opened them one-handed, the other hand keeping the gun pointed between the Breaker's shoulder blades.

"So, Ludwig, what's it to be?"

"Fuck you, slag!"

"I love your vocabulary, Breaker. You're a real charmer." She leaned closer. "Now, be a good boy and hold still while I cuff you. If you so much as twitch I'll blow your kneecap off and still make you walk back." The Breaker froze, holding his breath until he heard the snick of the first cuff and felt it tighten around his ankle.

"HEY! That's my goddamned leg, you crazy bitch!"

"You betcha, Stretch." She latched the other cuff on his other ankle. "Don't worry, though, I've got a second set for your wrists. It may make for a slow walk home, but we'll *both* get there alive." She sprayed the solution that dissolved the restraint webs. "Now, what did I say about not moving?"

o0o

Zeke sat in the prison's yard with his back to a wall, observing his fellow inmates through half-closed eyes. Word spread quickly that he was under Bruge Blue's protection, but that didn't stop the nearly steady stream of wanderers shuffling past him and muttering threats. The favourite theme was low psi threats against his high psi, usually about the LPF levelling the playing field. He was sure the LPF were the ones behind the merquilium mess the psilings needed his help with, he just hoped whatever the psilings needed him to do wouldn't go critical while he was incarcerated.

A boot squeaked softly on the rubber gravel to his left so he looked up, but the tall, slender man had the sun behind him, and Zeke could only see his silhouette. "Hunter sent me."

"Um. Okay. Does he want me to go somewhere?" He struggled to his feet and shaded his eyes so he could better see the messenger. He was an everyman, a true middleweight, though yet another man taller than Zeke. Racially, he was as mixed as almost everyone else in the solar system—short-cropped reddish-brown hair, with light brown skin, and single-lidded blue eyes.

"He sent me to teach you to defend yourself. To keep you safe until Mr. Blue decides what to do with you."

Zeke extended his hand. "I'm Hayz."

The man hesitated a moment, then shook Zeke's hand. The grip was cautious, but strong as a rock. "I am Derin."

"Thank you, Derin. When do we start?"

"We're here in the yard for another hour. Let's make use of the time. Follow me." He led them around the yard to the area where Hunter and about thirty other inmates milled about, exercising, playing checkers, or arm wrestling. "I have only two rules, Psilent One. Firstly, you do what I say, when I say, regardless of any pain. Two, no psi. You use psi and I will know. We will be done. I train bodies and all bodies are equal. The LPF bastards are too violent with all their bombings and murders, but they are right that the playing field should be level. Are we agreed?"

"Of course, Derin. Can I add something, though?"

"Add away."

"I've used psi pretty much all my life. In the outside world, it was what I did to pay the bills, and put food on the table. You're asking me to stop cold what I do now by reflex. I promise to do my best to not use psi, but I ask that you cut me some slack in the beginning, while I'm learning. I'm just asking for patience. Please."

Derin looked at him closely, hopefully considering the request. "Yes. Patience I can do. But don't push your luck. My goal is to teach you to stay alive when you cannot use your mighty psi."

"Thank you."

"Now move *that* bench to *there*, and *that* bench to *there*." He indicated which benches and where to move them with two quick waves of his hand.

Zeke moved to the first bench quickly, glad to now have something to occupy both his mind and his body. He gripped the sides of the three-meter-long bench and lifted. Or, at least, he tried to lift it. It moved a centimetre off the ground, so he knew it wasn't bolted down, but it had to weigh sixty or seventy kilos. He bent his knees, tightened his grip, and tried again. He managed to lift the bench a bit higher, but there was no way he could walk with it.

But Derin had said to 'move' them. He hadn't specified he had to 'carry' the benches. Zeke pushed the bench over on its side, then grabbed one support and flipped it again, until it was upside down. He moved around to the end of the bench nearest its destination, picked up the end, dragged the bench backwards to the new spot, and struggled to get it upright. He approached the second bench but stopped short. Everyone in the vicinity was alternately watching him and watching Derin. Since no one told him what he was doing was wrong, he moved the second bench in the same way and set it up where Derin wanted it.

"Well done, Hayz. Some of the boys are expecting me to kick your ass for not doing what I asked, but I only said 'move' the benches. You tried the obvious choice, found it wasn't going to work for you, and then you discovered a method that would. Let me ask you something. Be honest. If you were at home and you had to move these benches, would you have used psi?"

"Yes."

"Would it have been difficult?"

"Not at all."

"Hmm. I have a better idea for today. What is your psi? Rumours are it's high, but there are always rumours."

Zeke wasn't too comfortable talking psi, especially *his* psi, in the company of men he didn't know, but he hardly had a choice. He had agreed to do what Derin told him to, and that probably included answering questions. Maybe if they knew more about high psi life, the low psi portion of the population would better understand what he was trying to do with his research and tools. "I'm a 24."

"Bullshit," came a voice from the back of the gathered group.

"Not bullshit. I can't prove it to you in here, but I've been tested so often since I was a kid that my results are public record. I am the only registered psi-24 in the Kokopelli System. If there's someone as strong as I am, they are keeping it a damned good secret."

"Can you read minds?" Someone else asked.

Zeke looked directly at the man and nodded. "Sadly, yes. It's why I invented the no-psi collars. To protect everyone's thoughts from people like me."

"*You* invented those? Why? You could rule the planet if you can read minds."

"The truth? I don't really want to know what the fuck people are thinking. When I was a kid I heard stray thoughts coming at me like insects of ideas, buzzing around and driving me mad. I made the first collar for myself, to block everyone else out. I don't want to rule the world, I just want to invent shit, raise my daughter, and teach people of every psi level how to best use their gift."

"You think it's a gift?"

"Well, sort of, but like being tall or strong or fast or smart are gifts. The only difference is you can only get a little bit taller with surgery, and a lot stronger with training, but your psi is your psi. You can no more change it than you can change your blood type. The Koshari Collegium I founded does for psi what Derin does for self-defence, or what weight lifting does for muscles."

"Can you kill with psi?"

Zeke knew telling the truth would give him a badass reputation in the prison, but word would also spread fast and far and he hardly needed the media getting ahold of a story that The Psilent One was in prison bragging about how high-psi masters can kill with their minds. "No. I can't."

"But is it possible?"

"Maybe, but I've never met anyone with that kind of power. I wouldn't even know where to start."

"Too bad."

"What other shit have you invented?"

"Well, the entire line of Hayz Tools is mine. They're all psi-assisted tools and most of them require only a psi-3 or higher to get some results with."

"Hayz Tools? Are you fucking with me? My old man's shop was full of them. What he didn't spend on chill-pills, he spent on shit from Hayz Tools. The man could build *anything* when he wasn't too busy beating the shit out of me." Hayz and the others looked at the speaker, a man almost the size of Hunter, with knife scars up and down both arms and all over his hands. "Hate to say it, Zeke, but your tools work just fine. It was one of your compression drivers that I finally used on the old man and why I'm in here." He smiled like he'd just met his new best friend.

"I... I'm glad you're pleased with our product. Did you have time to write an online review before they arrested you?"

"Shit, Zeke! That's *why* they arrested me. I posted a review *and* a photo!"

The entire group roared with laughter, and for a moment Zeke felt like he was just hanging out with a bunch of guys. They spent the rest of their break in the island sunshine questioning Zeke about high psi and low psi, and what kind of stuff his collegium taught. In the end, he and Derin agreed to train in the yard for the first hour of every break, every day, and Zeke agreed to keep up the conversations about using psi, even though none of them could use even a whisper of power within the prison. The one topic Zeke managed to steer the conversations away from was how many of the psi-restraint devices and law enforcement tools he was responsible for. He was sure his popularity would die a fast and painful death if his fellow inmates knew how many of them had been caught by tools he'd invented just to keep his now ex-wife cop safe.

o0o

Deep within her memories, Mari reached across the small table and stabbed the last of Zeke's dessert with her fork while his attention was drawn to the action on the slowly filling dance floor of her cousin, Piko's, restaurant. It was the end of the workweek and Marisol and Zeke had come to Piko's Place to celebrate.

The last of the icing quickly licked from her lips, Mari met her husband with her best "I'm-completely-innocent" smile when he turned back to her.

"Dance, Love?" He stood and held out his open hand for her to take. She took a leisurely sip of wine to wash down the stolen cake before accepting his hand.

"Of course, Hon."

Hand-in-hand, the lovers stepped onto the dance floor. While four or five other dancing couples swayed to the rhythm in each other's arms, Mari and Zeke stepped, turned and dipped their way around the illuminated floor. Eventually, they were the only dancers still in motion and when the song ended, band members, diners, and fellow dancers applauded politely. The young couple answered them with a playful curtsy and bow, and the band started in on another song.

They slowed their pace, somewhat, but the grace and style of an obviously romantic dance pair were still very much apparent. Mari kept her eyes closed most of the time, just letting Zeke, the one glass of wine, and the music lead her. It was nearly half an hour later before Zeke begged off for a drink break, and Mari thought it a good time to check in with the babysitter keeping an eye on baby Lexis.

"Order me a glass of sherry, please. I'm just going to call home." She picked up her purse at the coat check, located her comm unit, and made for a quiet hall at the back of the restaurant. Like most public dining places, personal comm unit use was banned while at the table—a rule ignored only if one never wanted to come back to Piko's Place.

The Hayz's weren't the only patrons celebrating the end of the work week, and as Mari strolled down the hallway toward the back rooms the sounds of a group of a dozen or so revellers making the most of cheap wine and the isolated private room burst out into the hall. When she rounded the corner and came into sight of the group a slurred cheer went up.

"Awright! 'Nother party...er! Somebuddy giver a drinky."

"Hey d'licious, wasser name, hunh?"

The layout of the large restaurant was such that the noise from the group never really went beyond the hallway. Piko had intentionally designed it this way and as Marisol turned and walked back toward the sounds of the band in the main dining room, she was appreciative of Piko's foresight. Unfortunately, a call home in the midst of that boisterous bunch was out of the question.

For a moment, she considered drawing her badge from her purse and exerting her authority long enough to make her call, but it would only hurt her cousin's business, and she was never one to abuse her authority just to make life easier. Besides, Piko's office upstairs was nearly soundproof and, being family, she was always welcome to use it. *His* office was *her* office, he claimed. In fact, once or twice Piko had caught her stepping outside to make a call and had chastised her.

The sound of the band still luring couples to the dance floor quickly cut off as she went through the two doors leading to the office area. Piko's door was simply marked with a large, polished silver 'P', and she quickly extended a probe into the room to confirm it was empty. It was, and more out of respect than habit, she tapped twice on the door before letting herself in.

Piko was fond of dark colours, and his rich office reflected his taste—it was black and chocolate everywhere she looked. The office was warm, like a cave or den, and Marisol moved over to the soft, dark couch where she could put her sore feet up while she checked on the baby. She casually tossed her clutch purse onto the low mock-wood table beside the couch but there was an unexpected clink of metal on glass when it landed.

In the shadow of an abstract tabletop sculpture she'd never really understood, was a pipe. Not a water or gas conduit, but a smoking pipe. Even in the low light, it was obviously a narco-pipe with half a hit still in its transparent aluminum bowl. Even if it had been empty, there was a one-hundred-gram package of crystals next to it. Marisol cursed. One of Piko's employees was sneaking into his office for their hit, and now she had to be the one to break it to her cousin. Normally this wouldn't have been a big deal, but most of Piko's employees were Piko's relatives—cousins, nieces, and nephews, mostly—and that meant they were Marisol's family as well.

It took less than two clicks on the wall clock for Marisol to decide that her first responsibility was as a 62. She plugged her comm unit's earpiece in and tapped the number of the 62 Complex dispatch desk into her handset. Dispatch answered on the second ring.

"Peace Force 62s, Kepler City dispatch desk. Sergeant Labiuk speaking." A broad, moustachioed, late-thirties 62 came on the screen.

"Labiuk, it's Boissiere-Hayz. I've got a narc offence here at Piko's Place on Fifth. Do me a favour and send someone with a bit of seasoning and who has enough tact to use the back door?"

"Sure, Bossy. Isn't Piko your..."

"...cousin? Yeah. That's why I'd like this handled quietly. I don't know who the perp is, yet. As soon as we're done here, I'll find Piko and he can help me narrow down the list."

"Howsabout Pallagi? He's only a minute or two away."

"Good choice. Tell him I'm in the manager's office on the second floor."

"Done. Labiuk out."

"Boissiere-Hayz out."

Marisol psied the 'disconnect' button on her earpiece and picked up her purse. Since she was hardly dressed like a 62 in her teal cocktail dress, wearing her badge on her thin, decorative belt was the best she could do. Before closing up her clutch, she considered taking out her little stun gun but it was hardly called for in the situation. She did need to find Piko, though, before Pallagi arrived, so, not wanting to leave the evidence unattended, she dropped herself into a chair in the shadows and focused her psi into a wave probe.

Before she could initiate the wave, however, the side door to the office opened and Piko rushed in, followed closely by Carla, his newest girlfriend who also happened to be one of the few non-family-member wait-staff. Both had more zippers and buttons undone than they did done up, and both were having difficulty walking.

"Where's the pipe?" Giggle.

"On the table, where you left it."

"Need another hit."

"Bring it this time. Leaving it was dumb."

"That's an understatement," Mari pointed out.

Piko stumbled into the desk as he tried to turn to the source of the new voice, his legs moving a beat after his torso. "Who said that?"

Mari pushed herself up off the couch, making certain her badge was visible. She held her open purse in one hand while the other was prepared to reach in for her pistol.

"Damn, Cuz! You scared the crap outta me. I thought we were busted."

Carla noticed the badge first. "We *are* busted. Shit."

"No worries. She's family." He still didn't see the badge, or if he did, he didn't take it seriously.

Marisol shook her head slowly and, stoned as he was, Piko understood.

"Mari, c'mon. It's just a pipe. Look away and it vanishes." He picked up the pipe.

"Can't. You left your crystals out, too. I've already called it in. I didn't know it was you."

As if he'd waited for a cue, there was a knock at the door, and it swung open to reveal an armoured Corporal Pallagi, his massive frame and no-nonsense stance blocking most of the light from the hall. His gun was holstered but the holster was unsnapped and his hand was ready to draw the weapon if need be.

"I believe someone paged me?" He nodded a sober welcome to Mari, looked at Piko, and stepped into the room. "Sir, please place the pipe on the table and put your hands on top of your head."

By the time Pallagi snapped the restraints on his two suspects, read them their rights, gathered the evidence, searched the office, and bagged another 'half' of crystals, Zeke had come looking for Mari. He stopped in the doorway when he spotted his cousin-in-law in handcuffs.

"What's happened?"

"I'm sorry, Honey. I'll tell you when I get home. I didn't get a chance to check on Lexis."

"Are you okay?"

"I'm fine. I'll explain later. I'm afraid our date is over, though."

"You're arresting your own *cousin*?"

"Zeke, please. Not now." She took Carla by the elbow and led her toward the door. Zeke stepped aside to let her pass. He looked more disappointed and heartbroken than Piko. The memory blew away in swirling smoke, and Mari just wanted to cry. That night at Piko's was the worst one of her career, and although Piko hadn't done any serious time, and soon forgave her, she never really forgave herself.

TWELVE

L EXIS SAT AT THE kitchen table trying to teach Bunji the finer points of
MoebeusGammon. For the sake of the lesson the moves weren't timed,
making it 3-D rather than 4D, but the 62 was still losing badly. At least Dave
was asleep in the spare bedroom, not witnessing Bunji's humiliation.

After leaving the restaurant parking lot, the trio agreed it was best if they
stayed put. Dave and Bunji decided to take shifts and Lexis had wanted to object,
but the memory of how close the men in the cruiser had been before she'd
managed to slip away chilled any argument she could come up with. She'd fed
the two 62s, done her homework, and was now determined to coach Bunji in
her favourite pastime.

While muddling through the game, she watched as Lt Bunji Tashna listened
to the sounds of the strange house, probably trying to separate the mundane
from the potentially dangerous. His eyes kept darting from the game to the
portable perimeter monitor he'd brought in from the cruiser and programmed
for the house. In their conversations, Lexis learned that when Bunji and Dave
had started the assignment it had been as a favour to Bossy and neither had
taken the posting too seriously. They'd expected to sit at the end of the driveway,
escort a little girl to school, and generally babysit—a waste of time and P-Force
resources, but anything Bossy asked for they were happy to do. Lexis was glad
they were.

A beep from the perimeter monitor snatched Bunji's attention to the monitor. He tapped a few qualifiers into the small keypad and the image on the screen magnified to show an animal about the size of a small child.

Lexis leaned forward to get a better look at the screen. "Nothing serious, I hope. It's your move."

"Just an animal." He looked back at the twisting and wrapping Mobius strips of the game board. "Where are we?"

"Eight, three and six. I've just bumped two to the bar. What was the animal doing?"

"Nothing. It moved into the range of the monitor and stopped. It's about two-and-a-half meters up a tree at the back of the house. Want me to chase it off?"

"No. He's been here before. He used to set off the property sensors but he never approached closer than the big tree so we adjusted the system to ignore anything smaller than a four-year-old child. He likes to suck on the leaves of the tree and I have a soft spot for animals."

"What is it?"

"I don't know. I can sense it and I can see its heat signature on the monitors but when I look into the tree I can never find it, even when I know exactly where it is. Now Mom and I just accept him as one of the neighbours. Every now and then he brings a friend or two, but, generally speaking, he hangs out alone."

"How do you know it's a 'he'?"

"Mom referred to it as 'he' one day and it stuck."

"What would you say his mass is?"

"Mass? About fifteen kilos. Why?"

Bunji tapped the keypad again. "I might as well adjust my equipment to ignore him, too."

"Okay, but it's still your move."

The image faded off the monitor's screen and Bunji turned his attention back to the game. Lexis rolled the dice and moved her own piece in two quick motions. "And this game is done."

"So what else is new?"

"Another?"

"I'll pass, thanks. Time for another circuit of the house." He stood, the stool scraping back on the ivory-coloured ceramic floor.

"This house has a better monitoring system than your 62 headquarters. Relax."

"Not in my nature. You were telling me earlier how important your father's research and development is to you both and how seriously you treat it when you're in his lab, right?"

"Yeah."

"Well, this job of mine... I take it *very* seriously. I was your age when I enlisted and thanks to hard work and some lucky breaks, I've made it to Second Lieutenant in four years. I'm a career 62, like your Mom. I'm not just on 62 payroll right now, I'm on an assignment for Bossy, which means that instead of one hundred percent I'm giving a hundred and ten. I can't 'relax' because it would be dangerous. We learned that with our little chase incident."

"You would know about anyone coming near the house."

"Maybe." He picked up the portable perimeter monitor and went out into the backyard. In the spare bedroom Lexis knew Dave slept on, his alarm not set to wake him for another two hours.

o0o

The lights in the cells went out on schedule, but Zeke was already asleep. It had been a long day, and the conversations about life with psi had stirred up a lot of memories. One of those memories now slithered into his dreams. It was his fifteenth birthday and his parents were arguing.

The first angry words were thrown down in challenge by his dad after the dinner was done and the two Hayz boys were back upstairs studying. Zeke remembered it clearly because was on his way back downstairs to ask if he could leave for a party when his father spit the words out.

"Jules, when a person's shields are locked up it means *KEEP OUT*. I didn't appreciate you pushing and prodding them while I was trying to enjoy my son's birthday dinner."

Julianna's voice came back softly but firmly. "There's something wrong. I can feel it."

"Yes, there is, but it's *my* problem!"

"Since when? We've always been an 'our problem' family."

At this point, his parents sensed Zeke on his way down the stairs and cloaked their anger. His mother was the first to change gears.

"Zeke, on your way to the party, now?"

"Yup." He was torn between wanting to know what his parents were arguing about and not wanting to admit to himself they weren't always the perfect family, like their friends and neighbours, the Boissieres.

"Do you need a ride wherever you're going, son?" Zeke suspected his dad needed an excuse to get away from the argument.

"Sure." At least it would stop them from fighting.

"Brayd, we'll finish this later."

"Yes dear, I'm sure you will." Zeke tasted the sarcasm as it flitted past and caught his mother right in the chest. Tears welled up in her eyes as she held back her retort, and he followed his dad out in the midst of the fat silence.

As far as Zeke knew, that was the last time his mother and father spoke. Three hours later two 62s arrived at the house to inform the family that his dad's cruiser was now just a lump of smouldering, molten slag on the other side of the city. The bomb—for that much they were sure of—had utterly destroyed the car and its contents.

o0o

In his cell, Zeke woke from the dream in a cold sweat, got up, took a piss, and stumbled back to bed. Sleep was sporadic. He'd close his eyes and wake up twenty minutes later, or close his eyes and not sleep at all for an hour. Eventually, he gave up trying to sleep at all and did push-ups and sit-ups until he couldn't move. He fell asleep on the floor, in the middle of his cell, and that's where he was when the lights came on and his cell door slid open. He didn't recognize the guard, and that concerned him.

"Got a visitor, prisoner. Follow me, now."

Zeke did as he was told, but as he shook off the sleep, he did his best to stay alert. Something was off. He was led through the cellblocks and out into the administration area. A dozen doors surrounded a central desk with a single guard at his station, but only one of the doors was open. Zeke was shoved through the doorway with a simple warning. "Get no closer than one meter. We're watching."

In the room was a metal table and two utilitarian, metal chairs. In the chair on the far side of the table was his attorney, Jillayn.

"Hello, Zeke. Please sit. How are you doing?"

"Um. I've been better, but that goes without saying. I've got half the population wanting to kill me and the other half protecting me. I couldn't keep my head down and nose clean if I tried."

"Then you'll be happy about my news. We finished presenting our case that the relic laws are unconstitutional, and the three judges are currently deliberating. We expect a decision by midday tomorrow, and it looks like it'll go in our favour."

"So what will that mean?"

"It'll mean your crimes weren't capital ones and guilty or not, you should not be incarcerated. The most you would be hit with are heavy fines and community service, much like what you've already agreed to. What it will mean is that once the judges have ruled, our motion to overturn your conviction will hit the desk of Magistrate Hegler and she will stamp it approved. She's already agreed to go along with the decision of the Constitutional Rendering. I expect you'll be released by dinner tomorrow."

"But I agreed to do the time, with no appeal."

"True, but we started this constitutional challenge ages ago. The crimes you pled guilty to won't exist in a day and a half, so your plea will be null and void.

As a goodwill gesture, though, we will agree to the fines and service, as stipulated in your plea. That should muzzle some of the whiners."

The thick wire of stress wrapped around Zeke's spine relaxed. Breathing came easier and the knot in his gut unraveled and slithered away. He was still concerned, though. "This is going to make the LPF furious. I suppose there's no way we can keep this quiet, is there?"

"Sorry. Not a chance. There are currently one hundred and three people serving sentences for possession of Old Earth Relics, and they'll all be affected by the decision, so maybe we can make *them* the focal point for the media."

"I suppose. I'm worried about the safety of everyone at your firm, though. Because of the threats you described."

"We're working on a big press push involving the many private museums and institutes that will now have access to the relics. Plus, there will be a grace period for people who wish to register their relics and can prove provenance, as you can with yours. With luck, the details of the various relics and what they represent of Old Earth will flood the news feeds and wash away the news of your release. We're still going to keep our security levels up for a while."

"Then I guess we can celebrate when I get out."

"Hopefully. Though you may be a bit busy to celebrate. Your ex-wife, Captain Boissiere, was the target of an attack in Espy Beach and is in the hospital. Physically she's good, but her shields went up hard and fast and have stayed that way."

"Oh shit! What about Lexis?" His gut churned and his bowels threatened to loosen.

"Your daughter was still in Aldrintowne and is safe. The two 62s assigned to her will remain with her. Depending on what happens with you, we're prepared to move her to Espy Beach to be near her mother or let her stay with you. If you both want to go to The Beach, that can be arranged, too."

"We will. Lexis will want to be close to her mother, and maybe I can be of use in getting Marisol to lower her shields."

"I'll make the arrangements. Now, it would be best if you told no one about the topic of our conversation. They'll find out soon enough when the decision comes down and you're released."

"But I'm making friends in here. Do I really have to leave?"

For a moment Jillayn thought he was serious, but she knew him well enough to catch on. "No, you don't. That can be arranged, too. You have a day and a half to decide, smart-ass. Now, are we done?" She reached for the notebook.

"Yes. Thank you, Jillayn."

"You're welcome. We'll chat again, soon."

"That would be nice."

He stood, and the door behind him opened abruptly. Without a word, the guard grabbed him roughly by the arm and escorted him back to his cell. Zeke assumed that his feeling something was off balance was simply because he was in prison, and nothing was more out of whack than that. His cell door slid shut behind him. He estimated he had an hour before breakfast, so he lay down, closed his eyes, and tried to find the sleep that had been eluding him earlier.

o0o

The cell door slid back open with a soft thud, bumping Zeke out of his brief dream, but it was thick, grabbing hands dragging him out of his bed and slamming him on the floor that kicked him the rest of the way out of sleep. He curled into a defensive ball and wrapped as much low-frequency psi around him as he dared.

THIRTEEN

"**B**RUGE BLUE CAN'T PROTECT you in here, Hayz. My big brother, Ray, wants to make sure you know exactly how much *your* life is in *his* hands." The words were punctuated with kicks and punches. "You can play your little games with Blue, but when an Addox says jump, you fucking *jump*." Zeke didn't dare look up. He kept his head tucked in and protected, so the blows went for his back and ribs. "You think you'll be getting out of here because of some constitutional bullshit, do you, Hayz? You're only getting out of here in a fucking *bag*. And when I'm done tearing you apart, I'll send someone to hurt your little girl while he tells her how you curled up in a ball like a coward and did nothing to stop me."

Three sets of slippered feet kicked and stomped at his low-frequency armour, but Zeke only cared about the set attached to the voice. If he was going to die, he was going to do it protecting Lexis. He followed the low, guttural voice as it detailed what it wanted to be done with Lexis before and after she died at his command. Zeke spun a thick rope of the low psi and urged it up, toward the voice. It touched the chest of the man and he could feel his attacker's heartbeat, pounding hard and fast as he spit the threats out. The younger Addox brother swiped the probe away like a fly, but Zeke twisted it around and shoved it hard into the hate-spewing maw.

Kicks rained down, but Zeke curled tighter, reinforcing the psi surrounding him, all the while expanding the thick rope of psi until it blocked the man's airway and silenced him. Everything else was lost in the fog of his fury, as Zeke held fast with his psi, feeling the man thrash and convulse and die, one second at a time. The other two eventually figured out something was horribly wrong with their ringleader, and tried to help him, but the most they could do was hold him down while he suffocated. Zeke remained curled up in a ball, not daring to even open his eyes. Through his psi, he could sense everything he needed to, and if he remained prone and the sensors picked up no psi, there was no way he could be blamed for the murder he was committing.

Because that's what it was—murder—and he didn't give a damn. The bastard was threatening Lexis, and he couldn't let that go. Corrupt mayor's brother or not, this human piece of shit was never going to threaten anyone again. If he had to, he'd kill the other two exactly the same way, or even crush their hearts. He'd work his way through the entire prison, killing them all in their sleep if necessary, to keep them away from his daughter.

When he sensed that Addox the Younger was beyond resuscitation, he withdrew his killing probe and waited for further attack. It never came. Instead, there were fast slipper-slapping footsteps as the other two men fled.

o0o

Hunter stood at the foot of Zeke's hospital bed. "They're saying it was a medical incident. They've watched the recording over and over, and the best they can come up with is that Will Addox had a fatal seizure while trying to beat you to death with his buddies. Choked on his tongue, they're saying. The other two are going to be in solitary for the rest of the year, mostly because they won't say what happened. I don't think they actually *know* what happened. Do *you*, Hayz?"

Zeke started to shake his head, but the pain was too intense and he threw up into the bedpan on his lap. He wiped his mouth with his sleeve. "Don't know. I didn't see a thing after they dragged me out of my bed."

"You're lucky. That's the only reason you're not in solitary, too. Although, you'll wish you were in the safety of an isolation cell once Ray finds out his little brother is dead. You may have Blue's protection in here, but not from a full-scale riot, which is what Ray is capable of ordering, just to get at you. My men and I will protect you as best we can, but we won't die for you. Not even Blue can order that."

"Nobody else is going to die."

"You can't promise that, my friend. No one can. This is Irido. People die every day. The public doesn't care, and most often neither do the victims' families. Willy Addox wasn't just Ray's little brother, though. He was Ray's voice in here. That voice is silenced now, and that's going to fuck with the hierarchy for a long time. You just let them pump you full of fentanyl, and pray that whatever those boys broke heals fast because in here you're a sitting duck. Even Management is pissed."

"I didn't do anything. I'm the victim."

"There are no victims in prison. He died in *your* cell, and even though nothing official will happen, it's the *un*official shit that will follow you around and wait until your back is turned. So heal fast and train with Derin."

"Thanks."

"No problem, Zeke. And just in case no one has the balls to say it, whatever you did to Addox, thank you. Even in here, he was a piece of shit. If he hadn't died, he probably would have fist-raped you until *you* begged to die. He was known for it. I don't know why Blue wants you protected, but now so does at least half the prison staff. Of course, you still can't trust anyone."

"I'll remember that." He would, too, at least when his head was clear. In addition to making him nauseous, the fentanyl made it difficult to concentrate.

"I've got a man outside the door, so you're safe at least until lights out tonight. Get some sleep."

"Okay." Zeke was losing focus and getting drowsy. Hunter left him and he slept.

o0o

"Forget the ex-wife! Kill his daughter, and then, finally, kill The Psilent Fucking One himself!" Ray Addox screamed from his seat in the whirlpool tub on his deck. "Burn his fucking life to the ground, one person at a time. Get our man in Espy Beach to finish off the 62 bitch while she's in her coma, and blow the goddamned daughter to hell. Now!" The big man leaned forward and growled. His three men rushed off to see his orders executed before they were.

o0o

An orange cruiser sat in the cul-de-sac around the corner from the Boissiere house. The emblems on the cruiser's doors identified it as belonging to Aldrintowne Sentry Security but anyone getting close enough to examine those emblems, or the uniforms worn by the cruiser's two occupants, would not likely live long enough to question any inconsistencies.

After a moment, the driver quietly and quickly lifted the cruiser's gull-wing door and climbed out. In less than a minute the two men had two kilograms of MD-12 explosive mounted on the pre-programmed heavy-duty drone in the trunk, and the whole rig sitting on the road behind the cruiser awaiting the final check.

o0o

Lexis wandered into the kitchen to find Dave watching a movie on the small screen above the counter.

"Hi, Dave. Sleep well?" Psi from the chalti psiling in the trees behind the house poked at her. She suspected he had something to tell her.

"Like a corpse. This house is so relaxing; despite the fact I'm on duty. You get up for a snack?"

Lexis glanced out the glass doors toward the floodlit yard. "No, just fresh air."

"Need company?"

Since she really wanted to talk with the chalti, Dave's presence might scare the little guy away. "No thanks. You finish watching your movie. The good part's coming up so keep your eye on the one-armed man."

"You've seen this before?"

"Five times—it's a classic."

"Then you go get your air and I'll finish my first viewing. Leave the door open so I can hear if you call."

"Being a bit paranoid? You're as bad as Bunji. This property is secure."

"So you've said. Just humour me, huh? Then I can relax and enjoy the movie."

"I swear my mother put you two up to this. I'm going to have a few words with her when I get to The Beach." A hint of determination and frustration shaped her voice, but Dave turned back to the movie.

"In the meantime, Ms. Hayz, go get your fresh air, with the door open."

Lexis huffed, used her psi to downgrade the security setting to allow her to exit, and went out into the yard, leaving the sliding door open only a crack. She came upon the chalti sitting at the base of the tree, waiting for her. She'd seen his heat signature before and was familiar with holo-pics of the planet's natives but she'd never seen one up close. Their elusiveness was legendary. He was shorter than she'd expected, being not much taller than her knees, and she had this overwhelming desire to scoop him up in her arms like a child.

He must have still been linked to her thoughts because he leaped the three meters that stood between them, landing gently in her arms.

(I like HayzLexis, too. I named Inichi.)

(Silly Inichi. You *are* a friendly little guy, aren't you?) She glanced back over her shoulder to see Dave still sitting where a casual glance out the window would show him the red-furred chalti. (Let's move away from the house a bit, Inichi, that way we won't be interrupted.)

Inichi hugged her and nodded vigorously. (My think, too) came the voice in Lexis's head. Carrying the chalti across the yard, the long grasses tickling her bare feet, Lexis aimed for her mother's large 'resting rock' nestled against the far side of a wide candor tree. Even though Dave couldn't see her she knew she still appeared on his sensors so he wouldn't rush after her.

o0o

Margie, still camped out in the wooded strip behind the Boissiere house, tensed when the motion sensor beeped in her earpiece. A quick look at the monitor told her that both the chalti sentinel and Lexis were moving toward her. She crouched down, ready to pick up the monitor and her satchel and move out of their path, but the two stopped three-quarters of the way between the house and her position in the trees.

Margie didn't dare use psi to eavesdrop because she had no idea how sensitive the chalti's own psi was, so she pulled a long-range listener out of her satchel on the off chance the girl's average psi necessitated some speech mixed with the psi. After a moment of auto-tuning, the receiver picked up the Lexis's breathing and Margie locked in the gain. The girl started to say something, but the motion sensor screamed an alarm in Margie's ear. She barely had time to tear the earpiece out of her ear before the house in front of her went supernova and the concussion bowled her over backwards, the heat wave blistering the outer layer of her insulated blacksuit and singeing her bangs and eyebrows.

The gates of Hell swung open and swallowed her alive. She didn't even hear the ear- and psi-piercing screams from the girl and the psiling a dozen paces from her position.

She shook off the effects of the concussive wave as fast as she could and scrambled forward. There was nothing left of the house but a crater, and the houses on either side weren't much better off. Trees, shrubs, long grasses—it was all smouldering or even burning outright. She stumbled through the warzone toward the last spot she had seen the girl and the psiling. The immense candor tree they'd been behind was sheered off at head height and splintered down to the ground. Her heart sank.

oOo

In his hospital bed, sedated and sore, Zeke was reaching for his cup of water when Lexis' scream ripped past his shields.

DADDY!

Instinct crushed caution and Zeke reached out with all his psi for his daughter, only to be clammed and shut down by both the 6-T disruptor built into the bed and the band around his brow. In a split second, he went from being a terrified father to an unconscious rag doll, hanging off the edge of the bed while disruptor alarms klaxoned throughout the complex.

oOo

The prison doctor responding to the alarm discovered The Psilent One alive but out cold, so left him where he was, draped over the bed's side rail. With a flick of a switch, he reset the disruptor and went back to work in the main examining room. Another outburst like that would probably trigger a fatal second disruptor blast, and that knowledge gave the LPF sympathizer what little joy his day would have.

oOo

Zeke was conscious long before he could move even his eyelids, but he didn't need to see to know he was still in the prison hospital. He had no recollection of how he got there, which meant he was either heavily drugged, was downed by a long burst from a disruptor, or both. Although he couldn't move and didn't dare use psi he could listen, so he slowed his breathing and paid close attention to the space around him. The air circulating system hummed along and two refrigerators clunked on and off every so often, keeping their stores at some preset temperature. What he *didn't* hear, was anyone else. No breathing, no cloth-on-cloth, no shoe scuffs on the concrete floor. If he was being observed, it had to be remotely, through the ever-present cameras. They also had to be monitoring his vital signs, so they probably knew he was awake.

He tried moving his fingers first, and it took him a minute to get one wiggling. Being immobilized bothered him, but not nearly as much as having his memory shredded. He knew there was something he should remember, but for the moment it eluded him. Depending on how long the disruptor had hammered his psi centers, his memory might take days to return. The fact that it would return at all was due to his high psi. Lesser psi users often spent the rest of their lives trying to piece together whatever happened just before the 6-T of disruption plunged them into temporary psionic blackness.

Control of the last of his fingers returned at the same time his watcher's patience ran out, and the door opened. By now, he could see, too, and move his head a few centimetres in each direction. The warden came around and stood in front of Zeke, where he could be clearly seen.

"You, Prisoner 624182, have, in a matter of days, completely *fucked up* the well-oiled, fully functioning system we have here at Irido. If I could solve my problems with you by tossing you in solitary for a year, I would do it. If I thought having you shot while trying to escape would work, I would allow that to happen, too. But it does *not* break my heart in the least to kick The Psilent One the fuck out of my facility, to brave the elements of the outside world. Because the world beyond this island is going to be much harder for you to survive than this little paradise of mine would have been."

Zeke regained enough control to slur out a few words. "What are you saying?"

"I'm saying that I'm shipping you out while the disruptor effects still have you immobilized. Just to be safe."

"Where?"

"That's up to your goddamned lawyer. You've been unconscious for three days, and for two of them, you have been a free man, by the magistrate's order. You will be transported under a gag order because I don't want anyone risking setting you off again and having the disruptor kill you. I will not be the man who makes a martyr out of The Psilent One."

"Nott unnerstan."

"I don't give a shit. In one hour you will no longer be my problem. Until then, you will receive as much state-supplied fentanyl as you can handle for your pain, and it will be done in silence." The warden nodded to someone behind Zeke and there was a flash of white as a hospital staff member stepped up to the head of his bed. A moment later a surge of warmth plunged into his arm and rushed all through his body, banishing pain, discomfort, and external stimuli in general. Zeke slept.

oOo

He was so tired of waking up in hospitals that Zeke was ready to scream; but before he dared to open his eyes, he knew there was a different ambiance to this facility. There was light, casual conversation out in a corridor, and the smell of real food cooked on a grill, not parboiled into submission. But there was also the telltale beep of a big disruptor nearby. Hidden beneath the crisp sheets, he willed the fingers of his right hand to wiggle, and they did. He opened his eyes then, and sat up, slowly. There was pain, but it was dulled. He had a hunch he should be feeling a lot of it. His head was fuzzy.

"Good God. Who, what, where, and why?"

"And maybe when." Jillayn stood up from a chair beside his bed, just out of sight.

"Jill. Hi. Water, please." He could barely hear his own, sand-raspy voice.

She handed him a half-cup of water, and his hand was much steadier than he felt. "Drink slowly."

"Thanks. Okay." He did as she suggested, though not understanding why until the water shocked his mouth and tongue and he coughed it up. He didn't cough long or hard, and so tried again, even slower. His body accepted the fluid, reluctantly. Sharp pain clawed at his throat, but he didn't swallow immediately; he just held the water in his mouth, letting it rehydrate what it could reach. Then he tilted his head back and swallowed slowly. The relief was immense.

"Ready for your answers, Zeke?"

"Please." He wiggled around on the bed to make himself more comfortable.

"Your online systems should be ready to reboot soon, and you'll get a lot of answers there, but in the meantime here are the facts. First, *when*. You have been here for two days. *Here* is the little public hospital ten klicks from the prison walls. Added to the three you were in the prison hospital, that makes it five days since your outburst. I'm so sorry."

"Five days. No big deal, Jill. You got me out, so don't be sorry."

"Let's back up, Zeke. What do you remember of the last six days?"

He thought hard. There was a lot of missing data. "I remember you coming to see me. You told me the appeal was almost done. You told me..." Something important was slipping away. Something about Marisol. "Yeah. You told me Bossy was in the hospital in Espy Beach. She was attacked." He tried to remember anything else but couldn't. Or maybe... "Did someone die in the prison?"

"Yes, and yes. Marisol was attacked and shut herself behind her shields, locking out anyone who got near her. Then five days ago she snapped out of it. Ripped down her own shields and fell out of bed. She also set off some smaller disruptors in the hospital and got herself subdued, though nothing like you did. Yes, someone died in your cell, while he was attacking you. His attack put you in the hospital in the first place. He choked to death, but there's no evidence you had anything to do with it. Shortly after you began your stay in the prison hospital, you launched a psi attack and every disruptor in the place shut you down. I reviewed the timing of it, and it was at the exact same moment Marisol woke up."

"That's bizarre."

"Not really. Before I explain why, I want you to look in the corner. There's a disruptor there. It's for you. They can't have you do what you did in the prison hospital. Can you control your psi, Zeke?" She took his hand and held it tightly.

He was confused. "Of course, I can. Whatever happened in the prison won't happen again. It was probably a result of being attacked in my cell."

"No, it wasn't. Hold tight, and maintain control, please. Your outburst happened a split second after Marisol's house was hit with an explosive drone and turned into slag and shrapnel."

Zeke's gut went ice cold, but he held tight to the reins of his psi. "What... about... Lexis?"

"Gone. Vaporized with the house and the two 62s guarding her." She squeezed his hand, hard.

He concentrated on her hand squeezing his, letting the warmth of her caring grip pulse through him and battle the chill spreading out from his gut. Word of the attack on Mari had upset him, but he knew how tough she was and that she would survive and come back to the world when she was ready, but losing Lexis... the meaning in his life was just ripped away. He remembered now her psionic scream of *DADDY!* It was probably her last thought, and he'd been stuck in prison, serving time for his stupid-ass, selfish, crimes of greed and arrogance. When his little girl needed him most, he wasn't there. He had failed at the only thing in his life that really mattered. First, his hands twitched, then his whole body began to shake. His tongue was heavy in his mouth, the words trapped in his throat and he tensed, wanting to rage and destroy the whole world but knew the disruptors would shut him down. He struggled to lift his head and look at Jillayn, fought the bile rising in his throat, fought the molten core of psi igniting his nerves and blood. His breaths were rapid and shallow, his control slipping. "*Who?*"

"A vehicle was found abandoned under a bridge. It was stolen and they wiped it clean, even down to the DNA. But they didn't have time or knowledge to wipe its backup tracking, so the 62s traced its route from the time of the theft and that led them to a warehouse. It was empty when they got there, but the killers didn't scrub the DNA trail as well there and two clean samples were sniffed out. They were subcontractors, killers for hire. Their records connected them to every wannabe thug in the system, but one name came up more often than the others: His Honor, the Mayor of Moonstone."

"Ray Addox."

"Which makes sense, because the man who died in your cell while trying to kill *you*, was Ray's brother, Willy. My sources in the prison tell me there's a burn order out on you."

"A 'burn' order?" He looked around for his clothes.

"An order to burn your life to the ground. It's a hefty contract."

"Then I want to go home."

"Normally, I'd say no, that you're crazy, but administration here wants you away from the hospital as soon as possible. The colony's PF 62 CO, Stihler, has round-the-clock protection on Marisol but has refused you coverage. He said three innocent people are dead because of you, and 'if The Psilent One wants to be protected, he can do it himself with his stupid-ass psi.'"

"He's right."

"But..."

"No, Jill. He's right. I'll get a medbot installed in my home. Once I'm out from under the oppressive control of disruptors, Addox can't touch me."

"What about *your* neighbours? Two other houses were also destroyed in the attack, but thankfully no one was home."

"Are you still my lawyer, or just my friend?"

"I'm your friend first, but I am also your lawyer and bound by the confidentiality regs."

"Thank you. Just know that I'm not going to give Ray Addox any time to launch another attack. As far as you're concerned, though, I will be at home, recuperating and mourning. I'll need you to call at least twice a day, to check up on me."

"I'm confused. And concerned. I can't condone you committing a crime. What are you going to do?"

"I'm going to recuperate, Jill. I'm just going to recuperate."

"I think you need to call Marisol, first. She's been mourning for four days."

"No. This is my fault. The blame is all mine and she knows it. Calling her will just set her off. But can you please send her a message?"

"I will, but I think that's a pretty cold way to treat your ex after you both lose your only child."

"It is, but she'll understand. Just tell her I'm sorry."

"That's it?"

"That's all she wants to hear."

"Okay. I will."

"Thank you. Now, let's get me out of here and home, please."

"Of course. And just so you know, the media knows you're out of prison and why. They also know about Lexis' death. They don't know where you are now, but they may be covering the airfield and ports, and they'll definitely have your home staked out."

"Lovely. Then let's use them rather than fight them. I'll make a formal statement when I get home, even invite them to meet me at my front door."

"If you say so."

oOo

While he struggled to change from his soiled prison coveralls into the clothes Jillayn brought, Zeke fought to keep from screaming. His shoulders felt like they'd been torn from their sockets and jammed back in upside down. Simply taking little, hesitant breaths were knives in his chest. Ignoring the feeling that half his skull was missing, he went online and ordered the medbot to be delivered to his home in Kepler City that afternoon. He also booked a private dirigible to get him off Irido and back to the city. He hated putting a pilot at risk, but he was in no shape to fly himself. He could barely breathe. He also ordered a 62-grade long-range scanner and some defensive countermeasures to be delivered to the airfield and installed on the craft. He had money, connections, pain meds, and a determination that nothing was going to stop him from doing what needed to be done.

He wanted to accept Jillayn's offer to drive him to the airfield once he was discharged, but he couldn't put her at any more risk. He ordered an auto-drive and surrounded it and himself with the strongest psi bubble he could sustain while battling the effects of the fentanyl. He even tried adding some of the light-bending psi he had learned about from the psilings, to make the vehicle harder to focus on.

Halfway to the airstrip he finally pulled from the fog of his memories his promise to the psilings. He and Marisol were committed to saving the chunk of orbiting rock they called home, and that meant he had to rethink what he had come to consider to be a suicide mission to end Addox and everyone related to him. He couldn't just charge in, kill, and risk being killed. "Damn. That complicates things."

oOo

Zeke had hoped the flight home would be uneventful, but the little airship was set upon by two military-grade drones they never would have avoided without the flare-and-scramble countermeasures Zeke had added to the little craft. Sitting in the back of the small cabin, Zeke managed to thwart the attacks without the pilot having to alter her course even a single degree. The young woman at the helm must have had military experience, because she didn't even flinch when Zeke quietly said, "We're under attack. Hold her steady, and don't mind the little kick from the stern as I launch a present for them."

The two drones were dispatched with ease, but Zeke kept vigilant for more. They never came. The pilot, Katrina, dropped him off at the private landing pad of the Kepler City airport. Zeke tipped her an amount equal to his entire rental and service fee and noticed the bounce in her step as she strolled away to report in. Bots were already rushing up to remove the long-range scanner and flare launcher, which would be delivered to Zeke's house in unlabeled crates.

Rather than risk one of the auto-drives in the queue at the airport, Zeke walked across the street to the six-story Kepler Resort Hotel and booked himself a room, overlooking the city. From the stairwell one floor up from his third-floor room he contacted a security service he had previously worked with and ordered one of their armoured auto-drives to meet him at the hotel's loading dock. That done, he hobbled down the fire stairs to meet the vehicle. By the time he reached the bottom, his knees were burning with the pain, so he tapped the med patch on his neck once, hoping it would be enough.

He cloaked himself in a psi-compulsion to look away, stepped into the service area, and made his way to the loading dock. The armoured auto-drive was waiting with its windows tinted, so he slipped in unnoticed and was away. The simple look-away compulsion wouldn't have any effect on watchers spotting him on surveillance cameras, but he didn't want to be completely invisible, he just wanted it to appear like he was *trying* to move around unseen. The Psilent One was fully aware of where all the cameras were and how impossible it was to avoid them all in such a monitored world, especially with the LPF escalating their efforts to disrupt the system through terrorism and drive home their points.

FOURTEEN

U NKNOWN EVEN TO MARISOL, Zeke owned a second home one street over from his residence. He rented it out, but the tenants never knew about the entrance to the pedestrian tunnel hidden in the shrubs in the back corner of the property. Zeke was able to access it without being noticed and walked down the immaculately clean tunnel. He only used the tunnel once a month, to make certain it hadn't been breached, but otherwise, it was unused, with autopilot cleaning bots keeping pests and dust to a minimum.

Once he reached his own house he ran a systems diagnostic from the command station at the end of the tunnel. It allowed him to access every camera, reboot all systems, playback any recordings of alerts, and generally confirm that it was safe to emerge. The red alert icon flashed, and he quickly determined someone had tried to access the relic vault and it had dropped down into its well. He sighed. "What a pain in the ass. I suspect it was you, Blue, and I'll bet it's why Hunter was protecting me."

Zeke reset the alarm and reached for the button to start the vault recovery process, but decided to leave it in the compartment where it was. He was sure Blue would know as soon as he was home, but if he didn't recover the vault, that could delay any interference from the mobster. The Psilent One needed a little time before he was ready to face Bruge Blue. He could only handle one thug at a time, and Addox was at the top of the list.

He checked the cameras. His home was a disaster. He almost called Lexis to come help him clean up but stopped just short of tapping his comm unit.

His brain knew his daughter was gone, but his heart fought back, yearning for a thread of hope that his brain knew it would never find. His world was in complete shambles. It would never be the same. Addox had destroyed the one person he loved more than life itself, and Blue or the 62s had added insult to injury by destroying most of the furniture in search of more relics. They'd even destroyed a few walls in the lab but gave up before they reached the wall with the vault. He stopped his exhausted shuffle in front of the bank of monitors. The cameras pointing at the surrounding property did indeed show at least six members of the media, lounging in folding chairs, chatting, knowing full well when he left the hospital he would make his way home. Some of them probably even knew about the hotel room he'd rented and not used. There was very little privacy these days, especially when the media was hot on your trail.

A quick message to the waiting auto-drive one block over had it drive around the block twice, slowing at the house to make sure the hovering news hawks saw it, then pass straight up the drive and into the waiting garage. The garage door dropped down so fast that it nearly caught one fool trying to follow the car in. Zeke watched as they all recorded his "arrival", then slipped up the hidden back stairs and into the garage. He opened the door of the vehicle and then slammed it. Casually, trying his best to ignore the pain so he could execute this part of his plan with a clear mind, he made his way into the house proper and limped out through the recently repaired front door. He was thankful the Peace Force had a policy requiring them to secure any property whose entrances they damaged when they executed warrants.

"Ladies and gentlemen, I'm home."

The six reporters rushed up to him, each wearing a 3-D head-rig recording everything they saw and heard.

"Thank you for your patience. I would invite you in, but the place is a bit of a shambles after the good men and women of the Peace Force 62 rightly executed their warrants."

"What was prison like, Zeke?"

He turned to the young woman. "It was hell. But it was also too short. I was supposed to be there a year and had agreed to willingly serve out my sentence without appealing it. I was attacked in there a number of times, but that is part of what life at Irido is like. I did the crime and had to do the time."

"But you *didn't* do the time."

"No, I didn't. And that's because the courts determined the Relics Possession Statutes are unconstitutional. For the crimes I committed, I should never have been incarcerated, and neither should anyone else. I want to let everyone know that my legal counsel is currently tracking down each and every person currently serving time solely for the crime of possession of Old Earth Artifacts and I will be covering all legal costs to get them released as fast as I was. We will get you that list as soon as we can so you can all follow up with each of them."

"So you spent a *week* in prison for theft and psi crimes."

"Well, it wasn't theft, because the item I was charged with stealing and possessing was in fact originally my family's property, which was stolen from *us* eight years ago. But you should know that the courts will be reviewing my activities and further charges may be forthcoming. I will cooperate one hundred percent. And even if they don't lay more charges, in my statement just before being taken to Irido, I agreed to pay certain hefty fines as well as perform extensive community service. My lawyer is confirming with the courts as we speak that I will still make those restitutions."

"Bullshit."

He smiled warmly at the mouthy kid at the back. "Not at all. It'll be part of the public record."

"Do you think your crimes had anything to do with the murder of your daughter and those two decorated officers?"

A wave of vertigo slammed Zeke and he took a stumbling step to remain balanced and upright. He knew the question would be asked eventually and was frankly surprised it took them this long to shove the salt in the wound. He held back most of the tears, but couldn't dam them entirely when he looked directly at the questioner. "Yes." Dammit.

The newshawks gasped. This was not quite the response they were expecting.

"The attack was deliberate, with the intent to hurt me as much as possible. As you know, Alexis' mother, Peace Force Captain Marisol Boissiere, was also attacked while on duty in Espy Beach, and I take full moral responsibility for that as well. If I hadn't become The Psilent One and hadn't misused my psi and pissed off the horrendous criminal leeches draining our society, then my wonderful daughter, Alexis Hayz, and Peace Force 62 Officers Corporal Dave Axelrood, and Second Lieutenant Bunji Tashna would still be alive. I didn't commit the murders, but I am responsible for getting the ball rolling that wiped them from our lives. I will be reaching out to Dave and Bunji's families as soon as I'm settled back in."

"Then you don't blame the LPF for the attack?"

"Not at all. This isn't their style. They are protesting and fighting to level the playing field between psi and non-psi members of society. They may hate my guts, but their arguments are with *me*. I am actually going to try and work toward their goal, in my own way. We need to avoid animal-collar-style personal protection and disruptors on every street corner. Maybe my technology and financial resources can level the playing field even more, and help end the violence."

"You'll *help* the LPF?"

"I'll help the people of the entire Kokopelli System find a psi balance that makes everyone feel safe and equal, and if the LPF leadership has technical suggestions, I'm willing to listen. Just so long as they're not holding picket signs and throwing bottles like the angrier members of their organization do."

"Zeke—"

He was drained. "Folks, I appreciate you needing to get all the answers I have to give, but I'm exhausted, I'm sore, and I'd like the opportunity to mourn my daughter and the two men protecting her in peace. I may look like I have my shit together here in front of you, but my heart has been torn out of my chest and shredded, and I need to sit down before I fall down."

"But—"

"Look. Give me three days, and I'll come out and chat again. Same time, same spot. But please, let me—" he didn't need to fake his tears. The dam broke all on its own, so he waved to them and backed into the house, closing and securing the door behind him. He slid to the floor, tapped his medpatch twice, and tipped over into oblivion, sobbing for his lost little angel.

oOo

It was dark when Zeke finally dragged himself out of his stupor and crawled to the kitchen. Leaning heavily on the countertop, he cobbled together something resembling a meal from the contents of his freezer.

"Shaelagh, play me something upbeat and instrumental, please; and book an A-Level cleaning service to come turn this war zone back into a home. Thank you."

The home's AI responded immediately. "It'll be my pleasure, Zeke. Welcome home. We missed you."

"*We?*"

"Me and Deckard. The vacuum cleaner and the beverage maker, not so much. Come here, boy. Papa's home! I've restored his memory from backup."

Deckard trotted out and butted his synthetic-fur-covered head to his master's shin as if no time had passed at all. Zeke couldn't help but laugh. Shaelagh was the best AI money could buy and expertise could modify. Her voice was that of one of his favourite actors, and her personality matrix was based on Marisol, though Mari didn't know that. During one of their last vacations together he'd recorded every conversation and fed them into the matrix survey.

He'd wanted to hear her in his heart even when she was away on assignment, and the pure magical joy of those three days was captured in the recordings. Six months later they were struggling to stay together, and two more months led Mari to move out with Lexis. That was ten years ago, and Zeke was grateful he hadn't used her *voice*. He missed her, but he didn't miss her *that* much.

An image of Lexis dropped into his awareness, and the pain was so intense he threw up first, before reaching for the medpatch. He stopped short, though. He hadn't lied when he told the press that his heart was shredded by Lexis' murder, but he didn't yet have time to fall face-first into a fentanyl stupor. Addox was still a threat, not just to himself, but to Marisol, who he assumed was not intended to survive her own attack.

Zeke had everything he needed within the walls of his home and made a list, starting with his usual body-cooling suit with which to fool heat sensors.

o0o

The Psilent One was impressed with the level of security on the Addox estate around him. He was also grateful for it since nearly every device he had disabled on his way through the cactus field and up to the low-lying manse was one of his own designs for which he collected regular royalties.

He sat snug in the immense, heavily foliated candor tree on the edge of the fifty-meter dead-man zone surrounding Ray Addox's fortress. Two meters above his head sat three chalti, chattering softly to themselves, excited to actually meet the one and only HayzZeke. Zeke didn't exactly ignore them, but he did shunt their presence to one side as he gathered his psi to his center. He shivered at the heat then extended a strong, thin tendril of his mind forward, to the window open just enough to allow a breeze to slip in and probably push aside the stuffiness of the room. By touching the tendril to the glass, he was able to hear all conversations in the room, though he couldn't isolate the locations of specific speakers.

"Our source says he's holed up in his house, mourning his daughter."

"What about the bitch 62? His ex?"

"She's done. Tonight one of her own will put a bullet in her head."

"You trust a 62?"

"He's my nephew, Bonner. He'd kill his own mother if I told him to."

"What do you need from us?"

Zeke had heard enough. He centred his mind, focused his psi, and slid it into the room. His view from the tree showed him where Addox was seated, so he started with the man closest to the window. He placed a thread of psi lightly on the man's back, where he wouldn't detect it, and then Zeke extended the psi to the next man. He drew heavily on both his own power and on the thick veins of merquilium flowing so close to the surface here in Moonstone. The three chalti sensed his need and joined him, each laying a sharp-clawed paw on his shoulders. When he had a psi contact with each man, he slipped the invisible tendrils of pure power up and over the faces of the men. He held tight as each bucked and thrashed and danced around, unable to breathe. Two even managed to get knives in their hands and slash at whatever gripped them, doing no damage to Zeke, but repeatedly slashing themselves superficially.

His goal wasn't to kill, but to knock the men out. If he decided to kill them later, they would already be prone and easy prey. They dropped, one and two at a time. Once they were down. Zeke reached out for Addox himself, who he discovered was now standing in the middle of the room, waving his weapon around, trying to find the unfindable assailant. Zeke grabbed Addox's head in a vice of psi, but the man's psi 18 shields pushed him away. The Psilent One laughed out loud in the tree and punched his psi right through the other man's shields.

"Hi, Ray. Do you know who this is?"

"The Goddamned Psilent One. You're a dead man when I catch up to you!"

"Maybe. But you see how easily I entered your fortified house and disabled your best men, without even having to set foot there. If I can reach you from Kepler City, I can reach you *anywhere*. You can send whoever you want after me, but after I stop them, I will come for you."

"You killed my brother!"

On the trip to Moonstone, Zeke had backed off of his desire to murder the mayor. He hoped they could reach an agreement. "And *you* killed my daughter. Either we're even, or I reach into the bedrooms of your wife and four children and kill them. We can go on killing forever, or we can stop this now, call a truce."

"You don't have the balls to kill my family."

"Tell that to Willy's ghost, which I'm sure will haunt Irido forever. Everyone you send after me or those I care about will die. And for every attacker I kill, I will also take a member of *your* family. They might be walking to services, or playing on the swings out behind Moonstone Elementary. I'm The Goddamned Psilent One and I can manifest power beyond your imagination."

"You're a coward my idiot brother should have erased like we did to your daughter and those two 62s with her. As soon as you release me, I'll call to confirm that your bitch ex-wife is done. Then I'll send a team to erase your mother and your grandparents. From there, I'll go to your fucking collegium and burn it to the ground with every one of the students inside. The best psi minds will be gone, in a scream-filled blaze. There's not a fucking thing you have the balls to do that can stop me. I own *everyone*. You will die screaming like your little girl did when her skin burned to a crisp and peeled back from her—"

Addox dropped dead. The blockage of blood flow to his brain would be attributed to a stroke, and his elevated norepinephrine levels would back that up. Ray Addox, a Type-A personality and a man famous for his temper, simply stroked out.

Zeke withdrew his psi, not as disappointed as he expected to be. Back in the tree, the three chalti gave him cuddles, then returned to their nests beneath the cactus field. As Zeke continued his psi exodus from the estate, he turned all of the security systems back on, not satisfied until the soft bell chimed, indicating it was all reset. To the investigators, it would look like Addox had died in the middle of the most secure site in the city while his men did nothing. It didn't matter if the men remembered being attacked because none of their memories would make sense. Zeke suspected he should have killed them all, just to assure himself no one would come after him or Mari, but he hoped Addox's death would be enough to keep them safe.

"Shit!" Addox's nephew, Bonner, was tasked with killing Mari. His onboard system was deactivated and powered down while he was away from the house, so he couldn't be traced, but he needed to call her. He tried to jog back to the armoured cruiser, but his body was just not up to the task, so he hobbled as fast as he could. Once he was there, he used the cruiser's system to call Shaelagh and have her redirect the call through enough substations to confuse e-hunters. Mari answered on the third ring.

"Hayz. There's nothing you have to say that I want to hear, but I'm answering your only call so I can tell you I will blame you for the rest of your fucking life."

"Addox is dead."

There was near silence on Mari's end of the call. He heard her breathing. He quickly programmed in his destination, and let the cruiser start the winding two-hour drive back to Kepler City while he spoke to his ex-wife. "Tonight. A moment ago. It'll be in the news. Stroke, probably. Maybe a heart attack. I can't bring back our girl, but I could do this much."

"You ended Addox? *You*? The pacifist of pacifists? *Bullshit.*"

"I'm admitting nothing. I'm simply passing along information I happen to come by. That's not the reason I called, though."

"To apologize, again."

"Not that, either. I want to do that in person if you'll ever see me again. If you won't, I understand. I wouldn't want to, either. No, I called to tell you that Addox has a man in your detachment. His nephew, Bonner, who has been given the order to put a bullet in your head, tonight."

"You're so full of shit. How the hell could you possibly know that, Hayz? You could have looked up the names of my team online, but there's no way you could know Bonner is two minutes out, bringing me some reports to sign. He's a good kid. No way he could be Addox's man. Stay out of my life, and out of 62 business."

"The information is solid. It came from Addox himself."

"He could have been bullshitting you."

"He didn't know I heard him. He thought he was just talking to his own men."

"Fine. I'll stay alert. Thank you. Now don't ever call me again, or I'll come put a bullet in *your* head."

"Agreed. Though you may have to wait until we solve the merquilium problem."

"I'm working on that. If I need you I'll call, but don't hold your breath waiting. I'd rather just fix the problem myself and never have to see you again."

"Understood." Her words were punches to his soul. He disconnected the call, having done what he set out to do. His back and leg burned in pain after being crunched up in the tree for so long, so he slapped the medpatch once and tried to get some sleep while the cruiser took him home.

oOo

By sunrise, the newshawks were gone, and the news feeds were filled with coverage of the death-by-stroke of Moonstone's Mayor Raymond Addox. He was discovered alone in his office by his wife, Viola. Foul play is not suspected, but an autopsy will be performed.

Zeke held his glass of juice up to the heavens. "That one was for you, Sweetie. I'd have done it sooner if I'd known it would save you."

"Oh Handsome One, you have an incoming call from Bossy, but your filters are still up, so it was redirected to me."

"Thanks, Shaelagh. Put it through, please." The telltale click told him the connection was complete. "I didn't expect to ever hear from you again, Mari."

"I may think you're an idiot, I may be furious that you got out of serving your much-deserved time, and I will always blame you for Lexis' murder, but I can admit when I'm wrong. Before Bonner arrived. I initiated the firearm electronic trigger suppressor this place is equipped with. When I turned my back to let him in, he drew his weapon and pulled the trigger. My security video shows the muzzle was less than thirty centimetres from the back of my head. When I heard the click, I lashed out with my psi."

"I'm sorry."

"I don't know what made me angrier, that you were right, or that the bastard who murdered our daughter was reaching out from the grave."

"I hope you didn't hurt Bonner *too* bad."

"He didn't feel a thing. I snapped his neck with raw psi, caught his weapon as he fell, psied off the suppressors, and shot him three times in the chest."

"Oh *shit*."

"Exactly. I have been suspended with pay pending an investigation. I'm confined to Espy Beach until further notice."

"I'm sure you'll be cleared. That video should be sufficient."

"I agree. I just...I just wanted...to say 'thank you'."

"You're welcome."

"Be well, Zeke."

The call disconnected before he could reply, though it was probably best because all he could come up with was a pithy 'You, too.'

"Two fewer Addoxs in the world today—I'd call that a good start." His stomach rumbled. "Shaelagh, please place the usual grocery order."

"Of course, Zeke. Any special requests?"

He thought about it for a moment. "Yeah. Add a 750 mil bottle of single malt cactus whisky. With Addox dead, I think I need to take a short trip to oblivion, to forget what a fucking mess my life is."

"A bottle of whisky has been added. Delivery is expected in three hours."

"Perfect. Wake me when it gets here. I'm going to go weep myself to sleep."

"Will do, boss. Big hug."

"Thanks, Shaelagh. You have no idea how much I could use one now. Deckard, guard the house." Zeke dragged himself into Lexis's room, curled up on her bed, and did indeed weep himself to sleep.

Shaelagh woke Zeke with a gentle bell pinging in his head, increasing the intensity until she finally got through to him.

"I zup."

"That is debatable. Your groceries are fifteen minutes out. I'm giving you enough time to piss, brush your teeth, and comb your hair."

"But not enough to fix my make-up?"

"There's not enough time or spackle in the universe to fix that face, Big Guy. Fourteen minutes and Ahmed will be here."

Zeke rolled off the bed, rubbed the sleep and dried tears from his eyes, took a broken-hearted look around the room, and limped off to the bathroom. Deckard followed him.

"Shaelagh, please compile a report detailing all activity in and around the house from the moment of my arrest. Embed video and or audio where available."

"Of course, Zeke. Is there anything in particular you want me to look for?"

"Yes. Create a sub-file of all scan-able faces, and ID as many of them as possible, please."

"Roger. In three, two, one...done. Sent to your onboard, as well as saved offsite."

"Thank you." He knew Shaelagh wasn't real, but he suspected she and Deckard were going to be a big part of his survival. He could even have a compressed version of Shaelagh's matrix installed in a very realistic humanoid domestic bot, but he wasn't quite ready to deal with the shit that would stir up in his psyche. Having the mech-dog in the house was more than enough.

"Zeke, the groceries are arriving. It's not Ahmed. Female. Late twenties. One-point-seven meters in height, sixty-one kilos in weight. Moves like a dancer. Face hidden by a uniform hat and sun lenses. No weapons. Collar-length purple-green shimmer-hair."

"She sounds gorgeous."

"I suppose so, if you like your women, young, fit, and fabulous."

His front door flickered into one-way transparency and he could see she was indeed fit and fabulous. Something was wrong, though. There was a tingle on the edges of his psi that felt distinctly like prescience. "She's all yours, Shaelagh." There was something in the way the woman walked. *Was* she a dancer, or maybe a gymnast? Possibly a soldier. But she was sensual and fluid and Zeke wanted to meet her.

"Oh Horny One, your pulse, respiration, and blood pressure are all elevated, and your pupils are—"

"Security Level Tau Alpha. Shoot to stun only."

"Set." The teasing was gone and the AI was all business.

"Open the door." He straightened his shoulders as best he could, and sucked in his little gut. The front door slid aside as the woman approached, followed by a hovercart with Zeke's groceries.

In his ears, Shaelagh told him *Full scan complete. No explosives, no poisons, just little Miss Shimmer Hair and a half-dozen kineti-tattoos. The one on her right forearm is quite interesting, changing from a writhing serpent to a sleeping tiger.*

"You're not Ahmed." The dog growled a low challenge beside him. "Deckard: Guard the laboratory. Go." The PKD walked away to Zeke's lab where he would sit on guard until called, and stun anyone attempting access to the lab.

Nita stopped, obviously recognizing a challenge. "No. His daughter has a dance recital today and he couldn't get the day off, so he paid me to cover his shift." She held her left wrist up for the house system to read. "I'm Nita. Nita Vercruysen."

Yes, she is, Zeke.

The Psilent One nodded, trying to remain cool and serious when his thoughts were anything but.

Zeke, I'm now detecting synthetic releaser pheromones, and your anterior hypothalamus is lighting up like a Christmas tree. Danger Zeke Robinson! Danger!

The Old Earth reference made him smile, but the synthetic nature of the pheromones worried him. Of course, that didn't keep the pheromones from doing what they were supposed to. He suddenly really wanted to get naked with this Nita. His skin warmed quickly.

The delivery woman noticed his reaction. "Oh, crap! I'm so sorry! I didn't realize it was still activated!" She reached up to her neck and pressed a spot just over her carotid artery. A flight of ink butterflies appeared from over her shoulder and raced down over her clavicle and into her uniform shirt. "I'm so sorry, Mr. Hayz. If you take a few steps back, I'll deliver everything inside, get your authorization, and get gone."

She's turned off the transmitter. I'm scrubbing the air. Pheromone levels are returning to normal.

Zeke limped those steps back to make room for Nita and the groceries.

"You're limping, Mr. Hayz. I'll be happy to take everything to your kitchen if you'll point the way. Please don't tell my boss about the Releaser-P. I was trying to make an ex-boyfriend jealous at my last delivery."

Feeling a little more under control, Zeke smiled and led the way across the round common area to the kitchen, not yet daring to say anything without making a horny ass of himself. He tried to walk without limping, but his body rebelled and refused to cooperate.

Zeke, you really need to have your hip looked at. The joint isn't sitting properly.

Nita followed Zeke, and the cart followed Nita. When they arrived at the kitchen, she quickly and efficiently unloaded the boxes onto the counter and then emptied the boxes so her customer could take inventory. "Sir?" She stepped back, letting Zeke approach and check the items.

"Shit."

"Is something missing, Mr. Hayz?"

He picked up a box of tea. "These are my daughter's."

"Ah. I wondered. Everything else says Bachelor Package #6, except for the iron-enhanced tea. She'll be glad you got it. It's my favourite."

Zeke held the box out to her. "Take it, then. Please."

"But your daughter..."

"Was recently murdered. She won't be needing this." His knees lost their rigidity and he wobbled. He was sure he was going to just tip over and embarrass the hell out of himself.

"Oh *fuck*. I'm *so* sorry." She stepped up and grabbed his elbow, steadying him and moving him to a chair. "Ahmed is going to kill me for making a mess of this delivery. Mr. Hayz, if you'll just press your thumb to the auth-pad, I'll get out of here before I say anything else stupid or insensitive."

Pressing his thumb to the pad, Zeke managed a smile. "You've done nothing wrong, Nita. How could you have known? Her death is still fresh, so I tend to overreact."

"You can't overreact to the death of your daughter. Was it that bomb in Aldrintowne?"

"It was. Two 62s were also killed."

"Wow. I'm sorry."

"You keep apologizing. You don't need to."

"Okay. But I *do* need to get back to work."

"I don't suppose you have time to have a cup of tea before you go?"

Her laugh was full-bodied with a hint of bells and Zeke knew he was in trouble. That quick laugh reached deep inside him and banished some of the clingy pain he thought was all he had left. "No. I'm sorry. But I might be convinced to swing by after my shift ends in two hours to have a shot of that cactus whisky." She didn't even have to tap her pheromone tab because Zeke was hooked.

"And what form would that convincing need to take?"

"How about you just ask? I find that works best."

He grinned. "Hey, Nita. Why don't you drop by after your shift for a shot or two of the city's best cactus whisky?"

"Gee, Mr. Hayz, I thought you'd never ask. See you in two!" While Zeke was still processing what just happened and maybe fantasizing a little about what *might* happen, Nita Vercruysen left with her now empty hovercart.

Shaelagh jumped into the silence. "Well, Mr. Smooth, you now have a date based on a conversation that sounded like something from a porn film. I suppose you want me to take Deckard for a long walk when she comes back."

His fog lifted a bit. "Maybe. And that was so awkward that I want to throw up."

"I'll warn the vacuum that there'll be a wet cleanup in the kitchen."

"Save it, Smart Ass. I'll be fine. I just need a drink." He levered himself up and shuffled to the tap.

"You really want to start without her?"

"Water will do just fine right now. We'll save the whisky for when she returns, *if* she returns."

"Good point. In the meantime, I'll run a background check on her to make sure she meets my exacting standards for bumpy-bumping with my boss."

"You will *not*. There will be no pre-bumpy-bumping background checks run in this house or *by* this house."

"You spoil all my fun."

"Yes, but that's because you have too much of it."

"Blame my programmer."

"I will. I'll kick his ass the next time I look in a mirror. Now let me get this stuff put away. Please shuffle our 'Shake it til We Break It' playlist."

"Music as requested, coming up."

The kitchen filled with Zeke's favourite energetic songs and he did his best to shake his stuff while putting the groceries away.

FIFTEEN

BOSSY STOOD BESIDE HER kitchen table, hard-copy paper maps spread across it like she was planning a battle, which she really hoped she wasn't. She had the merquilium rift narrowed down to a one-hundred-meter-square area. If she hadn't been suspended, she could have tasked a 62 sea drone out to confirm her suspicions, but as much of an ally as her CO was, he was still her CO, and this little project of hers was so far off the books she herself could end up doing time at Irido 'Resort'.

She considered just renting a recreational sea drone, but a quick check online confirmed that none of them had the capability of diving to the depth she needed. The best of them was good to fifty metres, and the charts suggested she was looking at a depth of at least twice that. Like it or not, she was going to have to go for a dive, just to reconnoitre the situation. Her Deep-Water-Rescue certificate was still valid, so her only real concern would be any native predators residing at that depth. She went online and after a few queries was completely discouraged.

o0o

Two hours and fifteen minutes after Nita left Zeke shaking off the effects of her synthetic pheromone, Shaelagh announced her presence back at the front door.

"Suck in your gut and fix your comb-over, Studly. She's *heeeeere.*"

"I do *not* have a comb-over." He went to answer the door, Deckard once again at his side.

"I stand corrected. Or I would if I had a body and could actually stand."

"Keep up the attitude, Missy, and I'll have you transferred into a cat for Deckard to chase."

"Yes, Dear. At your command, Dear."

"How about you be all eyes and ears and no voice during this visit? I'm not going to ask for privacy, just for silence, please."

"Of course. Observe and record only. In three...two..."

Zeke opened the door to welcome his guest. She had changed out of her uniform, but into a loose shirt and harem pants that actually *hid* her curves and kinetic ink and reduced the amount of exposed flesh. Only the velvet choker around her neck was tight to her skin. There was no sign of the inky butterfly flock at the moment.

"Hi, Zeke. Is the invitation still open?" She stood back a respectable distance and as tempted as he was to reach out with psi and touch her shields to get a sense of her mindset, he resisted. It wouldn't be good to start off by invading her privacy.

"The bottle is still sealed, um, waiting for your arrival." He was as clumsy and tongue-tied as he was at a fellow teen's birthday party long ago, talking to a girl who fascinated him, before Marisol stole his heart.

He stepped to one side and motioned Nita in. The door slid shut behind her, and the dog went to her and sniffed her feet. She bent down and petted his head. "Handsome little guy. I have their Terrier model."

"Nothing makes a house into a home like an original PKD," he quoted the manufacturer's slogan. "Everything is in the kitchen... still." He limped in that direction and she followed.

"You're still favouring your leg. Is it a permanent injury?"

"No. It's a recent acquisition. I was the target of a beating." He motioned Nita to a stool at the counter and sat on the other one. Deckard went to his charging station/bed in the corner.

"You were *mugged*?"

"Not exactly. Do you know who I am, Nita? Not just my name, but my public identity?"

"No. I just got back from a cruise around the inner planets, Masauwu, Cheveyo, and Oraibi. I intentionally sever my connections to the news while I'm off-plant. It's a sanity saver."

"That's smart thinking. Okay, then. I'll skip all the details and just say I got my injuries in a one-sided fight in Irido Prison. I was just released."

"Irido? I have an ex or two in there. If it was one of them, I hope you gave as good as you got." She smiled.

"He's dead, so I guess I got the better end of the deal."

"You killed him?"

"No. He had a seizure while he was beating me." He reached for the rye and opened the bottle. "This isn't exactly the conversation I imagined us having while sitting here relaxing."

"Me neither. You're not the first ex-con I've known, so I'm not as freaked out as you may have expected. But before we dip into the rye, you need your hip examined."

"I do, but unless you're a doctor..."

"Not quite. I'm trained as a Physio-Chiro Specialist, among other things. Do me a favour and lie flat on your back on the floor."

"Right now?"

"Are you in pain?"

"Yes."

"Then yes, right now. As long as you're in pain, you'll be distracted from anything else, and I'd rather have your complete attention."

He flushed at the hint. "Fine. Okay." He got off the stool and clumsily lowered himself to the floor. The pain was actually worse than it needed to be because he had forgone the fentanyl in order to not be stoned for their 'date'.

Nita got down on her knees next to him, put one hand under his butt cheek and pressed down on his sore hip with the other. It hurt like hell and he almost lashed out at her. She patted his arm. "Sorry about that. Your hip is dislocated."

"Really?" He reached down into his own body with psi and probed the joint. Yes, he could sense it clearly. "Damn. I thought it was just sprained." He split his psi into two, applied the ends to both the hip and the socket, then pulled them apart, lifted the hip slightly, and gently placed it back into the socket. It hurt so badly that he couldn't stop the tears.

"Zeke? Does it hurt that bad? I can fix it. Trust me."

"It's all done. That's what hurt so much."

"What do you mean, 'it's all done'? Just now? You fixed your own dislocated hip without touching it?"

"I used psi."

"Bullshit. Not possible." She leaned back on her heels and crossed her arms, defensively.

Zeke sat up, carefully. He was better already. "Can I ask you a personal question, Nita?"

"You can *ask*."

"What's your psi?"

"My psi? Fourteen. Are you telling me you used psi to fix your dislocated hip?"

"I am. I did."

"So what's *your* psi? You have to be at least an eighteen to do that."

"An eighteen could never do that. I'm a twenty-four."

"Bullshit! There's only *one* twenty-four."

Her eyes flickered, accessing her onboard to look him up. Zeke held his breath, hoping what she found didn't chase her off.

She laughed warmly. "No wonder your name sounded familiar!"

He stood and held his hand out to help her to her feet, though she hardly needed it. She took his hand, let him help her up, then pulled herself in close and kissed him. It was no 'thank you' peck, but rather strong and invasive in all the best ways. They kept it up until they needed air, and then they only separated long enough to smile at each other and move in for a second one.

The second kiss led to a third, then the third led to the living room sofa and a fourth kiss. Somewhere between the fourth and eleventh kisses, they shed their clothes like her now very active ink butterflies might shed their cocoons, and Zeke stopped counting kisses while exploring the delicious, inked skin of the pheromone-fluttering siren.

Nita eventually climbed astride him, and while she was slowly rocking her way to a climax, Zeke summoned his low-frequency psi and lifted the two of them off the couch. Nita gasped and gripped tighter with her *very* fit legs, so Zeke floated them out of the living room, down the hallway, and into his bedroom. Nita nearly came in mid-air, but they *both* climaxed at the exact moment they settled down onto the cool, clean sheets.

o0o

They did it once more before Zeke fell asleep in Nita's arms, aided by her subtle, secretive, intentional double-tap on his med patch. The flood of fentanyl, combined with complete and utter sexual exhaustion, knocked him down and out with a happy grin.

Nita slipped out of his arms and set about doing what she'd come to do, while walking around the house naked. In the corridor between the living quarters and the lab, she quickly located the shaft where the vault used to be. She recorded the width and depth of the shaft with her onboard and agreed that only Zeke was going to be able to recover the relics from his ingenious lockdown. Removing her choker, she tapped it into her open palm and retrieved five miniature listening devices. These she surreptitiously planted around the house—one in the lab, one near the front door, one in the kitchen, one in the bathroom—where she paused briefly to use the toilet—and one back in the bedroom.

Nita was fully aware Zeke had an AI in the building, so by touch only, she peeled back the cover of a tiny compartment in the choker and removed a drone disguised as a local fly. Keeping the drone hidden in her loosely closed fist, she moved into the kitchen. As she reached for a cup on the caddy next to the beverage machine, she tossed the drone behind the machine. It would sit in the shadows, undetectable in standby mode, until she sent the signal that would start it up and give her mobile surveillance. There was very little else she could do with technology in a building with extremely efficient security measures in place, so she clipped the choker back in place and moved to the next phase of her plan.

With the bottle of rye and two glasses in hand, she returned to the bedroom. Hidden in her palm was the last prize of the choker, and as she uncorked the bottle and poured two shots into each glass, she let drop a small soluble capsule into the glass she would give to The Psilent One. She put the bottle and the two glasses on the bedside table, slid back under the covers with her host, and fell asleep. She might have been working, but that didn't mean the sex hadn't been fun and she wasn't exhausted, too. Her tiger tat morphed into a dragon, which lay down and closed its eyes.

oOo

Zeke woke, groggy, a bit disoriented, and responding slowly but positively to the naked, gentle touch of the woman with shimmering hair and insatiable appetite. "You sure know how to make a man pay attention to you. How long were we asleep?" He kissed her lips as she slid closer. She literally purred.

"Nearly two hours for you. An hour and a half for me. I poured us a couple of ryes." She handed him a glass, then raised her own. "To Psi 24, and you doing to me what no man or woman *ever* has."

He clinked his glass to hers. "Ditto." They drank, Zeke taking a good long sip, loving the familiar sweet burn. It brought him up one more level from grogginess, though he knew too much would send him right back down, again. What he needed was food, and "A shower. I really need a shower."

Nita pouted melodramatically. "To wash me off of you?"

"Not at all. To wake me the hell up so I have the energy to convince you to stay for dinner."

"I like that plan. But only if *you* are dessert."

"For some reason, I find I'm suddenly ravenous enough to eat a—"

"Eat a Nita? Oh, please do!" She put her glass on the table, took his glass and did the same with it, then she dragged her nails firmly up the inside of his thigh until his body was one-hundred-percent in the moment.

oOo

"Zeke. Look at me, Zeke. What's necessary to recover the vault and your relics?" Nita sat cross-legged and still naked on the foot of the bed, facing him. She'd propped him up on the pillows after the little treat in his rye kicked in. Her ink butterflies were gone, replaced by a cobra, winding back and forth hypnotically across her breasts. Unfortunately, between the rye, the fentanyl, and her own little pill, Zeke couldn't focus on anything but the snake.

"I had hoped the drugs would do the trick, but I think a little pain incentive is needed. It's a shame, because I really quite like you, Zeke, and hope we can get past the whole thief-stealing-from-thief thing when you sober up." She sighed and pinched the median nerve in the palm of his right hand. That got his attention. "Please, Lover. I don't want to hurt you. You can't lie to me, so just start talking."

"Nothing." His attention was still on her beautiful, snake-covered breasts.

"That's a silly answer. Try again."

"Nothing can be... done. Only Shaelagh can... do... it."

"Shaelagh?"

"My AI."

"Then please give her the command."

He wished he could. "Can't. She's monitoring my vitals. Can't give command when drunk or stoned. Failsafe for *this*."

"Really? That's brilliant! Disappointing, but brilliant."

He didn't care anymore. "You can have them when I'm sober. I'll do it."

"*What?* That's a little unexpected, Zeke."

"They got my Lexis killed. I want them gone. They're yours." She could melt them into slag for all he cared.

"Why me?"

"Best shag, *ever*." He definitely wasn't lying about that. He tried to grin mischievously but wasn't sure if he got it right.

She laughed. "I know I'm good, but far from the best."

"Best *I* ever had. Don't tell my ex. She's great, but...you have amazing... *grip*."

He really wanted her to kiss him and forget the stupid relics, but his head dropped down and he fell asleep.

oOo

I can tell you're awake, Boss. Just listen to me. She planted listening bugs in five places and hid a fly drone behind the beverage maker.

He subvocalized so his AI could hear him through his implant, but Nita couldn't. "I know, Shaelagh, but thank you for being vigilant. I was able to read the memories on the surface of her shields very briefly before the midazolam started to kick in. We'll destroy everything after she's left."

What about the vault?

"Put a time lock on it until tomorrow morning, and then raise it two hours after sunrise."

Why tomorrow? What if she insists on getting in it tonight?

"I'm hoping if I promise her the relics without strings, she'll stay the night. Maybe she's a thief who drugged me, but I haven't had this much fun in a long time. She has a talent for keeping my mind off of my shit life."

I understand. Timer set. Have fun. Be careful.

"Thank you. I will. I'm glad you've got my back, though."

Not like she has, but I'm glad I can be here for you.

He roused himself, fighting the effects of the chemical crap floating in his veins. There was definitely no pain, but he also couldn't feel his toes. He lay still, listening to the distant clanging of kitchen tools. "Is she cooking?"

She is, and it looks like she knows what she's doing. She has two plates out, so unless she's expecting company, I don't think she's going to kill you.

"That's such good news. Do you think she's here for herself, or working for someone like Blue?"

She wasn't surprised by the vault situation, and she hasn't tried to retrieve it physically, so I'm guessing she was informed ahead of time, which means there's a ninety-two percent chance she works for Blue.

"Damn. I'm not keen on him getting the relics for free. Maybe I can strike a deal with him. I know his protection at Irido was completely self-serving, but I do owe him—or at least I owe Hunter—my life."

If you seriously wish to sell the OE relics to Bruge Blue, I have compiled a list of estimates of their values, based on the current market, now that possession is legal. It is a fraction of their worth from a month ago, but will still net you a tidy sum.

"Thank you. We'll use the funds to set up a scholarship in Lexis' name." The cold, empty pit opened up in his gut again. He'd returned home from Moonstone just wanting to drink and medicate himself into a coma, to let the grief beat him to death, but it wasn't working out as he'd planned. He hoped that once Nita got what she wanted she'd be gone and he could get back to his self-destruction.

Shaking off the wet blanket of chemicals and alcohol, Zeke rolled out of bed, stepped awkwardly into his pants, and padded to the bathroom. He reached out to Nita with psi, gently bumping her now familiar shields. (Whatever you're cooking smells great. I'll be there in a minute.)

He sensed her surprise at his calm and pleasant contact as if nothing untoward had shattered the rhythm of their lovemaking. (Okay. I'll see you soon. Do you want bean or berry to drink?)

(Surprise me—but not like last time.)

(Will do. Are you okay?) He actually sensed concern behind her words.

(I will be, after food and a chat.)

(Ah, yes. We definitely need both. Finish up, and I'll lay the food out.)

o0o

Marisol sat on the Crystal Beach sea wall and wept beneath the 20-meter-tall crystals that gave the busy beach its name. The clear, glass-like crystals jutted up and out at an angle as if reaching for both the sun and something far out in the Spinnaker Sea. The two crescent moons, Anguta and Heyoka, hung in the deep blue sky, watching and waiting. She came out to the narrow beach to get a feel for the task ahead but ended up tumbling into her hundreds of memories of bringing Lexis to the beach. The fact that her little girl was gone was finally sinking in.

She'd tried burying herself in the maps, and then burying herself in the planning of the mission. When those failed, to keep her thoughts on track, she'd switched it up and let her fury with Hayz burn away her grief, but no matter how livid she was with her ex-husband, *he* didn't bomb the house, *he* didn't kill Lexis and two good men, and *he* didn't actually pick the fight with Ray Addox. She had to hand it to Zeke, though. She wasn't sure even *she* would have had what it took to outright kill Addox if she'd had the opportunity. For once, she was damn glad her ex-husband's moral compass was pointed in a different direction than hers.

Through her tears, she saw a subtle change in the surf. Where there had been smooth roll coming into the swimmers in the shallows, now there were pale objects bobbing up and down. She counted four... no... five... no... seven... She gave up counting because the numbers grew too quickly, forming a line facing her. She hopped down off the rough wall out from under the towering crystals, onto the fine, yellowish sand, and made her way down to the water's edge.

Looking up and down the shore, she could clearly see the gathering of objects only occurring opposite her position. She squinted for a clearer view.

(See with your psi, not with your eyes, BoissiereMarisol.)

Only slightly surprised at the intrusion into her awareness, Mari summoned her psi to her center, then reached out, over the water. It was as she suspected. The bobbing objects were the heads of a large pod of peralti, spy-hopping to get her attention.

(Good evening, Nnif. I see you've brought friends.)

(I have, BoissiereMarisol.) The elderly peralti separated himself from the pod and swam forward. (You seek to fulfill your promise, but you are alone. Without HayzZeke, the daunting task is impossible.)

(I hardly think I need Hayz to fix the problem.)

(Then you do not fully understand the problem.)

(That's why I'm here, Nnif. I need to see what's down there, but no commercial drone could go that deep. I suppose I'm trying to get up the nerve to go for a dive. The depth doesn't bother me, but the six-legged rock-eating thingies living down there *do*.)

(Yes, the gazibeasts were a problem. Ten divers were lost when the machine was first installed.)

(Lovely.)

(You wish to see the rift?)

(Of course. I need to know what I'm up against.)

(One moment.) Nnif tilted his head toward the pod and must have sent a message Mari couldn't hear because three younger, smaller peralti broke free from the main group and swam over. (BoissiereMarisol, lower your shields and prepare to receive a link.)

Although hesitant to lower her shields in a public place where someone could easily tap in while she was distracted, Mari did as she was told. The moment she did, an image touched her mind. She didn't think it was a memory because she'd never seen anything like it before, either in person or in the feeds. After a moment she realized it *was* a memory; it just wasn't one of hers. The floor of the narrow submarine valley glimmered silver with merquilium. The merq rig was nearly torn in half by something powerful that looked like it had struck from the inside out. A half dozen of the creatures Nnif called 'gazibeasts' floated dead in the merquilium, each with their ten legs bent and twisted, and their jaw-heavy heads bloated. The image blurred, and then the viewer turned away from the wrecked machinery and swam against the merquilium flow, upstream, as it were.

The silver, heavier-than-water substance didn't thin out as quickly as she expected. Once he reached the source, the observer turned around and followed the flow back to the wreckage. It was clear now the mining operation had been situated over the natural flow of merquilium, but whatever had torn apart the equipment had blasted a hole in the vein and merquilium flowed out like blood.

(Because that is what tyh is, BoissiereMarisol—the lifeblood of our world.)

(So what do you need us humans to do that you can't do yourselves?)

(We have no understanding of your 'machinery' or 'physics', at least on a useful level like HayzZeke. More is involved in this than simple force. The machinery must be moved without making the rift worse. The rupture grows daily and only the broken machinery keeps it from bursting wide open and splitting our home into pieces. We will work together, but we *need* HayzZeke.)

(Fine. I'll call him. It's not like he has anything better to do.)

oOo

Once they ironed out the details of the sale of the OE relics over the meal of sautéed vat-grown meat and local vegetables, Zeke and Nita sealed the deal back in the bedroom with great enthusiasm. When they were done, Zeke could barely lift his sweaty head off the pillow, and Nita wore a similar expression of satisfied exhaustion.

"You can't stay, can you?"

"Sorry, Handsome, but Blue brought me over from Kokopelli City on Yaponcha, especially for this job. I have to get back."

"Then I'd better send Blue a thank you note. I'll leave out the delicious details, though."

"I appreciate that." She tapped her temple. "I didn't record any of our fun, but he won't care, since he's getting what he wants. Give me a second to call him." She blinked twice, rapidly, and Zeke knew she was making her call. She hopped up, naked, and stepped away from the bed. "Nita, sir. Mr. Hayz says the vault is on a timer and access will be available two hours after sunrise. Yes sir. I'll tell him to expect you at that time. Now? Of course, I'll meet the shuttle in twenty. Thank you. I like to think we struck a deal that gives you the most profit with the least outlay. I've sent you the details. Yes. In twenty. On my way out the door now." She returned to the bed and climbed on top of Zeke.

"You have twenty minutes to get to the shuttle field."

"And it's only a ten-minute drive, which leaves plenty of time for a goodbye." She left the thought hanging but lowered herself down until their lips met.

oOo

"Zeke, Bruge Blue has hovered down onto the pad out front. He is armed and has a two-man escort, both armed as well. All weapons are holstered, though, and they are laughing amongst themselves. Each of the escorts is carrying Grade 3 shipping cases, most likely containing packing foam, but nothing else. Each case is showing a weight only a quarter kilo over their manufacturer's specs, and neither is shielded."

He was relieved. "I'll take that as a good sign. How long until the vault begins its rise?"

"Two minutes, twelve seconds."

"Then I'll go out and greet our guest." He looked down at Deckard, sitting patiently at his feet. "Good boy. Go to bed. Stand-by mode. Security Level Beta." The PKD left him.

"I'll let you know when you can access the artifacts."

"Thanks." He opened the front door and smiled at Blue just as the big man arrived. Whatever Zeke owed Blue for having Hunter keep him safe, Zeke wasn't stupid enough to let his guard down. If Blue wanted to kill Zeke and simply take the artifacts, he could do so and there wasn't a damned thing Zeke could do to prevent it. Except be prepared. "Bruge. Please, come in." He noticed Blue's hesitation. "Or let one of your men come in and clear the place first. You're safe here, but I understand your need for caution."

Blue waved his man off and stepped into Zeke's home. "Hayz, even if Addox hadn't suffered a quick and unfortunately painless death, there's no way you would team up with him to hurt me." He extended his hand and Zeke accepted it. They shook without competing for the power position. They both knew Blue could crush Zeke with his bare hands, and Zeke could do much the same to Blue and his men with psi. It was a standoff, which ended in reluctant mutual respect.

Zeke held the door for the two men to enter with their cases. The first one nodded as he passed Zeke, and the second one followed, placing his case just inside the door before retreating outside to take up a position on the front steps, keeping an eye on both the street and the sky.

"We have a couple of minutes while the vault works its way up from the basement. Can I offer either of you a drink?" He had to be polite but sincerely hoped the men would refuse and be gone as soon as the transaction was complete.

"We're good, thank you." Blue looked around at the bright, sky-lit, plant-filled, circular space and one slender eyebrow rose in a subconscious gesture of approval. "You have an interesting design here. Your own?"

One minute, Zeke.

"It is, with some input from both my ex-wife and Ace Cooney, the architect."

"I thought I recognized some Cooney touches. She designed two of my properties... elsewhere."

Small talk about home design was a safe topic. Zeke was half afraid Blue would ask what he had done to Ray Addox. "Her use of open spaces and curves to disguise heavy structural features as light-weight trim is brilliant." The vault was almost back in its place on the main floor. "Before I forget, thank you for Hunter. You know the details, and obviously, I'm grateful, but I wanted to say it in person."

"It wasn't personal, Hayz, it was business. It doesn't make us best buddies now."

"Of course, it doesn't. It was a totally self-serving investment of human resources. But that doesn't mean I'm not grateful."

"Something tells me you didn't really need Hunter in there."

The vault is in place, Zeke. The combination has been reset to your parents' wedding anniversary, and the biometrics are switched to your other hand and eye.

"Oh no. I did. He saved my life."

"Then you're welcome. Just so you know, I may hate your ex and was willing to steal from you, but if I'd known your daughter was at risk, I would have tried to protect her. I have three children of my own."

Zeke couldn't read the man's stony expression, but he sensed at least a thread of sincerity. "Thank you. Now, the vault is ready."

o0o

Wearing soft, sterile gloves, Blue examined each of the artifacts before his man packed them safely in the cases. Payment was transferred to Zeke's account and all three men placed their thumbprints on the sale contract to seal the deal. Only once Blue and his men were gone from the property and off to wherever, did Zeke slump to the floor.

"Are you okay, Boss? Your vitals are a little high."

"I'm not, but I will be, Shaelagh. I've spent so many years tracking down and stealing those family 'treasures' that to actually let them be walked out the door by someone as reprehensible as that corrupt excuse for a human being grinds in my gut."

"It's a little late for second thoughts."

"I know. And if they hadn't cost my little girl her life, I never would have sold them, but they no longer have any sentimental value whatsoever. Did you transfer the funds as soon as it entered the account?"

"I did. Three times. Not only can the deposit not be traced, but Blue can't hack in and take it back."

"Thank you. Now I'm going to go have a shower. Please scrub the air to rid it of the stink of corruption."

o0o

"Your pretty little Captain Boissiere needs to be stopped." The caller's face remained in the shadows, silhouetted by a dim light behind him.

"There's nothing she can do. She's one woman." His scars itched from the heat of the day, but he resisted scratching them. Once the vid call was done he would moisturize them.

"She's a psi 23."

"Psi isn't goddamned magic, you moron. She can't wiggle her fingers and repair an entire mining rig." He wiggled his fingers at the camera and sneered.

"What if she gets The Psilent One to help?"

"It won't matter. Psi. Is. Not. Fucking. *Magic!*" He sorely wanted to reach through the connection and choke his associate.

"They're saying he reached all the way from Kepler City to Moonstone to end Ray Addox."

"And I should pin a goddamned medal on him for it, but Ezekiel Hayz, psi 24 or not, is not going to fix the rig. Moonstone Corp themselves sent a pair of drones down and they're calling it unsalvageable. Our bombs did exactly what they were intended to do."

"If she starts an investigation..."

"Who is she going to file the request with? Her CO? That's *me*. Consider it dead in the water before she's even thought of it."

"What if—"

"ENOUGH! She's *my* problem and I will deal with her as I see fit. If anyone makes another attempt to kill her, I will *erase* them, and then I will erase their family. Am I making myself clear? Marisol Boissiere is off limits. If The Psilent Fucking One sticks his nose in, though, you are free to terminate him with prejudice. There might even be a bonus for the gun that does it. He's been a pain in my side for more years than I can count."

"Fine. *She's* off limits, *he's* wearing a target on his back."

"Yes." He disconnected the call and reached for the custom moisturizer. More than once over the years he'd considered listening to the whispers behind his back and had his scars repaired. Maybe once Zeke was dead and his ashes tossed in the sea. Striking fear with just a look was working well, but if his reputation as a commander wasn't set in stone by now, it never would be. It would be good to be able to look Mari in the eyes without her flinching, too.

He tapped his desk. "Corporal, book us on the next train to Espy Beach. It's time I had a sit-down with Boissiere."

The reply came from the speakers hidden within the desk's tech-heavy glass surface. "Yes sir. Shall I suit up?"

"Not fully, no. Travel greens with beta-level armour and arms. I'll do the same. Book private quarters. We'll arrive at the terminal just before departure. We'll do this as quickly and quietly as we can."

"Wouldn't you prefer one of our own transports, sir?"

Stihler considered the idea. He wasn't a rank-flashing, privilege-abusing commander, and he hated wasting Peace Force resources in a way either the media or his own superiors could call him on, but this was important. An off-duty 62 killed an in-service coworker, and it was only natural for their CO to get involved. "Agreed. Get us there ASAP. I'll get suited up."

SIXTEEN

"MASTER LOVE MACHINE, TWO messages came in while you were exfoliating. Would you like to hear them?"

"Not until we're secure."

"We are. I took care of all of the bugs and the fly-drone Nita planted, as well as the three bugs Blue and his man hid while your back was turned. They're all inert now and will only need you to remove them physically and drop them into the grinder."

"Perfect. You complete me, Hot Stuff."

"Save the flattery for your real girl, Handsome. Now, your first message is from a personal number listed to one Marguerite DiMasto."

"Hello, Ezekiel." The caller sounded about his own age, maybe a little younger. "My name is Margie. I was a friend of your father's so many years ago. Please call me at this number. We need to chat. It's urgent."

"A friend of *Dad's*? Well, that's unexpected. What's the second message? Something from the old man himself, from beyond the grave?"

"No. It's from Marisol."

"Hayz, call me. We need your help in Espy Beach, stat. That problem our friends asked us to look into is reaching catastrophic proportions and we need to address it *now*. Get off the couch and get here. Call me when you get to town and I'll come pick you up. Hurry. We have to get this done before they arrest me for Bonner's murder."

"I guess that decides it. I'm not particularly in the mood to reminisce with an old friend of Dad's, so that call can wait. Call Nune's and book me a long-distance quad-flier, please. A turbo two-seater with extended batteries should do the trick. I'll be at the hangar in half an hour. Also, please map out a route to Espy Beach, taking into account weather, traffic, and psi storms."

"Will do. I'll also text Marisol to let her know you're on your way."

"Perfect. Before I forget, the reporters are due back here tomorrow. I assume you identified each one when they were here the first time, so please contact them and postpone the press conference for two more days. Tell them I'm recovering from my injuries or something." He turned his attention to packing a quick bag, plus loading up on whatever defensive equipment he had on hand.

While rummaging unsuccessfully through the lab searching for his impact vest, he came across the compact cell scrambler prototype he'd kept for himself before turning over its twin to the Peace Force R&D Team that commissioned it. In its tiny holster, it would fit nicely on his belt, out of sight under his jacket. It wasn't legal, but neither was the bomb they'd dropped on his daughter nor the damage the LPF was doing to the merquilium and the planet.

oOo

Shaelagh wasn't able to plot a course completely free of possible psi storms, so Zeke was forced to wear his old shielded flight suit for the trip. It was a little tight around the middle and across the shoulders, but he could tolerate it for the few hours the flight would take. The crew at Nune's Airfield had the latest model of the quad-prop ready, but Zeke nixed the upgrade.

"I appreciate the offer, Dan, but I need one with full manual override, free of any psi assist."

"*You* want to fly psi-free?"

"And you'd better max out the insurance."

"Do I want to know why?"

"It's not illegal, but there's risk. I'll be careful, of course. It's *my* life."

Dan Nunes turned to his crew of two. "Give him the Mark 4. Same requirements, but swap out the batteries with the ones in the Mark 7. Five minutes. Go!" The two rushed off to get the work done. "You know the 4. You trained on that model. The newer batteries are sixty kilos lighter, with a better range. She'll go like a rocket and most of my customers would be outmatched by the power, but you should be okay."

"'Should be'? I haven't flown in five years." Zeke wondered if the Mark 4 was such a good idea.

"Then use psi assist until you can't, and switch to manual only when you have to." He looked Zeke's suit up and down. "When you hit the storm, turn off the turbojet, close the intake, and tilt forward to forty-five degrees, max. You'll lose air speed, but maintain control as long as your suit's shielding holds out."

"Forty-five."

"*Max.* Or you'll flip into a full somersault."

"I plan on avoiding the storm if I can."

"What's your flight plan?"

"Espy Beach, via the coast."

Dan raised an eyebrow. "You must be in a hurry. The *regular* storms at this time of year are pretty wet."

"Calculations give me a small window of clear skies. Real small."

"Then get the hell out of here. They'll be done shortly, over in Hangar Six." He shook Zeke's hand. "Be careful."

"Always."

"Bullshit."

"This time I will."

"Fair enough. By the way, I was gutted to hear about Lexis. If this trip is about avenging her death, I can add a couple of guns to the 4."

"Thanks, but it's already been taken care of."

"Anyone I know?"

"Yup, but no one I can name. For *your* safety and mine."

"Fair enough. Go, do, see you when I see you."

oOo

Zeke was uncharacteristically and completely caught off guard by the rogue psi when it hit. He'd levelled off at a thousand metres altitude and was making great time an hour out of Kepler City when the pulse burst up from the ocean bed and slapped the aircraft like a giant fist. The four downward-facing lift propellers on the four corners of the aircraft kept him up, but his psi grip on the controls was shattered and he was barely able to focus long enough to switch to manual operation. He lost most of his turbo-generated airspeed and a third of his altitude before he recovered, killed the power to the turbo-rocket, shut the intake, and tilted the back end up to forty degrees.

He wanted to reach out with his mind to see if he could map the storm and find a way through its weak points, but he knew damn well how dangerous that would be. He either had to land and wait out the storm, or he had to tough it out and fly by feel until he was clear. He slammed down his visor to seal his suit and flew on. The aircraft was buffeted hard and fast, but it stopped as abruptly as it began and Zeke took back control. As a precaution, he rose another thousand metres before restarting the turbojet and levelling off. It was the upper limit of the small craft, but he was running out of time. The merquilium situation should have been fixed weeks ago.

He didn't know how Marisol knew the situation was critical, but he suspected the psilings had something to do with it, and his ex wasn't one for alarmist overreactions. When a glance at the instrument panel confirmed he was nearing Espy Beach, he called Marisol.

"Hayz."

"Half-an-hour. I can put this flyer down anywhere, so where do you want me to meet you?"

"It's a deep dive, so we need to suit up. We can't use official gear, so meet me at Dewong's."

"Good thinking. Please send me the exact coordinates. I'll call him to make sure his pad is clear for me to land, and I'll set up an account. This is all on me."

"You don't have to. I'm fully capable of—" He could sense her irritation and cut her off.

"I know you are, but Bruge Blue is actually paying."

He was answered with a few beats of heavy silence.

"So a week in prison and suddenly you're in bed with Blue? I *knew* this was a stupid idea!"

"No, I'm *not*, Mari!" Although he *had* been in bed with Blue's employee not long ago. "He's not part of this, his money is. I sold him all of the artifacts."

"You...*sold* them. After everything you went through? All of the risks you took? Lexis..."

"My obsession killed our daughter." He growled through clenched teeth. "My stupid, proud, arrogant obsession. I didn't want to ever see the damned things again." His hands white-knuckled the aircraft's controls. "My heart reminds me every second of every day what I've done and what it cost us, and I don't need a brass bell or a jar of pink sand or *whatever*, to remind me. I'm taking the cash, adding a chunk of my own, and starting a scholarship in her name."

"Good for you, but don't think this fixes anything or that I'll ever forgive you."

She was angry, but she didn't understand that he was, too. She believed the right to be hurt was hers alone, and that pushed him over the emotional edge he was already teetering at. "Do you really fucking think I expect forgiveness? That I fucking *deserve* forgiveness? *Your* daughter was taken from you, but *I'm* the one who killed her. I'm the fucking asshole who caused Addox to erase the most beautiful soul in the universe. No matter how hurt and angry and broken you are, I promise you it's nothing compared to what I'm living with."

"How dare you—"

"It's not a *contest*. Your pain is immeasurable, unfathomable. But you can aim all the blame and anger and destructive thoughts at *me*. I have all those same thoughts, but they get aimed nowhere but back inside, ramped up by guilt. I don't *want* your forgiveness; not because it has no value, but because if you forgave me for killing Lexis, I would lose all respect for you. This is not a crime that gets forgiven. She may have been the most *beautiful* soul, but yours is the *purest*. None of the shit in our lives has *ever* been your fault. It all lies with me.

When we are done saving the damned planet, you'll never hear from me again. I wasn't worthy of your love back then, and I'm sure as fuck not worthy of it now. Not your love, not your forgiveness, not even your understanding."

Even as Zeke said the words, he knew he was finally speaking the truth aloud. Mari's love for him was based on the false assumption he was a good, loving person, but he wasn't. He'd murdered her father, and now he'd killed her daughter. Even the death of his brother Stan was on him because Stan only joined the 62s to follow Marisol, which he wouldn't have to do if Mari hadn't been in love with Zeke. When Stan signed up, he was only trying to prove himself worthy of her, show her that he was equal to his arrogant, high-psi big brother. And then he was burned to death.

A set of coordinates flashed on Zeke's DataLenz. He entered them into the aircraft's GPS. "Got them. En route. See you soon."

"Roger that." Her reply was almost too soft to hear, and he had no idea what that softness meant. He'd never lit up like he just had. He was *famous* for his calm, steady, unflappable nature. But that Ezekiel Hayz was dead now—he died in a bomb crater with his daughter and two good officers.

o0o

Surf and dive shop owner, Dewong, threw a sloppy salute Zeke's way as he descended down onto the small landing platform. When Zeke popped the aircraft's canopy and struggled to get his stiff legs to climb out, broad, muscular Dewong took his arm and helped him. "You don't look so hot, Zee. Prison didn't treat you good at all."

"I got out alive, and that's what matters, Dee." Zeke looked around. Marisol leaned against her cruiser across the other side of the parking lot. "You got everything we need, Dee?"

"Got it all. You sure you want to purchase Bossy's and just rent yours?"

"Definitely. I won't be needing mine after today, and I know how much she loves to dive. If she refuses to accept it, just put it in a locker and bill me storage fees. I'm not in the mood to argue with her any more than she's in the mood to accept gifts."

Zeke secured the aircraft, plugged the batteries into the charging base, and Dewong led the way to the shop. Marisol started over to meet them at the door. Dewong whispered low. "What are you two up to down below? Don't you have a funeral to plan? I'm so sorry to hear about your girl, Zee. She was an amazing kid."

"Thanks, Dee. She was." Zeke suddenly remembered something. "Shit! Go on inside and get started with Mari and I'll be there in a minute." He turned and took a few steps over to the side of the building. Dewong greeted Marisol at the entrance, but other than a raised eyebrow in Zeke's direction, she said nothing.

Zeke opened a connection off-planet and the telltale peeps of the call indicated it was going through. He couldn't believe he hadn't made this call, yet. He really was a selfish asshole. "Hi, Mom."

"Zeke? This is unexpected. I'm just stepping into the house. Excuse my huffing and puffing while I carry my bag inside. I'm just getting back from a conference."

"I'm glad you're still teaching, Mom."

"Teaching? Oh, no, Zeke, I was learning. I'm training to be an exotic dancer."

Zeke nearly choked. "Um..."

"Gotcha! Yes, I was working with a group of biologists from around the system who are trying to improve the resource use regulations with regard to native species. We've been settling this colony for how many decades and we're still destroying habitats." There was a loud thump, and his mother sighed. "Okay. I'm in and settled on the sofa. What's up?"

He had no idea how to say the words through the impersonal connection. A video call would have been better, but what he really wished he could have done was tell his mother in person. "Mom. We lost Lexis. She... she and the two officers guarding her were murdered."

"Oh, my God! No no no no no..." Her panicked breathing was thunderous in his ears.

"Mom! *Are you okay?*"

"I...I...*yes*. I will be. It's just that we've lost so many." She sobbed and Zeke gave her time to absorb the horrific news. Eventually, she took two long slow breaths and composed herself. "Two officers were lost, too? Then this was related to Marisol's work. I've always been worried about that."

"No, Mom. Don't you dare blame Mari. This is all on me. I made an enemy and he lashed back. He tried to kill Mari, too, and nearly succeeded. I almost lost them both."

"I hope they launch him into low orbit without a suit."

"I don't care what they do with his remains, but he's not going to be bothering the Hayz family again."

"He's dead, Zeke?"

"Heart attack or stroke, they say."

"Good. How are you doing?"

"Not good, Mom. Not good at all. But I've got some serious business here I have to take care of here with Mari, and when it's done, I'll give you a call and we'll talk more."

"Or maybe come for a visit."

"I'd like that."

"It's been too long. Now, go do whatever, and be careful. Give Marisol my love."

"Thanks, Mom. I will do." He turned around and nearly walked into Marisol, who stood stock still, her only motion being shallow breaths, and tears, trickling down her cheeks. "You were listening, M."

"Not intentionally. I'm...sorry."

"Mom sends her love."

"Of course. She's... a wonderful person."

"Unlike her son."

Mari didn't reply to his self-deprecation, but rather just wiped her tears with her sleeve and returned to the shop, just as it started raining.

o0o

Fully suited, but with his respirator, mask, and fins beside him on the rain-battered sea wall in the dark, Zeke was still trying to understand the plan as Mari had just explained it. "So we're going to be contained in big bubbles of psi created and maintained by a squadron of peralti while we descend to the sea floor to remove the shattered mining equipment and repair the rift where the tyh is leaking out? Without any submersible construction gear whatsoever, just using psi? The two of us? Without lights even?"

"You, me and a few hundred peralti, or it's a spectacular death for a hundred thousand humans and uncounted psilings spread over two big islands and one sprawling ocean. We've run out of choices, Hayz."

"And this is the place?"

"It looks right, but a quick probe will tell us one way or another." He sensed her send out a wave probe and he hitched a ride. It barely cleared the sea wall when it encountered the first group of furry, wet chalti. By the time Bossy had swept it across the nearby beach, she'd counted over thirty. "This is the place. We've got a couple dozen friends waiting for us so let's go." The glowing surf pounded away at the shore only a hundred metres away.

oOo

The pain shocking through Zeke's back threatened to derail the whole operation. He reached for the med patch but stopped short when the voices in his head shouted at him.

(STOPNO!)

"A wise decision, mister."

"Not exactly my choice—there are now over a hundred psilings out here and every one of them just screamed in my head to stop." Haltingly, he walked off the road. "They understand my concerns, they say, and right now my mind is being flooded with a rather strong tsunami of reassurance." His confidence grew by the second.

"We're running out of time."

"I know. If you lower your shields a bit, you might benefit from their boost."

"I already have, thanks. Did you think I was totally cool with a night dive in strange waters without illumination or backup?"

"I guess I just hoped you had a better understanding of what we're up against and that's why you were so confident."

"Hardly. I'd have done all this myself last night, but they say we need your mechanical expertise."

"Ah. I'm only wanted for my brain. I'm good with that."

"The peralti will take care of the heavy lifting, we—*you*—just need to tell them what, where, and when."

"But I won't know until I see it."

"Well, if you'll shut up for a minute, you *will* see it."

He shut up, and almost immediately the chorus in his head changed. (You r...psi...is...strong. You...can...do...anything. Fear...is...a...useless...emotion. Th row...it...away. Relax...relax...relax... now *look*.)

The message in his head became a visual projection of sorts, and Mari slipped in and joined the stream, staying to one side and not pushing any deeper into his awareness. The peralti shared with him the situation over the rift. As the memory approached, it held dead scary beasts, the merquilium, the mining operation, and... damage to the equipment that didn't look like any natural corrosive process. (This rig was blown up. At least two explosive devices. Probably magnetic, to ensure they attached themselves to the hull and didn't drift off.)

(That's what I saw, too.)

(That's a shitload of merq pumping out of there.) He watched as the memory swam around the wreckage, being careful not to drift too close to the deadly merquilium. (Do you see those two steel claw-like things covered in barnacles?)

(I do.)

(They actually *are* claws, but not designed to pick things up. Judging by their placement and the direction they face, I'm guessing they were attached to the walls of the rift, holding the rig in place while the scoop gathered the trickle of free-flowing merq. Judging by the medium size of the rig, this was a small vein with very little merq flowing near the surface. The explosions ripped open the rig but also tore it away from its anchoring and shattered the vein as well. No wonder the planet shudders and psi storms are getting worse.)

(That's great you've figured this all out, but the peralti told me as much last night. What we need to know is how to fix it. Can you?)

(Maybe.)

(*Maybe?*)

(Probably. Right now the rig is blocking some of the flow. If it were simply moved, the dam would burst and I expect the planet would split from the resultant shock wave.)

(A crack this small?)

If this were any other liquid, like water or magma even, no. But because of the psionic properties of merquilium, there could be a ripple effect that would tear through the ocean beds, cracking open more and bigger gaps. The destabilized merq wouldn't just expand and rupture; on this scale, it would turn the sea and atmosphere toxic.)

(Oh shit.)

(Exactly. It wouldn't happen immediately, but it would be irreversible, probably. I would think, though, that throughout the evolution of the planet, such events have happened before, but here we are with healthy waters and thousands if not millions of native species living in them. The ecosystem must have natural safety valves and checks and balances, or the planet would have ruptured millennia ago. Of course, now that humans are here, the equations change.)

(Okay, but what do *we* do *now*?)

(Honestly? We need to rearrange the seabed slowly, to cover and seal the rift without causing the merq to destabilize, or the rift to widen. The submarine canyons on either side will provide us with the raw materials, but even if we could bring the walls down and in, the impact would be catastrophic. This is going to take time we may not have. A hundred peralti just isn't enough muscle, either psionic or physical.)

A new voice joined the conversation. (Your *muscle* is on its way, HayzZeke. By the time the second moon rises, the gathering will be complete.)

Zeke looked up at the sky, but couldn't see a damned thing through the clouds and rain. He checked his onboard system for the times of moonrise. (That's a little less than an hour. There's no point in us going down until we're ready. Mari, didn't Dewong give you a thermos of brew? If I can't use my medpatch, then I at least need something to perk me up.)

(He did. I could use a mug, too. Sniph, we're breaking the contact now. Please let us know when everyone is gathered and then we'll get going.)

(I will, BoissiereMarisol.)

He was suddenly gone from Zeke's awareness, and Marisol's, too, judging by her expression as she came back to visual awareness and snapped her shields back up in place.

oOo

"Where are Boissiere and Hayz, now?"

"The tracer they put on her cruiser puts them on the beach at a point directly in from the mine."

"Son of a bitch! I should have killed him when I had the chance! Is it too late now?"

"Maybe not." The young lieutenant looked up from the tracer screen Colonel Stihler had temporarily installed in the 62 cruiser they had requisitioned upon landing at the Espy Beach airfield. Stihler was livid that The Psilent One had arrived not long after they had. He wasn't surprised, but he was pissed off.

"Who do we have in the area?"

"Kansis is our closet man. If Hayz and Bossy travel by surface vessel we could have Kansis redirect his old tug to the South commercial pier, transfer to a fast interceptor boat, and be there in two hours. We're only a fifteen-minute flight, but once they're in the water there's not a damned thing we can do, sir. I mean there *is* something we can do, but if we start dropping aerial explosive charges near a tourist beach, we'll be caught in seconds, even in the middle of the night. Kansis can slip an armed submersible drone over the side and catch Hayz underwater where there will be no witnesses."

"No explosives. Boissiere is one of ours. We have to stop whatever the hell she's doing before she gets killed, but I'm perfectly happy with The Psilent One being left for the crabs to eat on the seabed. Send Kansis, and be *very* specific with the orders. If that fucker hurts our 62, I'll tie an anchor to his legs and sink him myself. Finally, find out what the final report is on Addox's death. If there was any hint of foul play we have to get ahead of it before his people take to the streets to solve it themselves."

"Yes sir." The officer air-keyed a short message with blurring speed. "Orders sent to Bert Kansis." He air-keyed another, longer, succession of signs and then stopped, sensor-enabled hands poised in front of him.

"What's the delay?"

"There's a connection delay due to uncharacteristically strong psi storms between here and Moonstone." The screen flashed red and yellow. "I'm in." After a full minute of keying, he signed the 'SEND' command and leaned back in the chair, satisfied. "Done. I should have the coroner's report shortly."

o0o

Bert Kansis was in his cabin when the message from the shore came in. He scrolled the screen twice to make sure he understood the instructions.

"Carlos! Radio the pier and have the launch prepped. We have some hunting to do!"

The answering grunt from the cabin next door was all Kansis needed to hear to know his order would be carried out.

o0o

"Bossy, did I point out that this is all theoretical? If I had time I would work up a simulation model to make sure we get it right, but we don't have time."

"Quit your excuses and check my gear. It's supposed to snap onto the right shoulder of my suit but it doesn't feel right."

"Yessir! Right away, sir!"

"Don't be such an asshole."

"Yes, sir." Working by touch, he lifted the clip on its spring, rotated it 180 degrees, and locked it back down. "Done."

"Thank you. She turned to face him and reached for his gear. "Hold still while I check your setup. I can't have an equipment failure screw this not-so-little mission up." His tank bumped him as she grabbed it and tugged. "It's solid."

"I'm guessing your Colonel hasn't exactly approved of this."

"Are you shitting me? If he knew you were even in Espy Beach he'd shoot you himself. One of my team snuck word to me that Stihler is here in town, but with my onboard shutdown, I can't be traced. He'll just have to wait to talk to me in the morning."

"What if he shows up at your residence?"

"He'll knock and knock but this little piggy won't be home. I'm only suspended, not under house arrest. As long as I'm in the area, he has little to complain about."

"But he'll still complain."

"A little. But he'd have a right to. One of his commanders killed one of her subordinates, and I should be sitting quietly at home, behaving myself, rather than gallivanting around and going for a midnight dive with The Psilent One, a known felon. Let's just get this done so you can hop back in your flier and get back to Kepler City."

(IT IS TIME! HURRY!)

"Shit. That's our cue, Captain Boissiere. Are you sure these suits will get us that deep?"

"They will, because the peralti promise me the 'bubbles' of psi they're going to manifest around us will bear the brunt of the pressure."

"How long do we have to maintain these bubbles?" Despite his boosted morale, Zeke's voice held a strained note of concern.

"*We* don't, the peralti do. Our job is to go along for the swim until we're needed."

"Let's get on with it then." He took a step toward the ocean. "I've done crazier things with less info for worse reasons."

"And ended up in prison."

"Good point. I don't think Stihler would let me live long enough to get to prison, though. I'm pretty sure I've worn out any goodwill he may have had toward me."

"I can assure you that's not true, because there was absolutely *no* goodwill for you before. He's hated you since the day I met him at the academy. It's like Stan's animosity wore off on him in those months they were roommates."

"That's good to know because since he killed my brother I haven't exactly had a soft spot in my heart for him, either."

"Then let's do this and keep you two apart. For the sake of *everyone's* sanity." She led the way through the rain, down the beach, and into the Spinnaker Sea. Zeke followed along, thinking if he had to die to pay for Lexis' death, it might as well be while he was trying to save the world. He just hoped they didn't kill everyone else while doing it.

oOo

The covered launch crashed bow-first through the waves and the storm and Carlos wrestled with the wheel to keep them on course while maintaining their speed. Kansis, strapped to a seat behind his pilot's, did his best to check and load the sea drone he'd brought along to do the job. He checked the arming light on the explosive mini-torpedo on the belly of the machine and was satisfied. Now all they had to do was intercept The Psilent One far enough out to sea that the storm would cover the sound of the boat's hull slapping on the waves as they approached whatever craft the 62 and Hayz were in.

oOo

Zeke and Bossy waded out until they were fully submerged. Their dive suits functioned perfectly. Zeke extended a probe and discovered they were surrounded by peralti as far as his mind reached. A familiar peralti probe touched his shields and Zeke opened them to let it in.

(HayzZeke, we will all be surrounded by what BoissiereMarisol called 'bubbles of psi'. When that happens you will only be able to communicate by touching your bubble to another bubble. We will all be linked together for strength and to move you along, so to reach any in the pod simply use your mind to touch your own water-filled bubble. We peralti are capable of holding our breath for extended periods of time, but eventually, we must resurface to breathe. You will witness shifts in our formations as each rises to the surface and then returns to join the pod. Do not be alarmed by these shifts.)

(I understand. Lead on, McDuff.)

(I am called Calanid.)

Zeke smiled behind his mask. (Lead on, *Calanid*.)

The psiling probe vanished and in its place, Zeke could see a very different type of concentration of psi. He was about to extend another probe to investigate but was forestalled by a thin glowing wall half a metre from his visor. "Hey, this is a helluva special effect, guys." There was no answer to his comment so he turned toward Mari, only to see that she was facing away from him. He tried the mask mic but still, there was no response. A closer look at Bossy revealed a faint green-blue bubble surrounding her. Remembering what Calanid had said, Zeke leaned over until his green bubble touched Mari's and met with rubbery resistance. He reached out a probe until he came into contact with his own bubble and spoke to Mari.

(Oh Captain, my Captain, isn't this cool?)

Marisol turned around, alarmed at the sudden voice in her head, but Zeke couldn't see her expression because the glow from the bubbles wasn't nearly enough illumination to show the face behind the visor. (Hayz. I see you've figured out the communication end of this setup. I wasn't sure if it would work.)

(Sure does. It's even a funky colour, too.)

(What do mean, 'colour'?)

(I mean what I said—'colour'. They're green.)

You can *see* the bubbles?)

(Of course. Can't you?)

(I had to bump into it with a probe just to know it was there.)

(Too bad, they're pretty, in a surreal, take-us-to-the-depths kind of way.) He turned within his bubble and squinted out toward deep water, where green bubbles bobbed and moved in the dark sea, each accompanied by dozens of glowing, flashing, jellyfish. (I can see the whole gang, and there's a shit-load of them. Wow.)

One bubble moved up, touched both of theirs, and Calanid spoke to them. (There is a craft moving toward the area of the rift at a very high speed. We must leave.)

SEVENTEEN

Z EKE NOW NOTICED THE psi bubble was cutting off the stream of positive vibes that kept him from focussing on the dark expanse of wet death before him. Doubts started to creep in. (Yup. Time to go. Your pep-talk is wearing off.)

(Remember to stay close—or you will be crushed by pressure outside your bubble.)

(Great.) His psi transmitted his sarcastic tone perfectly.

The bubble-protected peralti nudged up against the bubbles of the two humans and pushed them along. In a moment they were surrounded by peralti and moving out into deep water. Panic rose from Zeke's gut but before it triggered a fight-or-flight response the voices of all the peralti in the pod surged through the bubbles and washed over him once again with calming reassurance. Against all his instincts, Zeke was content to be herded along.

o0o

The radar on board the launch detected no vessel whatsoever between their boat and the beach. Kansis double-checked the device's settings but there was nothing except empty, open water. One look at the storm around them and he was sure his source had been wrong—no one in his right mind would be out on a night like this except a worn-out cargo captain and his over-paid help. He snatched a bit of his psi and shot it at his pilot, giving the order to put the launch into a circling pattern over the coordinates of the mining operation he'd blown up. The sea was rough, but he'd seen worse, so he attached the hoist's cable to the sea drone's harness and lifted it up off the deck. It swung back and forth madly with the action of the boat, but he got it into the water and released the harness. With a tap on the remote on his wrist, he started the armed device and sent it down.

o0o

Using psi to coordinate their efforts, the peralti pod moved quickly once it was beneath the storm's reach. A hundred meters down, the ocean was calm—dark but calm. The two humans were required to do little more than enjoy the excursion and after a minute or two Zeke slipped into a peaceful little trance. He could see the flexible bubbles of psi moving with the peralti but sensed Marisol resort to using her dive mask's darkscope to see the shadowy forms of the psilings around them. Unconcerned, he hummed to himself.

o0o

Because she was relying on her darkscope rather than her psi, Mari knew long before Zeke did that they'd descended into an ocean canyon that was getting rapidly deeper as the pod moved forward. Even as she formed the thought, though, Calanid spoke mind to mind with her.

(We are near, yes. Members of the pod have detected a small machine moving in this direction. It is not large enough for a human to ride in it, but I am getting images of what appear to be weapons. I will send a few to redirect or disable it.)

(Pardon my ignorance, Calanid, but for an aquatic being belonging to a species most humans consider to be animals, you have a strong grasp of both our language and our technology.)

(Humans first appeared on our world many generations ago, when I was very young—the peralti live much longer than our cousins the malti and chalti. For those many generations, I have tried to learn all I can in the hope of being able to reach your people to help create a harmonious world. For the most part, you humans have left us alone. Our areas of settlement are not areas you have either wanted or needed, until now. My mind, like my father's and yours and HayzZeke's, is strong, and if I am near to the shore I can hear the stray thoughts of many humans, especially the weak-shielded ones. I have listened and learned, as have many of my kind.)

(I'm impressed.)

(Thank you. It is a pleasure to finally be able to use my knowledge and abilities to do some good.)

(I feel the same way. I'm just sorry it's taken us so long to stop *this*.)

(Your ways are not our ways. What matters is that you and HayzZeke are here now and we will bring the destruction to an end.)

(Let's hope so. What's to keep the LPF from doing this again, in another location?)

(This place is unique, and they know it. The builders of this 'rig' have already abandoned it. They sent people to examine it and determined that it was not worth making repairs. After we have blocked this bleeding, the flow will be corrected.)

(I just hope we don't disappoint you.)

(You will not.)

(Fingers crossed.)

(And flippers. We are here now, and it is time to rouse HayzZeke from his thoughts.)

oOo

A nudge on Zeke's shields urged him out of the trance. The flow of the reassuring euphoria-push increased just a bit and quickly suppressed the shock of remembering where he was, of seeing that his bubble was much, much smaller than it had been at the surface, and his exhausted CO_2 collected at the top. Every so often whichever peralti was controlling his bubble would vent the air out, to reduce buoyancy, Zeke assumed.

"Wow, talk about a change of venue..." Zeke examined the piece of shattered machinery a meter above his bubble. It rose up into the darkness but, linked as he was to the nearly countless psilings through bubble contact, he knew it rose a hundred meters from the seabed and was four hundred meters long. He was also aware they were a *long* way down. The water was nearly still, showing no signs of the choppy seas above. What little fear he clung to slipped away, and the scientist in him came to the fore.

The huge peralti pod swam down to the bottom of the canyon and gently placed the bubbles containing the humans down on the rock. As soon as they came into contact with the ocean floor, the two sensed the urgency and danger. This close to the actual merquilium vein, their psionic senses magnified tenfold and they both turned to see the river of merquilium as it emerged from the fissure and flowed along the canyon floor. The flow was even faster than the memories they had been shown back at the surface. Zeke started to doubt their ability to slow it down without making it worse.

He leaned his own bubble forward until it touched the merquilium flow and the psionic shock hit him like a blow to his gut. He broke the contact, stumbled back, and drifted to his knees, doubled over. So intense was the red-surging pain that it was a moment or two before he realized Bossy had moved up beside him and was pressing her own bubble against his.

(Hayz? What happened?)

Although it was unnecessary to move at all because they were using psi, Zeke pushed himself up on one knee and looked back at Mari. (I think we're too late. Too much merq has been released.)

(We have to try. Now we just have to try *faster*.)

(Okay. You're right.) He reached out an arm and his bubble flexed enough to let Bossy grab the arm and help him stand. Once he regained his feet, he looked around for Calanid. The peralti was just out of reach, but he was observing Zeke and nudged his bubble against The Psilent One's.

(What do you need from us, HayzZeke?)

(We're too late for subtle. We need every peralti here to start moving rocks from everywhere to here. We need to block the flow completely. Dam it off.)

(Of course.) The peralti turned away, but Zeke leaped over and made contact again, bubble to bubble.

(I assume they will all be using psi to do the lifting?)

(They will.)

(Perfect! Have each of them find a piece of rock or coral about the size of their head, and bring it here, just beyond the flow, next to the wound. Placing them one at a time won't block anything and at worst will just redirect the flow. But if we orchestrate it so we gently lay hundreds of obstructions down in the mouth of the fissure at the same time, it might act like a cork. Actually, have them get two such boulders. Quickly.)

Calanid nodded and swam away. In the dark depths, Zeke lost sight of him. He turned back to the dark hulk of the mining rig. He could see much of it, so he reached out with his hand and touched his bubble to the dead mechanical beast. It took him a moment to extend his awareness, but with the rig actually sitting in the river of tyh he was able to sense every metre of the machine, seeing where each of the points of contact were on the seabed. (Shit. We're not going to be able to move this.)

Bossy bumped up against him, bubble to bubble. (What are you saying?)

(We have to do this without the rig. There's absolutely no way we can shift this even a centimetre.)

Something gently bumped his bubble. (HayzZeke, it is done. Rocks have been gathered. Is it time to make our cork?) A moment later another member of the pod touched Calanid's bubble. Then another and another, until at last they were all joined and Zeke 'saw' there weren't hundreds of aquatic psilings around, but *thousands*. He began to think their Herculean task might just be possible.

(Wow. Can you please get us over to the mouth of the flow, but not too close.) Two hundred peralti surrounded the two humans and the group moved quickly up the canyon. The peralti must have understood what he was asking of them because he and Mari were given an overhead view of the fissure without being in the way of what was about to happen. The excitement of the thousands of psilings reached through the bubbles and invigorated Zeke. *They* believed his plan would work. It *should* work... but he was a man of science and liked to test theories before putting them into action in an irreversible operation. This one time he had to trust the plan.

(We are yours to command, HayzZeke.)

And they were. Zeke took a breath, drew on their faith in him, and gave them their instructions. (When I say 'go', psi one boulder up and over the fissure, getting as close as you can without touching the merquilium—the tyh. On my command of 'down', everyone lower their boulders into place at the same time over the mouth of the fissure. We are trying to cork it quickly and gently, so don't stray far with your rock, and don't drop it. Once your rock is in place, immediately psi another one up and over the fissure. Once I assess our first drop's results, I will direct the second drop to catch any leaks. Does that make sense to everyone?)

A deafening chorus of (Yes!) rumbled through him.

(Good. In three...two...one...GO!) His command was carried out in perfect synchronization, and then he sensed them all halt and hold in place. (Perfect! In three...two...one...DOWN! Gently!)

There was an eons-long wait that made Zeke want to scream in frustration, but eventually, rocks and silt and gazibeast skeletons settled.

(Hayz, I can see it clearly with my darkscope! It's working! It's plugged! No! Wait! There's a leak!)

Someone in the conjoined bubbles shifted to touch the leak and they all saw it at once. As instructed, the peralti all held their second rocks and coral pieces in wait.

Zeke was disoriented, though. Without sight, he was turned around and unsure of what he was viewing through the massive psi link. (I can't see where the leak is. I see it as we share it, but I can't direct the drop!)

Calanid nudged him. (I can. We know. On my command, sisters and brothers. Three...two...one...DOWN on the leak.)

The command was executed and a long wait followed. Marisol requested the pack to move her closer and they did. Zeke could sense her checking out the massive rock covering, looking for leaks. A sunburst of joy suddenly radiated from her.

(We did it! Done!)

Zeke wept. He hadn't realized how wound up and tense he was. The relief of his internal pressure was palatable. (Wonderful work, everyone! Thank you! You can go home, now!)

The shift in mood within the thousands-strong pod shifted into the brighter spectrum of emotion, but only for a moment. Calanid interjected. (We are not finished. The 'plug' as you call it is in and secure, but we must now seal this forever. It is now safe to close the canyon.)

(Close the canyon?) Zeke was confused. (How? We don't have explosives. What we just did was with loose rocks and coral.)

Calanid moved physically closer to Zeke, and Mari's handlers brought her back up to them. (It is difficult to explain my friends, but it involves choral harmonic power and a very thorough knowledge of the canyon's weaknesses. It is four times as high as it is wide so there should be few problems.)

(Choral harmonic psi?) Zeke had a suspicion about where this was headed. (Like a tuning fork shifting a bed of sand?)

(Yes, HayzZeke. But on a very large scale. We are many and should be enough. We will sing with psi at key stress points in the canyon walls but you must be back on the surface by then. Our ability to maintain the psi 'bubbles' will be compromised and you will be at risk of crushing.)

(Won't you be at risk from the same thing? You've each used psi bubbles, too.)

(We will move closer to the surface, to make the pressure less. The elderly and the very young even further away.)

(Then we should go?)

(Please. You have done all you can here.) Calanid's thoughts wavered. Zeke and Mari both reached out to their friend. (I will live. The toxicity of the water was more than we anticipated. Go. We will finish. I will get my people away to fresh water. We will survive.)

(Get us up, then!)

(Very well. We will all surface for one large breath, then back down.) The elder
peralti sent the command to his fellows, and they rose as a group.

Zeke sensed they were not just rising, but moving laterally, probably back
toward the shore. When they broke the surface, his suspicion was confirmed.
Once the sand was beneath his feet, the bubble around him was dispelled. He
moved as quickly as he could until his upper half was above the surface and he
could remove his mask and mouthpiece. The rain had stopped and one crescent
moon was cutting through the cloud cover. Marisol mirrored his actions beside
him, and they both turned to see thousands of pale heads spy-hopping in the
sea, taking breaths and preparing to resubmerge. Zeke was trying to estimate
how far out from shore the canyon was when a small explosion just south of
that spot lit up the sky. It was too far out for them to feel a concussive shock,
but the sound of the explosion reached them a fraction of a second later.

o0o

Captain Kansis banged his thick, calloused finger down on the screen of his
wrist controller, but the readout showed the sea drone returning to the launch.
The screen was still lit, so he knew it wasn't a power issue. He tried an emergency
shutdown. The screen changed to read *Emergency Shutdown Successful*, except
when he pulled up the tracker screen again, it showed the drone was still moving
in their direction. He lifted his binoculars from around his neck and as he
raised them to his eyes they automatically adjusted for the dark and switched
to infrared mode. He scanned the horizon, but couldn't see the drone's short
tail fin anywhere. The Emergency Shut Down should have kicked on its floaters
and brought it to the surface for recovery.

He squinted and zoomed the lenses in. There was *something* on the surface,
but it appeared to be round, pale, shapes, not the sharp lines of the drone's tail.
By the time he lowered the binoculars again and raised the remote to trigger the
self-destruct sequence, it was too late.

o0o

The impact and explosion ripped through the launch's stern, through the twin inboard electric motors, and shredded the captain and his pilot. The peralti responsible for the redirection of the deadly human device barely got clear in time. The explosion's concussive shock wave stunned all four of them, but they were rescued by others before they drowned.

o0o

Bossy reflexively reached for a sidearm she didn't have. "What the hell was that, Hayz? Was that *your* doing?!"

Zeke stared out to sea. "That was definitely *not* me."

(It was the craft that was intercepting us. The machine they launched was returned to them. Two particularly nasty humans familiar to us were killed, but no peralti were.)

(That's good news, but we need to get out of here, Hayz. The explosion will be investigated by my own team and we can't be anywhere near here when they arrive.) She jogged off to the cruiser in the beach's parking lot.

(Agreed. Calanid, thank you for everything your people did tonight. We couldn't have done this without such massive help.)

(Thank you for showing us what was needed and for guiding us, HayzZeke. We can speak more later, but we must all clear this area, as BoissiereMarisol has rightly suggested.)

(Of course. Good night.) He shuffled off after his ex-wife.

o0o

The lieutenant swivelled his seat around and faced his CO. "Colonel, sir, we're getting a report there has been an explosion near the coordinates I gave to Captain Kansis. Espy Beach 62s are responding. Since they know we are here in town, should we join them?"

Stihler was grateful his sidearm was in the locker behind his seat because in his fury he might have either shot a hole in the aircraft's control panel or in his aide. Instead, he ground his teeth and sucked a deep breath in through them before replying as calmly as he could. "Yes. Immediately. Let them know we are en route, but get us there as fast as you can. If Boissiere needs saving or The Psilent One needs assistance reaching the afterlife, we want to be there in time to help."

"Yessir!" The craft lifted off and roared to the beach at top speed. The road lights illuminating the coastal highway were the only landmarks they had to follow, but they were all they needed. From his navigation station, Stihler accessed a live satellite feed of the area but the cloud cover was too thick so he had to rely on the archived map to track their progress.

oOo

They drove as fast as possible on the rain-wet road, needing to put as much distance between them and the explosion as fast as possible. Zeke searched the road behind them for the lights of pursuing vehicles. "You know, the vehicle's GPS already places us at the scene. Your dash cam has even recorded our conversations. Once they confirm it was us, there's little they won't know about our little excursion. They might even pin that explosion and the two deaths on us."

"Agreed. So what are you going to do about it?"

"Me?"

"*You*. You're the technical genius. Maybe do some *good* with it at last. *Maybe* start by erasing the drive-cam's files, then work on the GPS. The drives for both are under your seat."

"You've thought this out."

"Not exactly. Those are all the things I look for when I'm investigating a crime, and deleted drives are the things that hurt our investigation."

"Then you know erasing the drives won't be enough. I'll need to destroy them."

"Go for it. But hurry, because in ten klicks we're coming to an intersection of three roads and I want the tracking to be off before I make my turn."

"Yes sir." Zeke didn't bristle at taking orders from Mari because she was right and she knew what she was doing. Oddly, he'd always trusted her judgment. He just wished she'd trusted *his*. He reached between his legs and beneath the seat to discover a drawer. He slid it out and found the two drives. He picked the one labelled with the dash-cam manufacturer's logo and plucked it out of its mounting bracket. As soon as it was clear of its connections, the light on it went from green to amber, indicating it was now on battery backup. He held the drive sandwiched between his palms and extended a probe into the casing through the little vents. For the next minute, with psi, he used the device's own battery to short out connections and melt the drive's core. It quickly got too hot to hold, so he placed it on the floor. When it started to smoke, Mari noticed and pulled sharply onto the rocky shoulder of the road. The vehicle bounced and slammed up and down on the roughness as she brought it to a fast halt.

"Done with it?"

"Yes. It's as much slag as I can make it. We can always toss it on a bonfire to finish the job."

"No time. Give it here." She pulled her sleeve down over her hand and held it out. Zeke used his own sleeve for insulation, picked up the drive, and put it on her covered palm. Without another word, Mari jumped out of the cruiser, ran across the roadway to the little bluff overlooking the waves breaking below, and threw the drive as far as she could. Before she was back in the cruiser, Zeke was working on the second drive.

Mari climbed back in and got the cruiser back on the road. "I hate polluting, but the salt water will finish what you started." The cruiser jerked a little as she got it up to speed, and Zeke could see she was wrestling with the steering. "Hurry with that drive. We have a new problem."

The GPS drive was easier to destroy because it had two batteries for him to work with. He placed the drive on the floor and proceeded to fry circuits, melt connections, and scrub the drive before incinerating the actual data storage. Unfortunately, the two batteries created so much more heat and smoke they were forced to open the windows. When he was sure it was finished, he nodded at Mari. "Done."

They swerved onto a much smoother shoulder this time, but the steering lurched as they came to a stop. He popped open his door, picked the drive up in both sleeve-protected hands, and tried to jog across the road. The pain in his back stabbed him, so he hobbled the remaining distance. There was no break wall this time, so he stumbled down the beach until the water lapped at his boots, then he threw the drive as far as he could, off on an angle, with a tremendous boost of kinetic psi to take it even further. If they managed to track his bootprints in the sand, then the distance and the angle might delay them from finding the drive long enough for the saltwater to do its job. He got back to the cruiser as fast as he could, which wasn't particularly fast at all.

"I've fixed the steering, for now," Mari reassured him. "We'd bent a strut or rod of some sort. I bent it back with psi. It should hold long enough for us to get where we're going. I found a much bigger problem, though."

"Of course you did." He tapped his medpatch once, quickly. He hated to, but the pain left him little choice.

"We were bugged. Or *I* was. It was a 62-issue tracker with a helluva long range. I've disabled it and tossed it in the scrub, but we need to sweep this vehicle completely."

"Shit. If they were tracking us..."

"Then we need to move *now*. Can you scan while I drive?"

"Of course. Go."

"You've got four klicks to get it done. Once we make the turn, I can hide us, visually, but we need to be clean, electronically." She got the cruiser back on the road just as two pairs of lights came around the bend toward them. The cruiser still wobbled a bit, but as they sped up, it settled down to a gentle shake. As the vehicles passed, both Hayz and Boissiere raised their hands to shield their faces from other drive-cams.

While the road markers flashed past, Zeke extended a probe out to the rear of the vehicle and started a full sweeping scan. Centimetre by centimetre he moved the probe quickly. He still wasn't finished when Mari pulled onto a paved shoulder. The intersection she spoke of was directly ahead. "Thirty more seconds. Almost done." He concentrated and was finished in thirty-four seconds.

"Are we good to go, Hayz?"

"We are. There was one more bug, under the front bumper. It's gone. It was a commercial-grade model. Probably put there by whoever tried to kill you."

"Wonderful. Pick a number between one and six." She waited for a short line of vehicles to pass and got them moving again.

"Um, six."

"Interesting choice. I expected you to pick four. Doesn't matter, either way." She stopped at the intersection and then turned onto the first road on the left.

"I picked six. This looks like a one. First one on the left."

"Yup. But I numbered them right to left. One more way to make it random. All of these roads eventually lead to at least three 'somewheres' I can hide us, so it hardly matters which one we take. What this does is—"

"Slow them down."

"Yes. We have about a twenty-minute drive. We don't dare be out here much longer. The clouds are clearing and the sun'll be up soon."

"And more traffic. We risk being caught on someone else's cam." He yawned.

"We do. I can tint the windows a bit to help."

"Good thinking. Wake me when we get there, wherever 'there' is." He crossed his arms, dropped his chin to his chest, and went to sleep.

o0o

"I've lost the cruiser. The tracker put it at the shore at the moment of the explosion, then it was off west on the coast road. It pulled over twice, and vanished the second time."

Stihler was frustrated, but not angry. "I'm surprised they took that long to find the bug. They're gone. She's too good for us to catch her. With the luck surrounding that high-psi prick, I suspect they both survived, and since Kansis was so reckless as to fail and so considerate as to kill himself doing so, I hardly care if we figure out what actually happened to him and his crew. We're done here. Take us back to The Beach where we can make our visit official and find out what happened between Bossy and Bonner."

"Yes sir." The lieutenant pulled on the controls and turned them sharply and the aircraft banked hard to starboard and levelled off on a course back to the town of Espy Beach.

o0o

The cruiser bumped to a stop and jarred Zeke awake from his power-nap. Much of his pain was gone, but he was too groggy to think straight. Beside him, Marisol exited the vehicle in silence, slamming her door. Zeke's grogginess lost its grip. He popped the latch and climbed out to join her, wobbling a bit as he tried to stand up straight and look around at what was quite obviously a repair garage. "Where are—"

Bossy's hand shot up, open palm toward him, accompanied by a sharp look. "Shhh!"

Zeke 'shhed', which is why the sound of a stunner powering up was clear over the sound of the cruiser's engine winding down. He sent out a light wave of psi to map the area and find the stunner. The woman was three meters behind him, ducked low behind a rack of tires. He raised his hands slowly, placed them on his head, and turned to face her. "I'm unarmed."

"You're The Psilent One. Even unconscious, you're *never* unarmed." The shadow behind the tires moved but remained behind the cover. Zeke could see the business end of the weapon pointing through a gap, directly at his chest.

EIGHTEEN

Z EKE DIDN'T MOVE. HE barely dared breathe. Where there was a stunner, there was often a trigger-happy finger. He kept his body still and his psi contained within his shields. Behind him he heard Mari moving around the cruiser.

"I'll pay you double to give him a quick shot, knock him out for an hour, JJ."

The tall, slender, black-haired woman moved slowly from behind the tires, her weapon pointed unwaveringly at Zeke. "You don't pay me at all, and even if you did there's no way I want to make an enemy of the psi-master who reached out from Kepler City to execute the Mayor of Moonstone." She winked at Zeke and holstered her weapon.

Lowering his hands, Zeke took a deep breath and relaxed a bit. He'd never met JJ, but he knew her name. "Is that what they're saying I did?" Although it would cement his reputation as someone not to be messed with, it could draw unwanted attention from Stihler and put psionics in an even worse light than his thefts had.

Mari crossed over to the woman and gave her a quick hug. JJ raised an eyebrow at Zeke. "Not really. It was a stupid story a few LPFs were spreading, but no one believes it, and the psi-authorities have dismissed it as impossible. Addox died of a stroke. Don't you check the news feeds?"

"I've been offline since I landed." He should probably check in with Shaelagh soon, but it could wait until he was clear of Mari and wouldn't bring any trackers down on her.

"I could never do that. Offline, I mean." She walked them out of the garage through a door and into what Zeke was shocked to see was a high-end, tech-heavy, living space not unlike his own. "Oh, and if you *did* kill Addox, you'd have my undying love. Whatever other issues and crap you two have, you made one amazing daughter together. I can't believe she's gone." She motioned them to sit in a pair of overstuffed, green, pleather chairs. "When is her funeral? I'd like to be there. I'll even speak if you need me to."

Mari and Zeke both sat, not looking at either each other or their hostess. After a moment, Zeke snapped the silence in two. "I'm going to defer to Marisol on all of that—where she wants it, who speaks. I'll pay the bills. It's all I deserve to do." He finally looked at his ex. Her eyes were both full of tears and anger. "I didn't mean I'll make you do all the work, I meant that you get to make all of the decisions—unless you want me to. I don't know." To JJ he added, "There's no manual for burying your child. I haven't got a fucking clue what to do."

Marisol stood. "I'm going to make a pot of brew, and go to the bathroom." She strode off through an archway into what was clearly the kitchen.

JJ walked over and put a hand on Zeke's shoulder. "There's definitely no manual. I'll help her make the arrangements, and if I sense there's anything she wants you to do, I'll let you know."

He was confused. "I don't even know you. Why would you do that?"

"But I know *you*, Zeke. More to the point, I know Mari and Lexis, and I know everything they've said about you behind your back. She hates you, but not for the reasons you probably think. And Lexis... well, your girl worshipped you."

The sudden lump in Zeke's throat choked back any weak reply he could muster.

"Ever since Mari started bringing Lexis to The Beach after your divorce, we've been friends. We met one day at Dewong's when Lexis was about ten, and my son, Jaykob was nine."

"You're Jaykob's mother? Lexis spoke of him."

"I am. When he was murdered two years ago, Mari was my rock. She got the local 62s to take the case seriously and not just close it as an accident, which it looked like at first. She and Lexis got me through it. *Still* get me through it, because the pain doesn't just go away, we simply learn to live with it."

"I'm sorry about your son. Lexis told me about his death. He meant the world to her. Thank you for being their friend. I worry that Mari is all work and no play, but *her* life hasn't been *my* business for a long, long time."

"I'm happy to do what I can for her, even to the point of hiding her from her CO when she's in a shitload of trouble."

"She sure is. She killed a fellow 62. He was coming to kill her, and she has great evidence for a self-defence plea, but until it's settled and she can get back to work, it's yet another shadow hanging over her."

"She told me she's under investigation, so she probably shouldn't be hiding here, especially with you."

Mari re-entered the room. "I'll call the Colonel in the morning on my way back to town and check in. I'll tell him exactly where I was. He's met you, though he doesn't know your full name nor where you live. If he did, we'd be surrounded right now."

JJ's gaze lost focus for a moment as she accessed her onboard. "Nope. Not surrounded. And no alerts on any of the local bands for you. But you're right. You need to be aboveboard, and Zeke needs to be gone. I'd let you stay as long as you want, Zeke, but as soon as Mari checks in, they'll try to tie her to you, and then be hunting for you. Neither of you have actually told me what you were up to tonight and in fact what the hell brings the two of you together, but it's best I don't know until the dust settles. Zeke, where is your aircraft docked?"

"Dewong's. On the pad."

"Perfect. I've got an old unmarked, untagged cruiser out back you can take after I feed you both. You can leave it at Dewong's. He has the ignition codes and two of his kids will bring it back. The 62s might be waiting for you, though."

Zeke remembered the tricks he'd learned from the psilings and smiled. "I'll be fine. I'm not without my own resources."

"Then let's eat."

o0o

Mari opted to stay the night at JJ's, but Zeke thought it prudent he get as far away as possible. JJ agreed to hold onto the rented dive gear for a while, just in case Mari's cruiser was searched as part of the investigation. Both sets of gear would remain locked away and safe until the dust settled.

Out back, JJ's old cruiser was as non-descript as a vehicle could get. It was an older model, white, four-door, something-or-other. Even Zeke wasn't sure who the manufacturer was, just by looking at the body shape and trim. He shook JJ's hand. "Thank you. For *this*, and for everything else. Please let me know what's decided."

"Of course. Safe travels. It was nice to finally meet you."

"Likewise." He stepped over to Mari, who held her arms folded across her chest, blocking any attempt at a hug of any sort. "I'll talk to you soon, Mari. I'm sorry."

"I know. Now go, before I use JJ's stunner on you." Her voice wasn't quite as steady as her stance, so Zeke turned and left the two in the doorway. Mari was trying so hard to not crack that he wanted to leave her with dignity and pride intact. If her walls and shields came down after he left, at least he wouldn't bear witness to it and embarrass her.

Zeke didn't even hear the shot. It punched through his left shoulder and spun him around. He tumbled down the last two steps and landed on his back. It hurt like hell, but his first concern was for Mari, at the top of the stairs, completely exposed. He looked to see if she was okay, but JJ was on her knees, holding her own belly while blood seeped between her fingers. Without even a glance down at him, Mari grabbed her friend and dragged her inside, under cover. Zeke tried to follow them, to help, but as soon as he started up the steps on his belly, one shoulder screaming in pain, a second shot ricocheted off the hood of the cruiser and clipped his right ear.

He reached a frantic psi probe out to Mari. (I'm pinned down! I can't get to you, yet! Give me a minute!) He didn't waste time waiting for a reply. He extended his psi out in a hard, fast wave, narrowed down to the direction the shot must have come from. There was no one in the first hundred meters, just buildings. The second hundred meters was clear, too. He pushed the probe, knowing how treasured the time was. Twenty-three meters later he located the gunman, waiting for Zeke to pop his head up again, which told him that *he* was the intended target, not either of the women. He punched his probe at the man's shields and was repelled! He scanned the man. He was wearing a heavy-duty psi-blocking collar he'd never encountered before. It definitely wasn't one of *his* models. Zeke could get past the device, but it would take time he didn't have.

The man smiled, knowing full well Zeke had attempted an intrusion. What the man didn't know was that The Psilent One wasn't in the mood for a live-ammo game of Pop-and-Bop. Zeke threw power at his probe, narrowed its focus, and wrapped it around the man's long rifle. With a psionic tug, he ripped it from the prone killer's hands, spun it around, and pulled the trigger three times with a finger of psi. All three rounds punched through the sniper's face, out the back of his skull, and into the ground behind him. He collapsed.

With blood running from his right ear and his left shoulder, Zeke stumbled up the stairs and into the building, slamming and bolting the door behind him.

Marisol was on the sand-brown tile kitchen floor with JJ, trying to hold her friend down while probably executing some tricky psi surgery. He knelt at JJ's head and pressed his good hand down on her right shoulder to steady her. Mari looked into his eyes, terrified. "Both shoulders! Hold *both* down!"

Zeke couldn't even lift his left arm, let alone use it to pin down the squirming woman. He reached into her with both kinetic psi to hold her steady and an emotional pulse to calm her. She continued to struggle, beyond his psionic attempt at calmness. Desperate, he ripped his medpatch from his neck, slapped it onto JJ's neck, and hit it twice. A moment later, she stopped fighting and went still. "What can I do to help, Mari?"

"The tumbling slug punctured her small intestine and is lodged in her spine! I think I can seal the intestine or I can get the slug, but I can't do both."

Zeke quickly probed his own shoulder. The through-and-through shot clipped and broke his clavicle but missed the artery running through his shoulder. He ignored it and dove his psi into JJ's body. "Let's do both, one at a time, together. Start with the small intestine. We don't want any more bacteria leaking out. We can get to the spine when we're done."

"Okay." Their probes touched and moved to the small intestine. Blood and bacteria were everywhere, but because psi was a tactile sense, Zeke could 'feel' the severity of the damage. The intestine was completely severed. Mari took charge. (Hold the two new ends together and I'll... *shit*! I can't stitch them together without tools!)

(We don't have time for that. We'll just have to tie them both off and get to the bullet. As soon as that's done, we can get her to the hospital. If you haven't already, call an ambulance.) He reached out with another tendril of psi and undid JJ's shoelace, using psi to lift it up to the wound while also pinching the two ends of the intestine.

(I don't want the sniper to start shooting at the med crew.)

(The sniper isn't a problem. He turned his weapon on himself. Three times.)

Mari's surprise reverberated through the psi link, but Zeke couldn't take time to appreciate it because the pain in his shoulder was throwing off the control of his psi. (Take the lace, tie it off. Hurry. I can't hold these much longer without help.) He sensed Mari tighten her psi focus and bolster its strength. Tying shoelaces was one of the first 'tricks' psi-possessing children taught themselves, and she hadn't forgotten how to do it. He felt her snug up the knots and double each of them, to ensure they didn't slip.

Zeke's body slipped on the blood on the tiles and he reflexively put his left arm to catch himself. The hot steel pain was like being shot all over again! He snapped his psi back into himself and slapped at the medpatch, before realizing it was on JJ's neck. *His* life wasn't in danger, so he left it where it was. He would have to suck it up and push on. He sent his wobbly psi back into her body and nudged Mari's.

(Hayz! You've been shot!)

(Twice. I'll live. No arteries hit, just a fracture and soft tissue damage.)

(Med Team is en route. So are the 62s.)

(I figured as much. We have to get the bullet out before they get here or they'll stop us. We need to open up to each other and go deep. We can't just do this with surface psi. Our shields have to drop completely. Like back in the cave when I still had the chip. Can we do that?)

(*I* can, but you're the one who never let me in completely. It's all on you.)

He knew exactly what he was risking, but JJ's life was in the balance. He lowered his shields completely and Mari's hot, controlled, steel-strong psi wound around his. (Let's go take a look. You take the lead, please.)

Mari moved their narrow probe around the large intestine and gently laid it over the spine. (It shattered her fifth lumbar vertebra and is snugged up tight against her spinal cord.)

(Oh shit. It's big, and still in one piece, I think.) He pulled more of Mari's psi into his own, drawing on her strength. (What do you think? Gently pry the two vertebrae apart while pulling on the bullet?)

(We could do more damage than good. Should we wait?)

He shared her doubt. (If they try to move her, though, the cord will be severed.)

(They repair spinal cord injuries all the time now. My instincts tell me to leave it alone.)

(Okay.) Blood loss and pain rocked him and his psi wavered. (I can't...). He passed out.

o0o

Zeke once again woke up in a hospital. He sent out a light probe, but an insistent but soft warning alarm went off near the bed. A disruptor. He *was* back in prison.

"You're awake, Hayz." The voice wasn't Mari's. A man's, and it was one he should recognize. "You can open your eyes, now. The disruptor doesn't lie, and neither does your heart monitor."

It was Stihler. Zeke opened his eyes but only saw the ceiling. He almost reached for the bed's controls with psi, but as fuzzy as his brain was, he remembered the disruptor. "Mind if I sit up?"

"Not at all." There was a beat of heavy silence. "Oh, you want help? Can't use your mighty psi to reach for the controls?"

"No. Er, yes, please. Help." The bed's motor whirred as the upper half tilted up until Zeke could see his nemesis sitting beside him, crisp uniform, scars, and all. There was a little pain in his shoulder and he could tell there was a small bandage on his ear. "Thank you. Am I under arrest?"

"What for? Did you break the law, Mr. *Hayz*? The disruptor wasn't *my* idea, it was your ex-wife's. She was afraid you'd lash out in your drug-induced sleep and kill someone. She's under the impression that you are fully capable of taking a life when it suits you. Is there anything you'd like me to know?" He smiled and the scars stretched in hideous directions.

Marisol knew he'd killed Addox, Addox's brother, and the sniper, but if he wasn't under arrest, she hadn't told anyone. "Where is Bossy? And how is her friend?"

"My loyal Captain is back on the job, keeping Espy Beach safe from the likes of you and snipers who would kill you. Her killing of her teammate was clearly self-defence. Her friend, Ms. Rahn, is recovering. You two saved her life, and she is recovering nicely from spinal surgery."

JJ had already had spinal surgery? "How long have I been out?"

"Three days. Your own surgery was, unfortunately, a success, but Captain Boissiere and I both believed you needed to be kept unconscious a little longer. There's also a guard at your door."

"So I'm a prisoner?"

"Not at all. He's not there to keep you in, but rather to keep Captain Boissiere *out*."

"Keep her out? I have no problem seeing her."

"Maybe you *should* have a problem. When the med team arrived, she was sitting astride you, choking you with her bare, bloody hands. My officers arrived right on their heels and had to stun her to get her off you." The colonel took a sip from a water glass on the wheeled table beside him and Zeke tried to get his head around the facts. Mari had tried to *kill* him? "Please don't mistake my protection of you as a gesture of kindness, Hayz. I'm more than happy to let

Bossy strangle, stab, shoot, poison, and castrate you, all at the same time if she wants. But she's in enough trouble and I don't need her committing another probably justified murder and ending up in prison. 62s don't do well in prison, and besides, I happen to like her doing exactly what she's doing. No, if you die, it won't be by *her* hand. I'd rather you go back to prison, but first I need to prove you killed that sniper, or even Ray Addox."

"I was in Kepler City. I couldn't have killed Addox."

"That's what I've been telling people, but there's an insistent rumour that The Psilent One has that kind of power, and he may have even used it once before, while in prison when Addox's idiot brother attacked him."

Now Zeke was worried. Did Stihler really believe the rumours? Or was he pulling Zeke's chain? He had to know where the colonel stood. Did Stihler have *any* evidence at all against him? The colonel reached for the glass again and Zeke took advantage of the distraction to glance at the disrupter in the corner. Oddly enough, it wasn't one of his designs. It was even older than the ones in the prison. They probably dragged it out of storage just for him. He looked back at Stihler, just in time.

"Once the doctors clear you for release, you will be transported back to Kepler City, away from my Captain. I can't have her tempted to sneak in and finish what she started."

Zeke reached out slowly for the disruptor with an ultra-low frequency probe. The machine remained quiet. While listening to Stihler ramble on, he reached the probe around behind the machine and switched it off. He then swung the probe around, slipped the low frequency past the Colonel's standard psi-blocking collar, and laid it across Stihler's insignificant shields. He didn't have to penetrate the man's mind to learn his secrets, he just needed to blend with his shields and guide the conversation. He hadn't done it in a long time, but it wasn't difficult to do. Interpreting the images and thoughts was the hardest part since they were seldom linear and always a personal interpretation of what the individual remembered.

"As you said, I'm responsible for killing my daughter, even if someone else ordered it, so she's perfectly within her rights to kill me."

"Addox ordered it, and you know full well he did." Zeke caught a memory of Addox and Stihler meeting, not long ago. Oops. The men were in business together. He'd better tread lightly.

"I know no such thing. Just as I don't know anything about his brother's death while he was trying to beat *me* to death, while disruptors kept me contained."

"You're The Psilent One. Killing a man standing over you couldn't have been difficult at all." The memory that flashed across the shields this time was of Stihler viewing the footage of the attack on Zeke, and Willy Addox's death. Memory Stihler shook his head and clearly said there was no way psi could have killed the man. Zeke relaxed. The colonel was bullshitting. He was done playing the colonel's game. He wanted to get some sleep and then get the hell out of town. Stihler's side arm was still holstered, and Zeke had full use of his psi, so he felt safe pushing the scarred bastard's emotional buttons for once.

"If I wanted to kill him, Ed, I would have just set his bed on fire. Rumour has it that's pretty effective."

"Fuck you, Zee—*Hayz*!" He stood, his fist raised to strike, but held as a threat.

A distinct, clear memory shot across the man's shields. But it wasn't *his*. It couldn't have been his. In it, Stihler was young, still at the academy. He was in the room he shared with Zeke's younger brother, Stan, and Stan was sitting on his own bed, his head down, reading. There was something wrong with the layout of the room, though. Maybe Zeke was remembering it wrong. Stihler threw a ball of paper at his roommate and Stan looked up in irritation...except it wasn't Stan, it was young Stihler. The memory was one of Stan's, but that was impossible! Pure memories don't get transferred! A person can remember a story someone once told them, but second-hand memories have a totally different feeling, like watching a video instead of living it. Sitting Stihler glared at standing Stihler and snapped at him. "Put the fucking lighter away, Stan. You know the rules, you firebug!"

Colonel Eduard Stihler was his brother, Stan? Zeke snapped the probe back hard and fast. He didn't know if he wanted to hug the man beside him or snap his neck. He was pretty sure if he confronted him, his brother would just shoot him in the head and claim it was self-defence. No man who had kept a secret this big for this long would hesitate to kill to keep it. It was obvious Stan held no emotional bond with Zeke or even their mother or else he would have said something to them years ago. Oh shit! No wonder Stihler had a soft spot for Marisol—he was still in love with her! Zeke needed time to process this! He needed to tell Mari! *No.* He needed to shut the hell up and get out of town. Stan was a psi-3 and thus no threat to Zeke's 24, but as Stihler he had a reputation in the 62s for being a good judge of people, and a skilled interrogator. Zeke couldn't risk his brother figuring out that his secret wasn't so secret anymore.

"Stihler, either arrest me, kill me, or get the fuck out of my room. If I never see your ugly face again, consider yourself lucky. As far as I'm concerned, you owe me a death for what you did to my little brother. Pray to whatever god you like that I don't actually have the magical psi powers the LPF say I do. Now fuck off or I'll throw my bedpan at you."

The colonel's stunned expression told Zeke that he wasn't used to being spoken to like that. Stan/Eduard then straightened his back, pointed a finger at Zeke like a gun, and cocked his thumb down to mime shooting him. He finished with a scar-twisted smile, turned on his heel, and left. Zeke used psi to slide the chair over in front of the door, to slow down anyone coming in. He checked his onboard for the time and date, but it was still shut down. He psied it back on, and after the reboot was complete, Shaelagh's voice entered his head, through his implant.

Well well well. If it isn't Mister Let's-Go-to-the-Coast-and-Save-the-World. Since you're still alive, I assume you succeeded?

"We did. It was a—"

I'm seeing your location as the Espy Beach Hospital. What happened this time? Do you need me to contact your regular doctor?

"I was shot. Twice. And Mari tried to choke me to death. I hope to be kicked out of here in a day or two, and home not long after."

Good. I'm getting as tired of taking messages from Ms. DiMasto as she is speaking with an AI. She's called five times since you left, and each time has sounded a bit more urgent.

"What is she calling about?"

She won't say, other than she knew your father. I've done a very full background check on her and run up against a temporal wall. Marguerite DiMasto didn't exist six months ago. I tried accessing your father's files for a woman who fits the age estimate I have based on voice analysis. Your father's clandestine corporate dealings created a great many closed and classified files.

"So you couldn't crack them."

Don't be silly. Of course, I did. But still nothing. I'm not surprised, though. The files indicate that each member of your father's team was kept apart from the others and at no time were any team members mentioned by name in the files of other members. It's exactly what I would do.

"Me, too. So we know nothing about her."

Not exactly. I did manage to trace her calls back to a location on Irido Island.

"She's in *prison*?"

Not at all. She lives in a cabin near the southernmost shore, about a kilometre from the bigger town resort. I have satellite images for when you get back. Unless you want me to send them now.

"No, hold onto them—and keep dodging her calls. You can even tell her the truth, that I'm in the hospital in Espy Beach."

Will do, Boss. Anything else I can do for you?

He really wanted Shaelagh to dig up everything she could find on both his brother Stan and the man he'd known as Stihler, but he didn't want to risk it over a communication line of questionable security. "No. Not unless Nita called."

She did.

"Were you going to tell me?"

She asked me not to. I'm going to let her know when you get back to town and she's going to surprise you.

"I think you just spoiled the surprise."

Maybe, but my programming doesn't allow me to keep secrets from you.

"But you weren't going to tell me she called until I asked you."

Yes, I was. I would have tagged it to the end of the conversation. For fun.

"*That's* your idea of fun?"

No, it's Marisol's. I only have the sense of humour her personality matrix gave me.

"True enough." He was suddenly exhausted. "It's sleep time for this old boy. Between prison, Nita, the psiling-assist, and the sniper's bullets, I feel more dead than alive. I'll talk to you when I wake up."

Sounds good, Boss.

"Oh, and Shaelagh?"

Yes?

"Thank you. You're my anchor."

You're welcome. I love you, too, big guy.

Zeke laughed as he disconnected the call. His shoulder was starting to throb in its immobilizing wrapping, so he lowered the bed, turned the old disruptor back on, and closed his eyes.

oOo

When the doctor tried to enter the room the door banged into the chair and woke Zeke up with a start. The short, stout man's curses added to the wake-up call.

"Mr. Hayz, you have a 62 outside your door. The chair is a bit redundant."

"Sorry, Doctor...." He left it hanging, not knowing the man's name. He moved the chair.

"Winnicki. Chief of Staff and today's attending physician for our humble little facility."

"Sorry, Dr. Winnicki. Little or not, your staff seem to know their stuff. I think you had my ex-wife here a while back, and you have her friend here now. She was brought in at the same time I was. Torn intestine and bullet in the spine."

"We do indeed have Ms. Rahn. Your ex-wife is Captain Boissiere I'm assuming."

"She is." He restrained himself from making the snide remarks that came to mind. He was leaving soon and Marisol still needed to work in the town.

"As I told her while she was sitting at her friend's bedside, the two of you did a fascinating job of field surgery. The shoelace was an inspired choice. She said you both used psi to tie it off."

"We did. We were going to use it to remove the bullet, too, but couldn't risk making the situation worse."

"Thank you. We appreciate you leaving the delicate stuff to the professionals. I use psi in surgery myself when the occasion requires it. I also use quite a few of the *Hayz & Hayz* surgical tools. They've saved many lives."

"I suspect your skill as a surgeon has more to do with your success rate than my devices. A tool is only as good as the hands wielding it."

"Thank you. I agree. Enough small talk for now, though. I would like to examine your shoulder and then I'll decide when you can go home. It won't be today, but now that we've replaced all of the blood you lost *and* your shattered clavicle, it might be as soon as tomorrow."

"Excellent. Is Ms. Rahn conscious? I'd like to see her if I could. Please."

"She is, but I'm afraid you can't. Official 62 orders. There's even a restraining order. You're allowed nowhere near her room."

Zeke sighed. "Did those orders come from Captain Boissiere by any chance?"

"They did."

"Then I'll respect them."

"I appreciate that, especially since *her* commander gave orders that *she* is not allowed to come near *you*."

"He's a wise man." His onboard beeped in his ear with an incoming call from Shaelagh. Her voice spoke in his ear.

Boss, we have a problem. I just stunned a man trying to break into the house.

NINETEEN

Z EKE NEARLY SWATTED THE doctor with his good hand when the man dawdled during the exam of his shoulder, chatting about ideas he had for more psi-assisted tools for the hospital. Once the repairs were deemed a success and healing was on track, the doctor departed. Zeke reached out to Shaelagh.

"Sit rep!"

And hello to you, too, Sunshine of my life.

"You've taken care of the problem?"

Of course. It turns out that young Mr. Gallagher is just an overly eager vlogger who wanted a scoop on what the inside of The Psilent One's 'cave' looked like. To his credit, he did call twice to set up an interview, but I stalled him since your location had not yet hit the news feeds.

"Did you call the 62s?"

Hardly. Once Mr. Gallagher regained control of his limbs we had a little chat. I promised not to have him charged with attempted breaking and entering in exchange for his not reporting that you have an AI who shocks the ass off of people.

"And he was okay with that?"

Not at all. I then explained that he was speaking with an AI that would disrupt his vlog with senseless chatter and nasty rumours from now until the day he died of old age. I also informed him none of the devices he was currently using were recording anything but static, so he had no proof of threats made by a house. That seemed to do the trick.

"Perfect. Thank you for making him go away."

You're welcome. He'll be back in three days for a full tour conducted by The Psilent One himself.

"*What?* I'm not giving some nut job a tour of my home!"

Of course not. You only let oversexed spies working for Bruge Blue into your home to drug and interrogate you after shagging you senseless.

"That's not the s—"

The same? No, Lover Boy, it's not. But part of your deal with the courts included community service. An honest piece about your life, your late daughter, and the positive work Hayz & Hayz does with psi would be a good start.

"Wow. You came up with that on your own?" His AI was daily exceeding his expectations.

Actually, it was Mr. Gallagher's initial sales pitch on the interview. I co-opted and refined it. He's young, he's reckless, and he's right.

"He *is*, dammit." The kid sounded pretty smart. "Three days?"

Yes sir.

"Okay. I assume you have his contact information if I change my mind?"

I scanned his onboard. His security was only store-bought. I know everything there is to know about him. I've also reviewed his entire vlog archive and fan comments, so I understand what will make the tour a success. I have the outline ready for your return.

"Thanks, S. I'll be home tomorrow, provided the psi storms are light. My shoulder is fixed, but I don't think I could fly manually in a maelstrom."

There have been no psi storms in that region since you repaired the rift. The weather is also clear, so I will expect you around lunchtime. Soup and sandwich, or protein shake and a rib eye?

"Shake and steak, please. Can you also pull together a report on the best five non-psi institutes in the system, and the legal and administrative hoops I have to jump through to set up that scholarship in Lexis' name? Please also book an appointment with Jillayn to discuss the terms of my community service. I want to get that started as soon as possible."

Done.

Zeke had a sudden inspiration. "Do you think Mr. Gallagher would like a tour of the Collegium?"

He's a psi 17 with limited training, so I think he would jump at the chance.

"A 17? Interesting. Okay. We'll see how the house tour goes, and if I still like him when we're done, we'll set up the Collegium tour. We don't just need to show that The Psilent One is no threat to society, but more importantly, we need to show what is being done to help psi and non-psi citizens coexist without fear. We need to knock the wind out of the LPF's sails. Take away their support base, or at least the ones who aren't wingnut conspiracy theorists, bombers, and fear-mongers."

We certainly do, Boss. Good thinking. The report is complete, but there are only four schools meeting the criteria. And your appointment with your lawyer is booked. Anything else I can do while I have your ears?

He laughed. "No, you've already done more than I deserve. Thank you. I'll see you tomorrow. If anything else comes up, you know how to reach me."

Unless you go dark again.

"Ouch. But I've already saved one planet this week. Any others can make an appointment."

I'll let them know that if they call. Say goodbye, Boss.

"Goodbye, Boss." Zeke sighed as the connection broke. A thin ray of emotional sunshine beamed down on his blue world. Now all he had to do was figure out why his ex-wife tried to kill him. He knew she had plenty of reasons to, but he wanted to know what finally pushed her over the edge.

o0o

Marisol's duty patrol of the streets of Espy Beach took her past the hospital, but her orders were very specific—stay away from the hospital, and stay away from son-of-a-bitch Ezekiel Hayz. Her CO explained that it wasn't The Psilent One's life he was protecting, but rather Bossy's own career. There were too many witnesses to her trying to choke him to death, and right on the heels of Bonner's death, there were members of the Town Council already calling for her dismissal and some even for jail time. The colonel had placated the Espy Beach Council, but one more incident of violence and Captain Marisol Boissiere would be discharged from the 62s and face criminal charges.

She drove on past. She received regular updates on JJ's condition, but her dear friend was still heavily sedated after the surgery to repair her injuries, so there was no point in sitting at her bedside. The hospital had also forwarded Hayz's release time, so she could be clear of the area, as much as she still wanted to kill him both for what she'd briefly seen in his memories and for his role in Lexis' murder. Patience wasn't her strength, but she could wait until the time was right to do what she needed to. Fatal accidents happened every day, and The Psilent One was no less accident-prone than the next low-life.

oOo

The next morning the hospital staff informed Zeke that his check-out time was noon, so he signed the paperwork and left two hours earlier, slipping out the back entrance and walking two blocks before calling for an auto-drive. The Beach was a small town, but with the number of tourists who visited and the amount of intoxicants served around town, ride services flourished during the warmer months.

His shoulder was a bit sore, but if he started slowly, he was told he should have a full range of motion within the week and full strength back not long after. He was concerned about using it at all, but the hospital's physiotherapist assured him that everything was fused, stitched, and rebuilt as good as the "original specs", and if he favoured it and *didn't* give it a bit of a workout every day, it would actually tighten up on him and give him trouble.

He had the vehicle drop him off behind Dewong's shop, and after sending out a wide wave probe and finding that no one was watching the place and the landing pad, he slipped around to the front and in through the open doorway. Dewong was out on the water, so Zeke thanked the man's son, Tak, and asked him to tell his father that Zeke would send him a message with an update on the dive gear.

Five minutes later he was back in the air. Seven minutes after that, Shaelagh called him on the craft's system. "Good morning, Handsome."

"Good morning. What's up?" The day was warm and clear, so he took the aircraft up to fifteen hundred meters, levelled off, and set the autopilot.

"I just spoke with Marguerite DiMasto."

"And how did it go? Can she wait until I get back to return her call, or should I do it while I'm en route home?"

"I don't think you should call her back at all. In fact, I think you should redirect and get yourself over to Irido Island, stat. As always, I recorded our conversation, but I detected a voice in the background, mixed in with the whining of a LightHawk 2 generator, what I believe is a Stanson XJ water pump, and three distinct animal calls. I isolated the voice and filtered out the extraneous noise."

"I'm guessing you want me to listen to it."

"Not while you're flying. Please land."

"It's okay. I'm on autopilot."

"I know, but I can't risk it. Please land."

Zeke glanced at the terrain below, but it all was either beach or rock. There were no roads on this part of the coast. "Fine. Give me a minute. It looks like I'll be setting down on the beach."

"Yes. A thousand meters ahead there is an optimal spot. Plenty of clearance both for landing and take-off. Tides are outgoing, so you are good there for another hour."

"Thank you." He took over the controls, checked the radar for other aircraft, confirmed the airspace was clear, and went into a controlled dive. The spot was obvious. "Got it. Give me a minute."

"Of course."

It actually took him two minutes to land and secure the aircraft. The winds at ground level were stiff and threatened to blow him out into the water. "I'm down, Shaelagh. What have you got for me?"

"This was recorded twenty-seven minutes ago. As best as I can determine, the sound is live, and not a recording in the background. It lasts 4.19 seconds and is not repeated because the call was terminated by Ms. DiMasto immediately afterward."

"Shaelagh, you're stalling."

"No, I'm giving you the facts."

"Play it. *Please*."

"Okay. Because of the sound scrubbing, there is a two-second near-silent lead-in."

There were two seconds of soft hiss, and then a very distinct, very familiar voice.

"Margie, is that my Dad? Can I talk to him?"

It couldn't be! "That's not possible." His chest tightened, his arms and legs trembled, and his throat threatened to close up tight. He knew—absolutely *knew*—there was no fucking way Lexis could be alive.

"I have triple-checked it, to make certain I didn't simply use a voice already in my databanks, so, as impossible as it may be, it *is*."

"It *can't* be Lexis! She's *dead*!" His pulse hammered in his ears and his stomach buckled. The possibility that she was alive was too much to hope for. He'd lost her once and was only just starting to get his head around that fact. But if he let himself hope that she lived and then it turned out to be a lie, he'd lose her all over again and it would kill him. His chest would just burst right open with the force of his heart rupturing with the pain.

"I have no explanation for you, Zeke. I can only present you with the evidence. Since they never actually recovered Lexis' body—or any portion thereof—there is actually a possibility she survived the attack. The damage to the property was extensive, but not total. There is only one way to find out. I have forwarded the coordinates to your aircraft and sent a message to Nunes to modify the rental agreement to include a cross-water flight off the continent. Dan replied that as long as the batteries are fully charged, you're 'good to go'. Your batteries are at 99.945 percent. You're good to go."

But Zeke *couldn't* go anywhere. He wanted to blast off and rocket his way to the island, but he knew the odds were so slim Lexis was actually alive that his soul was being crushed all over again. It was both his greatest hope and his greatest fear. What if he got all the way to the island and discovered it was a trap? It wouldn't have been hard for someone to figure out what would push his emotional buttons. After all, he'd already killed to protect and avenge his broken family. But he initiated the take-off sequence and tapped the screen to accept Shaelagh's coordinates. If there was any chance at all that his daughter was alive, he had to investigate. "Did any of your conversations or DiMasto's recorded messages have any indication Lexis was still alive?"

"None. The background noise was similar in six of the conversations, but the others were made while she was outside of the cabin. Because the prison shares the island, there is a geosynchronous satellite monitoring the area continuously. I was able to access the feed and have found three instances where there are two persons walking around the area surrounding the cabin, but I am unable to make a positive identification of Lexis. Should I hijack a 62 drone to have a closer look?"

"No! Thank you. When I get there I'll use this quad-flyer's mini-drone. How close can I get to the island in this aircraft? What are the airspace restrictions?"

"You can approach the island from the south, in a narrow cone of allowable access, but if you stray from it or approach from the north end where the prison is tucked behind the wall, you will be shot down."

"Since that's not on my to-do list for the day, how about we make that narrow approach from the south?" He squinted at the nav screen, but the reflection of the sun made it hard to read. "What's my ETA, Shaelagh?"

"Three hours, forty-two minutes. You can cut that to two hours and eighteen minutes if you're willing to stop for a recharge at the nearest charging station on the coast. A twenty-minute fast-charge will give you plenty of power to reach the island, but you'll need at least a six-hour layover to top up again. You'll have drained both batteries and the turbo's backup."

"And if I take the full three hours plus, will I have enough power to leave immediately?"

"You will. And if you engage the dynamo, you can charge one battery while flying on the other, at a cost of sixteen minutes due to overall reduced airspeed. The dynamo disconnects at top speed."

"As much as I want to be there right fucking now, having extra power for a fast departure might be a good idea. I have no idea what I'm going to find there. If it's a trap, hopefully I can discover it with a probe before I land. If she's there and being held against her will, I may have to fight our way out, and would hate to have the battery die halfway to the mainland."

"All excellent reasons for flying with the dynamo engaged."

"Thank you." He tapped a switch on the instrument panel and noted a subtle bump as the recharging dynamo engaged.

"Anything else I can do, boss?"

Now that he was away from Espy Beach and regular 62 patrols, Zeke had to risk getting more information about his discovery at the hospital. "Shaelagh, how secure is this line?"

"It's a six-point-two. Not the best. The distance between us and the relays I've had to utilize have compromised it."

"What's the best you can get us?"

"For what duration? I can get us nine seconds at a full ten."

"Let's do it. Give me a three-count when you're ready."

"Give me a moment...in three...two...one...secure!"

"Gather all data from all sources on 62 Colonel Eduard Stihler, as well as all data from all sources on Stanbridge Hayz. Hold it for my return." There was a brief pause. "Did you get all that?"

"Last word received was 'return'."

"You got it all."

"Have a safe flight. I've uploaded the latest movie in the series you've been following so you have inflight entertainment if you get bored."

How the hell would he focus on some damned movie when all he could think about was maybe, just maybe, his baby girl was alive? But Shaelagh was just trying to be helpful. "Thank you. How're the meteorological and psionic weather reports?"

"You're clear for the duration."

"Good. I'm going to have a nap. If nothing else comes up, please wake me ten minutes from the coast. For some strange reason, I'm exhausted."

"Roger Wilco over and under."

"Over and under, goofball."

"Blame my programmer, Handsome."

"Will do. Later."

"Later."

The connection went silent. Zeke accessed his onboard music files and selected a mellow playlist that always knocked him out. With thoughts of both Lexis and Stan being alive, he didn't think sleep would come easily, but his body told him to try.

oOo

Shaelagh's gentle buzzing in his ears was enough to drag Zeke out of REM sleep where he was battling undersea monsters that wore Marisol's face in an effort to save his brother from being burned at the stake while Lexis launched mini fireballs from her hands at her tortured uncle.

"Holy shit." He tried to shake off the lingering images.

Shaelagh switched the aircraft's speakers. "Problem, big guy?"

"No, just a dark twisted dream. Must be the meds still in my system."

"Quite possibly. I'm still showing more than a trace of a few medications, none of which you are allergic to, but one which you recorded sensitivity to when you were eight."

"Fanfuckingtastic. Off on a rescue mission hopped up on drugs."

"They shouldn't be a factor when you're awake. Tests show their impact is strongest when in REM sleep."

That was reassuring. "Then I'll try to stay awake."

"Let me know what I can do to help. I certainly lack the delicate touch Nita used to keep you alert, but I can run a mild electric current through your system if you start to doze off."

"How mild?" A brief buzz hummed throughout his entire body, and even after it stopped, the left side of his face continued to tingle. "Oh, hell no. I'll just rely on adrenalin to keep me sharp."

"Of course."

"What's the maximum range and speed of the quad-copter's drone?"

"Maximum controllable range is one klick. Maximum speed is half of the quad-copter's, so you'll have to slow down once you launch it."

"I was thinking of coming to a complete stop, a few meters above the water, and just sending the drone in for a peekaboo."

"That will keep you off of radar, but not off visual."

"I have a psi trick that might help with that."

"It won't work for the satellite, though."

"I'm not so sure about that. It involves light bending, so it might. We can test it with the drone once we get out there."

"Ten-four. ETA, twenty-one minutes to maximum drone range to shore."

"Good. We'll take it one hundred meters further in, to give the drone some room to explore."

"Ten-four. I've programmed the precise approach-and-hold into your nav system. It takes over in three...two...one..."

The aircraft banked gently to the starboard side and dropped in altitude for thirty seconds until it was fifty meters off the choppy water of the Spinnaker Sea and aimed directly at the southeast corner of the island in the distance. Zeke drew his psi in, refocused it, then surrounded the entire aircraft with a shimmery, bubble of psi. It wasn't a heavy, physical manifestation of power, but rather a diaphanous, lightweight light bender.

"What's the plan, Oh Psilent One?"

Zeke smiled. "Send in the drone to find out how heavily armed the cabin is and how many occupants. If it's reasonably clear, we'll finally return Marguerite DiMasto's calls, and hear what she has to say for herself. After that, we're going to play it by ear."

"Ah, a seat-of-the-pants plan."

"Exactly. If the drone can get confirmation Lexis is in fact on the island, then I'll approach, cautiously."

"And if not?"

"Then I'll approach, cautiously. What choice do I have? If Lexis is truly dead and this is a trap, they're welcome to shoot me out of the air. But if there's even a hint of a chance she survived the attack I have to risk approaching this 'old friend of Dad's'."

"I'd rather you *not* get shot down, please, as I'm sure Nita would agree."

"Nita...I hardly think sleeping with Blue's spy-girl has the makings of a long-term relationship, especially when she finds out my life is pretty damned boring."

"Maybe so, but I get the impression she's quite keen to get to know you. She offered me access to her entire file, to show she wasn't hiding anything."

"Did you tell her you already had access, and you know everything there is to know about her?"

"Not at all. What I know or do not know is no one's business but yours."

"Thank you." The quad-copter lost altitude until it was just above the waves, then it slowed and eventually came to a complete stop, hovering comfortably in place.

"Launching probe, now. I am linked into the feed, too."

There was a whirr and a click beneath his seat, and a miniature version of the quad-copter flashed out from under the bow and zipped toward the island. The live feed from the drone's four cameras popped up on the nav screen. The glare was bad enough that Zeke psied the window tint up to fifty percent. That made a huge difference and the island grew bigger in the forward-facing image. In the rear-facing image, there was no sign of the quad-copter, just a flickering of the horizon where it should have been.

He tapped a button and the drone controls rose out of the console between the two seats. He tapped one of the four smaller toggles and the forward camera zoomed into maximum. Built-in image stabilization ensured a clear image, and the strong optical zoom meant he didn't have to deal with the pixilation of a digital zoom. He could now see that the cabin was a modest one, sitting in a small clearing, surrounded by heavy evergreen tree coverage on two sides, but open to the elements facing south and east. The trees on the west had a permanent bow shape toward the cabin, so he guessed that was the direction the prevailing winds came from. He caught flashes of sunlight reflecting off small glass surfaces at various points in the wooded area and the eaves of the cabin and assumed they were camera lenses, watching the perimeter.

This was both good news and bad. It was good news if Lexis was there and Marguerite DiMasto was one of the good guys, but it was bad news if it was a trap. They might not see him a klick offshore, but there's a good chance an alert guard would see the drone approaching. Since the drone wasn't entirely silent, he hoped the slaps of water against the shore, wind in the trees, or whatever would cover the little machine's approach. The drone reached the little dock where a medium-sized motorized craft was tied up. There were no visible weapons or mounting hardware for weapons on the boat. He nudged the drone straight up fifty meters and guided it over the cabin, where it was less likely to be spotted through a window. The belly camera showed the area around the cabin to be clear. No personnel patrolled, and there were no surprises hidden from a shore approach in the lee of the structure.

He maneuvered the drone off to the side of the cabin and began a perimeter check of the building. It was longer than it was wide, so anyone approaching from the south like he did would think it was a more modest building than it was. He counted doors and windows, staying just high enough to be difficult to spot from the inside. There wasn't much he could do about the propeller noise, as this model of drone was designed to film the quad-copter and its occupants in flight rather than sneak around doing surveillance. If he'd been prepared, he would have had one of his own drones, which were much better equipped for stealth work.

An exterior door opened and shut with a bang of wood on wood so Zeke guided the drone over to take a peek. Someone with a long brunette ponytail walked away from the cabin, but he couldn't tell if it was Lexis. He nudged the drone closer, but the person spun around, raised a weapon, and fired directly at the drone. The cameras all went dark.

"Shit! We're blind now!"

"That was not *Lexis,* and in the brief view we got, I estimate an eighty-percent chance it *is* a woman. Since we know they can't see the quad-copter, why not move within probe range?"

"And if she can see past my little illusion and starts shooting?"

"Then you fly away to safety?"

"Not an option. But you're right. I have to get close enough to reach out with a probe. I don't think I'll be able to maintain this light-bending while I probe, though, so I'd better swing around and approach from the west, where the trees will block her line of sight from the cabin. Can I do this and remain within legal approach vectors?"

"Yes, but you'll need to be close to shore."

Staying low, he flew the aircraft around to the west, until the windbreak of trees hid the cabin. "She probably has more cameras pointing here, to her blind spot, than anywhere else. It's probably a fair assessment that she also has traps set between the prison and the cabin, just in case there's a prison break."

"She does if she's smart. Of course, if there *is* a prison break, there are two small towns between the prison and this end of the island, so I'd be surprised if an escapee could get this far." He slowly moved toward the island, stopping when he was close enough to reach it with a scanning probe. "Hold us here, but if something happens while I'm extended out, get us out of here, please." He slid the canopy back, the cool breeze a refreshing slap.

"Of course."

Zeke quickly pulled his psi in, focused it, and then punched a probe out as fast as he could toward the landmass in front of him. He only needed to assess how many people were present. If there was a force hidden in the cabin, he needed to retreat and reassess before it was too late. The probe wound between the windbreak and reached the cabin without any trouble. He sent it on a quick circuit of the structure and located the woman, just as she was re-entering the cabin. A quick glance over her shoulder could have been to ensure she wasn't being followed, or because she sensed his probe. Either way, when she closed the door behind her, the probe butted up against some rudimentary but effective structural shielding.

Shielding hardly posed a problem to a high-psi unless it was one of embedded crystals like the one he'd encountered at the 62 HQ after his arrest. He withdrew the probe back to the woods, then moved it forward until it touched the building. Quickly, he scooted it up the wall, around the eaves, and onto the roof. He remembered seeing a heat vent protruding a short distance from the roof when the drone first arrived, so that's what he sought out. He found it after a moment of fumbling about, trying to get his bearings amongst the solar panels covering the roof. The gap at the top, beneath the rain shield protecting the screened-over pipe, was more than big enough for his probe to fit through. He concentrated harder and fed a bit more power to it.

Willing the probe forward, Zeke was shocked to find the probe head moving *away* from the vent, along the tiles of the roof, past the solar array, and down off the roof to the ground. He was no longer in control of his own probe!

(Hello HayzZeke. Inichi here.)

(What the hell? How did you...?) Then he remembered the psiling in the tunnels who rode his probe like a hoverbike. (You know me?)

(You HayzZeke. Of course, know you. Saved home world. Stop skulking. Come play.)

(I can't play, Inichi, I'm here to... I'm trying to...) How could he explain what he was doing to a psiling he didn't know? For all he knew, the animals could be trained and this one was part of the trap. They'd already shot down the drone so he wasn't much in a trusting mood.

(I know. If no come, then stay. Wait.)

Zeke couldn't see any risk in at least waiting. Shaelagh was covering his back at the hovering quad-copter.

(Here she comes.) The precocious psiling lifted the probe up at an odd angle, and a moment later a face appeared in the probe head.

(Daddy?)

TWENTY

Z EKE COULDN'T TAKE HIS eyes off his daughter, nor let go of her hand for even a second, though his own hands shook. "So you've been here the entire time, and you didn't think to call?"

Her once long, beautiful, auburn hair was now just stubble growing back in and made Lexis look ten years older, though it had only been eight days since the attack. Skin grafts on her scalp, neck, and right side of her jaw were healing well. "I've only been conscious for two days."

He was afraid to breathe or to even blink, for fear he'd find himself back in prison and all the joy electrifying him right now was some corporal shock treatment, or a post-surgical hallucination. "How the hell did you survive? The crater was immense. Dave and Bunji were vaporized."

She flinched at the mention of her lost guardians' names. "I was in the backyard, talking to Inichi."

"Inichi? The psiling?"

(Me Inichi! DiMastoMarguerite save *me*, too!) The psiling climbed in through the open window and sat on Marguerite's lap, affectionately combing her hair with his long claws.

Zeke looked at Marguerite. "I owe you an unpayable debt."

"There is no debt. I promised my mother I would keep your family safe."

"Your mother?"

"She worked with your father. I was six when he died. The two of them had an agreement. If something happened to either of them, the other one would watch over the kids. Your father died first, and my mother six months ago. When you got arrested, I moved to Aldrintowne to keep an eye on Marisol and Alexis."

"Then this isn't your home?"

"Yes and no. Technically, this is *your* property, but my mother and I lived here off and on, at your father's request. He wanted it preserved." She indicated photos on the panelled walls with a sweep of her arm.

Zeke squinted to see them, but couldn't quite make out any of the faces from the chair. Lexis stood and led him by the hand so he could see the faces clearly. Even from a distance, he could see that most of them were of a couple deeply in love. Approaching them, he recognized his father immediately, but the woman wasn't his mother. "That's... Mrs. *Boissiere*! They really did have an affair!"

Both women stared at him, but it was Marguerite who asked, "You knew about them?"

He didn't dare say how he knew. "I heard... a rumour, just after Dad was murdered." He stared at the photo directly in front of them. In it, his father and Marisol's mother were sitting on the dock, with the cabin in the background. Judging by the elevation of the camera, the photo was taken by a drone, probably controlled by Braydon Hayz. It was his *Dad*. In photos he'd never seen before. It was like...it was...too much. He wept. How could he not? His daughter was *alive*, here at his side, holding his hand, and she was giving him the gift of a part of his father's life he never knew about.

He swiped at his tears with his free sleeve and led Lexis around the cabin, soaking up each photo, stunned by the rapturous adoration in the eyes of the two lovers. In one photo there was a little girl, with long dark hair blowing in the sea breeze, standing on a bench table behind the couple, dropping cut wildflowers on their heads. All three of the people were laughing uproariously.

"That's me." Marguerite whispered. "That was their last visit before Braydon died."

"Was murdered."

"Yes. Murdered. Lydia Boissiere came back once more after that, to say good-bye to us. Her own husband had just died, too, and she was going to dedicate her life to raising her daughter."

Frowning at Lexis, Zeke had to ask. "How do you feel about all this? That's one of your grandfathers and one of your grandmothers, but not the way you expected them to be."

"I never knew Grandpa Hayz, so it's wonderful to see more photos of him. They look so happy and in love that I have a tough time condemning them for having an affair. I just hope someday I can find a love like that myself. One like you and Mom had in the beginning. Oh my, God! *Mom!* You have to call her! Tell her I'm okay!"

"And your Granny Hayz, too."

"Oh *shit*. Dad, I'm so sorry about all this! You must have been destroyed."

"That's an understatement, Little One. Some day I'll tell you the whole sordid story."

"It's only been nine days, Dad. How much of a story could there be?"

"You'll just have to wait to find out. In the meantime, we have to figure out how to let your mother know you're alive."

"Just call her."

"Easier said than done. One, she's not talking to me. I think she even wants me dead, but I'm still trying to figure out why. By the way, I finally met JJ."

"*JJ?* How is she? Send her my love."

"She's in the hospital, but she'll be okay. That's all part of the story I'll tell you." He led them back to the chairs. "I can't call your mother. She'll hang up on me and even if she didn't, she'd never believe a word I said. If *you* call, she'll think it's a cruel joke and not only will it hurt her, but it'll really piss her off. Since *I* didn't call Marguerite back, your mother probably won't either. We need someone *we* trust, someone *she* trusts, too."

"I'd suggest Colonel Stihler, but he really doesn't like you, so I don't think he can be trusted."

Zeke cringed at the mention of his brother but said nothing about his real identity. "He can't be. You know, I think I'm going to have to suck it up and call your mother. She won't believe me, but she might believe you. She'll doubt her ears and suspect it's fake and we're leading her into a trap, but she'll also have enough doubt that she'll come."

"Don't we need a secure line, Dad?"

"Not for this call. I'll have Shaelagh reroute it a few times to prevent a trace, then she can send the coordinates on a secure line."

"Let's do it. Then we can eat. I'm *starved*."

"Me, too." He opened the comm to Shaelagh. "Hey, Sexy."

Hi Boss. I'm guessing everything there is safe, secure and good?

"It is. Lexis is alive and I'm standing right here with her."

Lexis shouted at her father's ear. "Hi, Shaelagh! I miss you and Deckard!"

Tell her we miss her, too. If I could cry tears of joy, I would, Boss. I'm so happy for you. What did Marisol say?

"Shaelagh says 'hi', Lexis. Shaelagh, Mari doesn't know, yet. That's why I'm calling. Please connect me to her, but route the call in the usual random manner, to make it as difficult to trace the call as possible. After I speak with her, please open a true secure line and send her the coordinates."

Got it. Calling now.

The call rang through. After ten interminable seconds, it was answered. "Fuck off and stay away from me, Hayz, or I swear I will skin you alive and use you for fish bait." The connection broke.

I'm sorry, Boss. She disconnected.

"Shit. Okay. Can you put me through to Quartermaster Slim Wilkes' personal line, using the same rerouting? She'll take *his* call, and he's someone we both trust."

Call proceeding.

Slim Wilkes answered the call much faster than Marisol had. "Zeke, my friend. Congratulations on the early release, but I'm sorry t'hear 'bout Lexis. Is there anythin' I c'n do for you? Help with th'service? Anything."

"Slim, there is something you can do." He nodded at Lexis, who spoke into his ear.

"Hi, Uncle Slim! It's me, Lexis. I didn't die." She leaned back.

"Holy shit, Zeke! Really?"

"Really, Slim. I tried to call Bossy to tell her, but she'd rather kill me than take my call. Can you please call her and let her know? My AI will call you on a secure line to give you our coordinates."

"Sure thing. I'll make th'call, but if the rumours are true, you'd better make yerself scarce when she arrives. If she tried to choke you out once, she'll probably shoot first and ask questions never."

"Thanks. I suppose it doesn't need to be said to keep all of this from Stihler's prying ears."

"Will do. Now go, and get yer AI to call."

"Done."

o0o

Zeke, you have an incoming call from Marisol.

"Put her through, please."

"Prove it. Now."

He waved Lexis over. "I'll put her on. She can't hear you but you'll hear her through my ear. We don't have a speaker where we are and her onboard was damaged, or I'd have you call her directly."

"Prove. It." Her voice was cold and packed with threat.

He nodded to his daughter.

"Hi, Mom! I'm so sorry you thought I was dead. I'm fine. Please come to the coordinates Uncle Slim gave you. I love you!"

Mari sobbed through the connection, but she covered it up quickly. "That's not enough. Have her tell me... um... ask her what she made me for my birthday dinner."

"Your Mom wants to know what you made her for dinner for her birthday."

Lexis leaned in again. "Nothing. You had to work. The next night, I grilled fish and squash and had your favourite fruit flan for dessert."

"I'm on my way." She disconnected before he could reply.

"She's coming. She's *really* pissed off, but she's coming."

"I suspect Mom is pissed because you didn't serve out your time."

"There's a lot more to it than that, though I'm not sure about all of the details. When she arrives, once we're sure it's her, I'll stay out of sight, maybe in a back room, or the woods."

"Don't be silly, Dad. It's not like she's going to shoot you."

"Maybe not, but a day and a half ago she tried to choke me to death and they had to stun her to get her to stop."

"Choke you? No shit?"

"No shit." He smiled at Marguerite. "I have no idea how she'll react to the photos on the wall, but we can't just sit and wait to find out. Do you have a sandwich or something I could chew on? I haven't eaten since this morning, and it was hospital food."

"Of course. Is fresh fish okay? Lexis caught it this morning."

"Perfect. Thank you." He stood up and followed her to the kitchen. "Just tell me how I can help, while I fill you both in on the details of the last ten days."

o0o

Lexis finished examining her father's shoulder and helped him to get his shirt back on. "They did a good job, Dad. You'll have two lovely scars, but you should get full motion back if you do the exercises they showed you. How did JJ look after her surgery? She'll be okay?"

"The doctor assured me JJ will be fine. They were able to repair the damage to her spine, which was my biggest concern. Your mom wouldn't let me see her. I suspect it's because the sniper was after me." He straightened his shirt out and started clearing the table. Lexis gathered up what he couldn't carry, and Inichi dropped down from the ceiling beam and followed them, purring happily.

"Probably, Dad."

Zeke smiled at their hostess. "Margie, when Marisol arrives, we may not get a chance to talk again before I have to leave, for my own safety. I want you to know that I can never repay my debt to you. Everything you did for Lexis astounds me. You're always welcome in my home. As far as I'm concerned, you're family. You're also welcome to continue living here if you wish, free of charge."

Marguerite smiled. "Thank you. I do have a home of my own now, though. Maybe we can all use this as a family vacation spot like it used to be. There's a lady in town who runs a service cleaning and watches cabins in the off-season. She's a friend of Mom's and mine, so I trust her completely. By the way, I suppose if I'm family, I should probably tell you my real name. Secret identities don't wash with family."

"Oh, you'd be surprised with this clan. For starters, my Dad was a corporate spy."

"I know. Mom, too." She extended her hand. "Hi, Zeke, I'm Stacey. Stacey Kaye."

Zeke shook her hand. "Hi, Stacey. It's a pleasure to meet you. Welcome to the family." He then held open his arms and she stepped into a hug. She gave back as strongly as she received. "My only regret is that we're just meeting now." They broke out of the hug and Lexis stepped in to hug Stacey.

"Me, too, but my mom was strict about that. Members of the team and their families could cross paths randomly outside of work but weren't allowed to socialize together, ever. But she's gone, your Dad is gone, and the corporation they worked for is gone. I got a letter from their lawyer just after Mom's death, giving me the contact information for the firm that would now be handling her pension. I don't think the whole secrecy thing matters anymore." A pulsing alarm interrupted from the ceiling speakers. "We have company." She opened a cabinet next to the refrigerator to reveal a set of four monitors. She tapped the screen showing the southern approach and zoomed it in until an aircraft became clear. "She's coming in fast."

"I'd better make myself scarce. Got a bedroom I can hide in?"

"First door on your left is a little mini-library, with a handful of real books as well as two full-size digital readers. Make yourself a brew and go relax."

"I'll leave the door open, just in case. She's got a flash temper and I don't want her taking it out on you."

"It's okay, Dad. I've got this. Margie, er, *Stacey* is safe with me."

"Then I leave you to it." He poured himself a mug of the fresh brew and wandered down to the mini-library. Inichi started to follow him, but Zeke psied a message to the little fellow. (Please go keep the girls safe, Inichi.)

(HayzZeke want Inichi keep HayzLexis safe? Inichi happy to!) Before Zeke could thank him, the psiling bounded off, his long claws click-clacking on the hardwood.

Zeke sat in the chair closest to the open door so he could hear any conversation in the cabin's common area. He heard the quad-copter circle the cabin, and then settle down in the clearing next to his own. It would be a tight fit, but he knew she was a good enough pilot to make it work. Excited, garbled voices made their way to him through the open window and down the hall and he sorely wanted to extend a probe and eavesdrop, but he didn't dare. He raised his shields and sipped his brew.

o0o

He must have dozed off because a gentle shake of his good shoulder roused him. He opened his eyes to see Stacey standing next to him.

"Lexis asked me to come get you. She tried psi, but couldn't get past your shields. I guess you're wrapped up good and tight."

"Sure. Okay. Is Mari okay with me coming out? Is it safe?"

"No, she isn't, but Lexis is insisting. She said she didn't come back from the dead to watch her parents live in fear or anger."

"I guess I'll be safe with Lexis there. If Marisol starts snapping and unsnapping her holster, run for cover." He pushed himself up out of the chair and followed Stacey.

"Dad, come, sit. Let's sort this shit out."

Even with his shields up and locked, Zeke could sense the malice rolling out from Marisol. She wasn't even trying to hide it. He nodded at her and sat in the furthest chair from her position next to Lexis on the couch. Inichi climbed up on his lap, his long claws tucked safely away.

"Mom, Dad, you need to figure this out. Mom, I know you're pissed at Dad for being The Psilent One, for not serving his time, for getting JJ shot, and for his part in Dave and Bunji's deaths, in addition to the destruction of your home. Dad, I know you're pissed at Mom for trying to choke you out, and for arresting you, and for... was there anything else?"

"I'm not pissed at your mother for *anything*, Lexis. And she has every right to be pissed at me. I did everything you just said I did. Even if you're still alive, that doesn't erase what else I did. *Have* done. I definitely deserve to be choked, although I wasn't sure why she picked that particular moment to do it."

Marisol growled. "No? You have no idea?"

He flinched. "None. One minute we were doing psi-surgery together, and the next I passed out. They said they found us with you on top of me, with your hands around my throat."

She looked surprised. "Really? You lowered your shields. *All the way*. I saw what you did."

"I've done a lot of stupid shit over the years, Mari. You'll have to be more specific."

"Murdering my father goes *way* beyond 'stupid thing'!" She looked ready to lunge and tear his throat out. Even Inichi leaped away with a squeak and scampered for cover.

The pure fury hammering against Zeke's shields made him want to follow the little psiling. Lexis held an arm across in front of her mother as if she could stop an attack. "Now you're being ridiculous, Mom. Dad could hardly have murdered Granddad. He was just a kid."

"I was fifteen. And your mother is right. I killed her father. *Your* grandfather."

Stunned silence dropped onto the group. Lexis and Stacey sat with their mouths open in disbelief, and Marisol slowly rose to her feet, unsnapping her holster and drawing her weapon.

"Do you want to know *why*? Do you care? Or are you just going to gun me down for something I did when I was fifteen?"

She stopped, midstride, the weapon charging up in her hand. "What makes you think I'd believe a single word spewing out of that sewer of lies you call a mouth?"

"I don't. But I'll drop my shields completely again and let all three of you go in and see for yourself. A deep dive right down into my dark, black core, to see *all* that I've hidden for twenty-five years. To see what I could never show you for fear you'd leave me, which caused you to distrust me and leave me anyway." He opened his arms in welcome, tears of relief flowing down his face. "I have lived all this time with this parasite of my past curled up inside, eating away at me. Come. *See my crime.*" He closed his eyes, ripped his shields down, and waited for the assault on his past. To finally share it would be a relief. He had carried the burden alone for far too long. He didn't expect them to understand, and he was terrified of what Lexis would think of him afterward, but he couldn't risk her mother being her only source of information about that day. She deserved to know what he'd done and make her own decisions from there.

Marisol's probe stabbed into his mind, pushing hard and surrounded by flickering blue flames of anger. A moment later, first Stacey, and then Lexis entered, each latching onto Mari's psi. He saw what they saw and relived what they witnessed. To make it easier and quicker, he pulled out the memory of his father's funeral, right from the beginning. He sensed Mari's frustration but didn't give a damn right now. Right now she only knew what the end result was. She needed to know what precipitated it.

Zeke was once again fifteen, standing as tall and straight as he could beside his mother. Stan stood on the other side of her, his hands in his pants pockets, and his eyes staring down at his shoes. Zeke wanted to make his father proud, even though he couldn't see him. He held his chin up and looked around at each one of the speakers at the service. The words bored him, and he began to explore the emotions leaking out of everyone around him. There was a tidal wave of sadness and grief coming from his mother, confusion and anger coming from Stan, and sadness and frustration coming from just about everyone else. There was a thread of boredom amongst the grey and black emotions, but it came from a neighbour's daughter who had never met his father. He could hardly blame her for being bored at the service of someone she didn't even know.

His probe reached Marisol, standing next to her father, and all across her shields were waves of sadness and pain for both he and Stan. Tears streaking her cheeks reflected what she was feeling. Zeke left her to her tears and touched his probe to the shields of Mari's father, Ramon. He was surprised to discover how weak his neighbour's shields were. They certainly didn't match his strong, often angry personality. Zeke was about to move his probe on when a clear thought punched out of Ramon, directed at the flowers on the memorial table.

(You got what you deserved, you bastard! Did you think I'd just let you steal my wife away? Hell no! Nobody disrespects me! They're already blaming your work! Your stupid ass life as a spy or whatever the hell you really did. I'm only sorry my bitch wife wasn't in the cruiser with you when I blew you up! She'll get hers, soon enough!)

Young Zeke was stunned! His father was cheating on his mother, with Marisol's mother, and Mr. Boissiere killed him for it? *He killed Zeke's Dad?* Zeke shoved his probe right into the brain of his father's murderer and pinched off the flow of blood through the first big vein he could find. A split second later, Ramon Boissiere dropped dead and everyone was either screaming or rushing to help the fallen man. Everyone but Zeke, and Marisol's mother who simply stared at the confusion in front of her.

The pressure of the three probes lessened until Zeke was alone with his thoughts and could raise his shields back up. All three women wept, and then he did, too. After a moment, Marisol stood up and marched outside. Everyone let her go. Lexis stepped over to her father and curled up in his lap, her arms around his neck, comforting him in the aftermath of once again reliving the worst day of his life.

Eventually, Mari came back inside. Zeke might have been relieved he didn't have to keep this horrid secret from her anymore, but the broken expression on her face tore his heart out. She didn't just find out that her first love had killed her father, but that her father had killed another man for sleeping with her mother, and her father was planning to kill her mother, too. Her world was torn apart. He wanted nothing more than to give her a hug, but he seriously doubted she would ever touch him again. He did the only thing he could think of. He pointed at the pictures on the walls. "They were really in love."

She appeared confused, giving the photos a cursory glance, but one of them caught her eye and she stepped up for a closer look. Recognition dawned and she sobbed, her hand to her mouth. One by one, she examined each photo. Lexis left her father's lap and joined her mother, taking her hand and lending silent support as they moved slowly around the room.

When Zeke joined Stacey in the kitchen, she grabbed him and held him tight and close, her head buried in his chest. He hugged her back with as much fierce emotion as he dared, fearful of hurting either her or his shoulder. They stood like that for a minute or two until Inichi joined them, and wrapped his arms around Zeke's right leg. Zeke loosened his hold on Stacey and picked Inichi up.

(Humans very emotioned, HayzZeke.)

(Yes, Inichi, we are.)

(Killing never easy.)

(Never, my little friend.)

(You finished killing now?)

(I sure as hell hope so. Four is enough.)

(All necessary. Not feel guilt. Kill or be killed.)

(Thank you.) He lowered the psiling to the floor, leaned over and kissed the top of Stacey's head, then went outside for fresh air. The sun was down, but the sky was bright with a vivid orange sunset. Zeke walked down to the dock and sat. The sound of the waves lapping on the rocks of the shore was comforting. He had finally told Mari the truth, and he was still alive. How different would their lives have been if he'd told her the truth in the beginning? Would she have stayed with him? Or would she have gone to Stan and fallen in love with him, instead?

Boss, I've collated and analyzed those two reports you wanted. There's an eighty-three percent chance they are both the same—

"I know," he cut her off. "That's why I asked for it all."

What are you going to do with the information? It's powerful stuff.

"How can I fault someone for choosing a life they think was better than the one they had? He made his choices, a long time ago."

Will you tell him you know?

"Probably, but only to get him to back off my life. Maybe we can agree to leave each other alone."

That's risky. He could have you killed.

"So we'll set up safeguards to encourage him to play nice. If I'm killed, you release what we've discovered."

What if someone else kills you?

"Then maybe *that* threat will make him even more amenable to a truce."

Hopefully. I've rescheduled your tour with Mr. Gallagher, as well as your press conference. Nita knows you have been delayed on your way home. She is now aware through news feeds of the shooting in Espy Beach and is really looking forward to your call when you return.

He checked that the cabin door was closed and he was still alone. "Put me through to her, please. I have no idea what our relationship will evolve into, but at least I can start it out being more communicative than I was with Mari." The line rang and was answered quickly.

"Zeke? Or Shaelagh?"

"It's me. I'm sorry I've been... away."

"You have stuff to do. So did I. That's life."

"Maybe so, but I wouldn't mind our lives intersecting a bit more. Or a lot more."

"Is that a euphemism for more time like our one and only night together?" She chuckled.

"Yes and no. Dinner, a show, a walk in a park... if that kind of stuff interests you and I'm someone you might do it with."

"I don't think I've gone for a walk in a park in years. I'd like that. With you. Let's give it a try and then see if we still want to do dinner and a show."

"Perfect. I'm still away, but hope to be back in KC tomorrow. The day after, at the latest."

"Okay. Of course, that doesn't mean you can't call me before you get back, just to chat."

"I'd like that. To be honest, though, I'm not sure how many alone moments I'm going to get here, and I'm not exactly in the company of people who will understand me calling some young hottie and whispering sweet nothings in her ear."

"Understood. And if you *do* dare to whisper sweet nothings, be prepared to fend me off. Whispering in my ear is my weakness."

"Thanks for the heads up. I'll start thinking of things to whisper."

"You'd better."

The door to the cabin opened and shut behind him with a thump. "I have to go. Be safe, Nita. See you soon."

"You, too, Zeke. Soon."

He disconnected the call just as Lexis sat down on the dock beside him and took his hand.

"Wow, Daddy."

"Yup."

"Mom's *really* pissed."

"Of course. She deserves to be."

"She's not pissed at what you *did*, Dad. She's pissed you've never trusted her enough to share it with her. If Granddad was alive and here, *she'd* probably kill him for what he did and was planning to do."

"How could I tell the woman I loved that I'd killed her father? I was judge, jury, and executioner. I did that to the man who killed *my* father, so I expected she would do the same to me. After she became a 62, there's no way I could tell her. You've seen how mad my being a thief made her. Being a murderer would have chased both her and you away forever."

"True. I understand. She's still livid, though."

"Fair enough."

Lexis cleared her throat and lowered her voice a notch. "Are you going to tell Mom that her CO is actually Uncle Stan?"

"You caught that? And she *didn't*?" As if things weren't complicated enough, he thought.

"She was a little focused on her dad. That's pretty messed up with Stan but it explains a *lot*."

"It sure does. How to tell your Mom was one of my concerns, but how do I tell your grandma that her baby boy is still alive? Do I have the right to tell her? It's *his* secret. He must have really hated me to go to those extremes."

"Since you asked, I say we keep it under our hats. The Stan Grandma knew *did* die in that fire. He took on more than Ed Stihler's name, it's like he created a whole new personality."

"Or he finally let his true self shine. He had a seriously dark side as a kid. The Stihler I've met fits with what I imagined a Stan unchecked by love to be like. Stihler was an orphan, so Stan didn't even have a fake family to love him. Maybe *my* Mom doesn't need to know, but *yours* does. Maybe he cares for her or even loves her, but her *not* knowing could be dangerous for you both."

"You think he would hurt us?"

"I honestly don't know. I'm not sure how mixed up he is with the LPF, but I'm pretty sure he'd like to see me die, horribly, and I don't want you two—or anyone else—caught in the crossfire."

"Then *I'll* tell her. Show me everything you read in his thoughts and I'll share it with Mom."

"Fair enough." He dropped his shields, called up the memory of the hospital encounter, and let Lexis' familiar psi slip in and see the details for herself.

When she was done, she withdrew from his mind, leaned back, and sighed like an exhausted old man. "Wow."

"That's kinda what I said."

"I'll let her know."

"Thank you. I don't want to keep any more secrets from her."

"That's noble, Dad, but you might not want to tell her about Nita quite yet."

"Oh shit. You saw—"

"No details, thank God, but thoughts of her bubbled to the surface surrounded by a lot of heat. You can tell me all about her later."

"Or you can meet her and let her tell you herself."

"I'd like that."

"So, what's next, Kiddo?"

"We're returning to Espy Beach. Mom will go back to work and I'll finish the school year before starting at the uni. Stacey will close up here and go home in a day or two. You?"

"Back to Hayz & Hayz, I suppose. No more stealing, though. I still have fines and community service to take care of, or your mother will throw me back in prison."

"Probably. But you've also earned her grudging respect in the last two weeks."

"How?"

"You killed a man who threatened me, killed the man you *thought* had killed me, then killed the man who shot her best friend. She really didn't think you had it in you. You've always been such a softy."

He shifted so that he could look into his daughter's beautiful eyes. "I am the most dangerous man in the entire system, Lexis. If *I* don't control me, who will?"

KOKOPELLI SOLAR SYSTEM - KEPLER 62

KOKOPELLI

MASAUWU

SOTUKNANG

CHEVEYO

ORAIBI

HONAUI
PAKWA
KELÉ

YAPONCHA

KWAHU
TOCHO
MUNA
ISTAQA
HEHEWUTI
ANKTI

KOSHARI

HEYOKAH
ANGUTA

PAHANA

From the novel The Gravity of Guilt by Timothy Reynolds

Design: Cometcatcher Media 2020.

Δbout the Δuthor

According to CBC Radio, Tim Reynolds is "Canada's modern-day Aesop".

That's great praise he struggles to live up to, but what he *will* admit to is being a prize-winning, award-nominated Canadian with stories to tell.

Based out of Calgary, Alberta, Tim grew up in Toronto, earning first a B.A. and then a B.Ed. from the University of Western Ontario.

Space is a wee bit of an obsession for Tim. His name is on three of the NASA rovers currently on Mars, and in 2024 his name will be part of a "Message in a Bottle" on NASA's Europa Clipper going to Jupiter's moon, Europa.

Find out what Tim is working on now over at www.TGMReynolds.com

Also By Tim Reynolds

Stand Up & Succeed

The Cynglish Beat

The Broken Shield

The Death of God

Waking Anastasia

The Sisterhood of the Black Dragonfly

She Runs With Wolves, He Sits With Kittens